Crime & C

by
The Crescent Collective

The Crescent Collective 2018 ©

Crime

Black Cherry Wine

Jan Jenner

Wiping her hands on her apron, Elsie looked contentedly at the gleaming bottles of wine against the end wall of the kitchen. She was fast becoming an expert in the science of oenology. In twenty-four years of marriage, wine making was her main achievement. She had lived her life just going through the motions. She had kept the house tidy and clean and put regular meals on the table. Wine making was different, it was her passion.

A single bottle of black cherry wine was on the top rack that was George's favourite, next came elderberry then blackcurrant and carrot. Below that were apricot, peach, wheat and barley with a few bottles of her special remedies on the floor.

Elsie was a plain woman to look at. Her thin pale blonde hair was beginning to fade to grey. She had a dumpy figure, well rounded with years of insufficient exercise. Arthritis in her hip gave her something of an ungainly gait, but she managed to get around. When her hip began giving her trouble four or five years ago, she'd started to collect books on herbal remedies and began cultivating different plants in the garden and greenhouse. Lately, she'd combined her two hobbies and had developed one or two interesting, medicinal wines.

She wiped down the kitchen counter tops and straightened one of the bottles.

She knew exactly how many were on each rack and how many of each kind. On occasion George would take it into his head to help himself, it made her cross, she didn't like his meddling. The kitchen was her domain.

Soon she would run out of space. Maybe she could put some more racks along the side wall. She would have to think about it, maybe next month, after the county show, when things had settled back down.

She was planning to put several bottles into the show. Blackcurrant, elderberry maybe a bottle of the peach. She hadn't decided; they were all ready to drink.

She was quite confident of winning at least a commendation, being a comparative newcomer to the show she couldn't expect to get much more than that. Perhaps next year she could set her sights higher, aim for the first prize. The thought sent a quiver of pleasure down her spine. She mustn't think of it. Next year was a long time ahead, so much could happen. For now, it was only a dream.

After lunch, she went into the garden. She frowned and shook her head as she walked past the narrow strip of untended garden by the garage wall, it was still overrun with weeds, how many times had George promised to clear it?

After a short while in the garden she had assembled a collection of leaves, berries and roots which she took back into the kitchen.

Picking up a worn and shabby book she'd bought from a second-hand shop the year before. She found the page she wanted and carefully read the instructions. Putting the plant material into a muslin bag she placed it with a cup of water into a small saucepan. It could well be the panacea for all her ills. She placed the saucepan on the stove on a low light and left it simmering while she prepared tea.

Elsie had another dream -- to live in a little bungalow by the sea. Pretty chintz curtains at the windows, polished wood floor in the lounge with one or two colourful rugs. A few delicate pieces of antique furniture. Her small collection of plates displayed on the wall, where they could be seen, instead of hidden away in a cabinet, in case they got broken. She would have lots of books in matching bookcases. In her bedroom, she would have soft, thick pile carpet and a king-size bed. She sighed, if only reality was so pleasant.

Last thing, before going up to bed, she took the bottle of black cherry wine down from the rack and added the dark red liquid from the saucepan. Then she washed the saucepan and put it away.

The next day was Saturday. George was up early and out of the house soon after breakfast. George's Saturdays were always the same, golf in the morning then football on the television in the afternoon. Elsie went into the kitchen to check on her wine.

She poured out a very small glass, it smelt good, but she had to be careful. She took a small sip, It tasted sweet, rather like an undiluted cherry cordial.

She put the bottle back on the rack and went to get her coat. Today she would treat herself to a day out in town. Perhaps lunch at the Alderney Hotel.

When she returned home, George was watching football on the television, he looked up guiltily when she came in. "Hello dear, had a good day?" he asked.

The half empty bottle was on the floor by his chair.

"Yes thank you George," she smiled, he would meddle. "I'll just go and start tea."

She went into the kitchen humming softly and started to peel potatoes.

During the evening, they sat and watched television in silence, the bottle of wine gradually went from half full to empty. After the ten o'clock news George yawned. "I'm off to bed," he said, stumbling slightly as he stood up.

"Good night dear," she said.

Elsie picked up the empty bottle and the glass and took them into the kitchen.

When she had washed and put them away, she locked the doors and went up to bed. "Good night George" she said softly. There was no reply, he always fell asleep as soon as his head touched the pillow.

The next morning Elsie woke at her usual time. She called to George and went into the bathroom to wash.

George still hadn't moved when she came back. She went to his side of the bed and gave him a gentle shake.

The doctor came at once. He had to call the police, of course. They were very understanding. A young police officer made her a cup of tea. She would rather have done it herself. She really didn't like anyone meddling in her kitchen, but it didn't seem right to make a fuss, he was only being kind after all.

The police asked a lot of questions. She told them about the medicinal remedies and her arthritis and showed them her book. She'd asked George not to meddle in her kitchen many, many times. They seemed annoyed that she had washed the wine bottle and the glass. They took them away anyway, to do some tests they said.

Of course, they found traces of Atropine at the post-mortem. They came and dug up the bit of land by the garage wall, taking away the plant with the pretty bell-shaped flowers. Maybe she would plant a climbing rose. It was a lovely sunny position; a rose would grow well there.

George died of respiratory failure, they told her. They were very sympathetic. The coroner said it was death by misadventure.

The insurance money was a bit more than Elsie expected. After the show, when she had more time, she'd put the house on the market and look for a small bungalow. Wouldn't that be nice?

Ok. It was a mistake

Maxine Patterson

"Ok. It was a mistake! I admit it. But those were the facts. A car with blood all over the tailgate and a gun with my finger prints on the handle!"

"For crying out loud Karen, what on earth possessed you?"

"I just couldn't cope any more. The never-ending noise, yelling, screaming. Doors banging, kids snivelling and shouting. And that bloody dog barking all day and night! I just flipped!"

"But, you've lived with it for nearly four years now? I don't know how, but you've coped with much worse."

"I know Jean. I can't believe what I did! I think it was because it was the Thursday night, Ian was on earlies and we'd gone to bed and actually managed to get to sleep."

"And?"

"Well, some great pickup drove up to next door screeched to a halt, hooted, started revving up. And if that wasn't bad enough the music started! It was so loud the front of the house was shaking. Well, I just flipped! I stormed out of the front door marched over to the pickup and snatched the keys out of the ignition!"

"What?"

"Exactly. It was like World War Three! The whole house erupted, they stormed out of the front door, round from the back door and from the other van waiting on the road!"

"I almost daren't ask…"

"I knew I was in trouble when I saw two of them carrying baseball bats!"

"OMG!"

"Then it got really bad!"

"What? Even worse?"

"Yup! Another one came from the back of the van on the road carrying a rifle. I thought – what have I done? By now I was screaming, they were screaming and yelling. Half the street was up and watching through the windows."

"Yes, they would – they all complain. But daren't do anything or back you up!"

"By this time, I was kind of pinned up against the pick-up, Then I realised I still had the keys in my hand. I jumped in – locked the doors and started it up. I was nearly deafened by the noise from the sound system. How they can drive with that going on defeats me. Honestly, no wonder they have to shout, if they listen to that all the time."

"Karen, get to the point! Get on with it. What happened next?"

"I thought they'd break the windows with the baseball bats – but they didn't! They just stood staring and shouting. Then I realised they didn't want to damage their own pick-up! So, I started it up, revved it up and put it into gear. I just wanted to get somewhere safe."

"When did the Police come?"

"I don't know… I was just hoping that someone had rung them – because of course I'd gone out in my dressing gown and fluffy bunny slippers! Hadn't thought I'd need my phone"

"So, who did ring them?"

"It was someone from number 68 – way down the street, all the local neighbours were too busy enjoying the show – bloody typical! Anyway – there I was in the pick-up – deafened by the music, revving the thing up like mad, sounding the hooter as well and my foot slipped!"

"What?"

"My foot slipped – I was just so stressed…. And obviously I hadn't ever driven something like this massive pickup before and my foot slipped!"

"So, you ran over the man with the gun by accident?"

"Well of course I did! I mean I was mad – but even I wouldn't actually choose to run the bloke over. I didn't realise it was in reverse and he was standing right behind the pickup – waving the gun around – I couldn't see him because the cab was full of equipment and boxes. All I felt was a slight bump and judder."

"Then, what happened?"

"They all stopped shouting and it all went quiet. Everyone just stood staring – not at me – at the back of the pickup. That's when I got out…… I thought they'd kill me – but they were all just standing and staring. I walked round the back and saw the bloke lying wedged under the bumpers. I just grabbed the gun. I've no idea why… it was an automatic reaction."

"So?"

"Well it was a really bad move, because by this time the police arrived. It was the armed response unit! You know- they shine those little red lights on you, and they're shouting to put the gun down and lie down. We were all made to lie down on the ground – I was dragged away because I had the gun.

Things went from bad to worse, they were all put in the back of the police van. I thought they'd kill me if I had to go in with them, but I was put in the back of a police car in handcuffs!

The most amazing thing was…."

"Well?"

"Ian slept through it all, even the ambulance and the fire brigade arriving with sirens blaring full blast! The police had to wake him up to tell him they were taking me down to the station. And...this really beats it all"

"There can't be anything else, surely?"

"A neighbour complained about the noise of the music... said they didn't see why they had to listen to the Bee Gees 'Staying Alive' at full volume at three in the morning! Even the police laughed!"

"I know when you rang me from the police station you sounded desperate."

"I was. I thought I was going to be charged with murder. But it turned out he'd said he'd fallen and that it had been an accident. Later, I found out – they were well known to the police, drugs and all that stuff. The family didn't want to press charges and just wanted everything dropped. That tells you a lot about them doesn't it?"

"So, are you going to move then Karen?"

"No way, they're so polite now, it's embarrassing. We're just enjoying the peace and quiet"

A Night to Remember

Anne Marie Phillips

"Right Lad," said Sergeant Roberts briskly. "Here's a nice easy one for your first night duty. You can even do the arrest and the caution."

Al Roberts was an experienced Sergeant and he took his mentoring duties seriously. He knew some older officers who belittled the young PC's as not being real coppers yet, but he wasn't one of them. He knew that while these kids were still a bit green, they only needed time and experience all of which they would get in due time. He thought it a pity that many of the older officers seemed to have forgotten when they were new. Mind you, they probably remembered only too well how they had been treated and were simply passing it on. Anyway, he could see that the young PC was extremely nervous, and he knew the only way to get him over it was to throw him in at the deep end and let him get a success under his belt.

This was a routine call out. According to their source, the little toe rag that had been seen dealing drugs on the notorious Mandela estate was now safely tucked up at home watching TV. All they had to do was go to his house, detain and caution him and bring him in for questioning. While they did that, a search team with a sniffer dog would enter the property and give it a right good going over. Hopefully this would be another link in the drugs chain broken.

PC David Johnson gulped. He had already had three weeks on day duty and that had been scary enough. Now he was starting his first night duty and he knew that was a whole different ball game. Most of the low life only came out and operated at night. During the day they were sleeping off the previous night's excesses and didn't give much trouble. Now he knew he was actually going to arrest one of them. He mentally went over the wording of the caution as he followed Sergeant Roberts out to the squad car. While he was nervous, he was glad Sergeant Roberts was his mentor. He had always been very fair with him and had taught him a lot. He knew he would be alright.

Al Roberts smiled to himself as he saw the young PC's mouth moving. He remembered how terrifying it was to give your first caution. Get it wrong and the suspect could walk free. Dave Johnson was a good lad. He listened and followed instructions and wasn't afraid to ask if he was unsure. Al knew he would make a good copper once he got his nerves under control.

Everything seemed quiet as they drove onto the estate. A few youths looked over as they went past but didn't pay much attention. They found the house, were admitted and cautioned and arrested their man. He was still drunk and didn't give them any trouble. Dave Johnson recited an impeccable, if shaky, caution and earned a nod of approval from his mentor. Al Roberts was puzzled as to why everything had gone so smoothly. He had expected the lad to put up a bit of a struggle, but he hadn't. Perhaps it was just their lucky night.

As they led him to the door, they became aware of a low murmuring from outside. Opening the door, they immediately saw what was going on.

A large crowd had gathered outside the gate. There must have been at least fifty people, mostly youngsters, but some adults too. As soon as the police appeared, they began to jeer and hurl insults. Some of the louder ones filtered through.

"Scum; Fuzz Bastards" There was a fair smattering of ripe swear words, but nothing they hadn't heard before.

"Don't worry lad," said Al Roberts, "they won't do anything. Just get him in the back of the car and let's get out of here."

As they reached the gate, it became clear that the crowd had no intention of letting them near the car. They had surrounded it and were now pressing forward.

"Quick. Back inside" muttered Al.

They turned their prisoner round and headed back to the house only to find the door firmly shut and locked.

Dave Johnson reached for his radio to call for back up. He had just pressed the button to talk when something hit him on the back the head and his world went black.

Dragging his prisoner down to the ground with him, Al lay on him and reached across Dave's body to grab the radio that was squawking irritably on the ground. Quickly giving his name and number and their location, Al called "Urgent assistance required, officer injured" repeatedly into the radio. He wasn't particularly bothered about protecting his suspect, but he still had a duty of care and it wouldn't do him much good if he let the kid get hurt. His real worry was Dave. He felt for a pulse in his neck and was relieved to feel a faint beat. That was a good sign but the fact that Dave was clearly deeply unconscious was not. He could only hope he was concussed and no further damage had been done. The crowd were confused now and had not advanced any further into the garden. They were unsure of themselves now that they had felled a policeman. This had tipped over from an angry confrontation into something much more serious and there were many people who did not like the turn of events.

The sounds of sirens approaching suddenly galvanised them into action. Very few of them wanted to be found out on the street at that moment. Al could see the fear in many of their eyes and knew that those were not the ones responsible for throwing the brick. Al had already recognised and memorised many faces. Those that had realised this now turned to face the oncoming police vans.

The vans that arrived on the estate were riot vans with their riot screens already in place. No-one was taking chances once a copper had been injured. Behind the vans was an ambulance. Al knew they would not be able to get to them until the situation was secure and it was safe for the paramedics to approach. He knew it could be some time before they got help.

Hearing a faint squawk from the radio, Al lifted it again. He pressed the button. "Go ahead" he whispered, not wanting to draw attention to themselves. His prisoner was wriggling furiously underneath him, but Al was not bothered about him. He had been the cause of all this and there was no way Al was going to be concerned about causing him a little discomfort. All he wanted was for the crowd to move away to allow the ambulance to come and get Dave.

"Ambulance is going to try and approach from the rear" said a calm voice. "The riot squad will draw the crowd away from you"

"Understood" said Al. "Dave is pretty badly hurt, He is out cold and bleeding very badly from a head wound. They need to be quick."

"Hang in there, mate, they'll get there as soon as they can."

Al now became aware of the shouting from the street. Enraged by the sight of the riot squad in full riot gear, the crowd were now advancing towards the vans brandishing whatever weapons they had managed to acquire. Al was aware of the ambulance quietly backing out of the street and around the corner out of sight. The crowd never gave it a second look.

It felt like an age but could only have been five minutes before a couple of paramedics accompanied by two riot police crept around the corner of the house. Certain that Dave's only real injury was his head wound, they quickly scooped him onto the stretcher and scurried away, back the way they had come. Al followed with his now sore and protesting prisoner.

"You can shut it for a start" snarled Al. "You're the reason we're in this mess in the first place" Your mates are now otherwise occupied with the riot squad, they seem to have forgotten about you"

The man was subdued by this revelation. Perhaps he had thought his neighbours had come out to rescue him when in fact as they had spotted the police car coming onto the estate, they had seen it as an opportunity for a bit of police intimidation. He was just a reasonable excuse. He was still a bit the worse for wear and in no condition to make a fuss. Al had a pretty good grip of him and judging by the way he had thrown him to the ground earlier he wasn't too fussed about hurting him. Sensibly, he went quietly.

Round the back of the house and out of sight of the riot, Dave was loaded into the ambulance and taken away quietly. Al bundled his prisoner into a police van and reluctantly went back with him to the station. Every nerve in his body was screaming to know what was happening to Dave, but first things first. He had to get this low life processed and then he would have to give a full report to his senior officer, Inspector Stevens. Only then would he be able to go and see Dave.

An hour later, Al was getting himself cleaned up to go to the hospital when his Inspector came into the changing room. One look at his face told Al that the news was not good.

"Dave?" he asked.

DI Stevens shook his head. "I'm sorry Al" he said. "Dave didn't make it. His skull was crushed, and he suffered brain damage. The lad would never have fully recovered."

Al sank down onto a bench. "Christ" he muttered. "It was only supposed to be a routine pick up."

He knew that a full-scale forensics operation would be swinging into gear right now. The crime scene would need to be preserved and he would have to identify as many suspects as he could. He would need to see Dave's parents as well. For the moment, though, all he could do was drop his head into his hands and wonder how something apparently so simple could go so bad in such a short space of time.

The Endangered Wheelbarrow

Muriel Claybrook

"Shot" shouted Geoff appreciatively, as Phil, his partner, advanced their score to twenty, by potting a difficult red. Roger and Al, were beginning to get impatient waiting for their turn, feeling sure it would come soon.

The four retirees met every Wednesday night in the snooker room of the village hall. They had all lived in Critchley for many years, and now, with less demands on their time, they enjoyed participating in community life. Geoff, being a keen gardener, enjoyed maintaining the hall's outdoor space. Only that afternoon he had been applying winter feed and moss killer to the front lawn and had left his wheelbarrow round by the side of the hall, away from prying eyes, when he had finished.

Roger had joined the board of trustees, who managed the hall, at the last AGM. Their average age was seventy plus, but it had been very difficult to attract new blood and in fact the last two new recruits had raised the average age. Playing snooker was a relaxing way to pass a winter's night, sharing a yarn and a beer with like-minded friends.

Phil chalked his cue and was lining up for his next shot when they all heard thuds, followed by a loud noise of a vehicle's engine revving. After looking at each other with puzzled expressions, the four quickly went out to the car park, expecting that there had been a car accident.

As Roger stepped outside a tall young man lunged at him, swinging a punch that caught him on the side of his head, causing him to stumble away. Al was right behind him and as he stepped forward shouting, he too was punched, this time full in the face. His spectacles went flying and he fell backwards, hitting his head. Everything was happening so fast, but Phil and Geoff were trying to keep calm, survey the general scene and take appropriate action

A battered white van, engine running, was backed up to the hall, a couple of metres from the double doors. Next to it lay Geoff's old wheelbarrow, with the bottom of it fallen through, and near to it two rolled up pieces of lead.

"So that's what he's been up to," said Phil.

The thief was now hurtling round to the driver's door of the van to make a getaway. Geoff turned the handle of the rear doors to pull them open, thinking that if they swung open it would slow the driver down. He was shocked to see, in the very back of the van, two young boys, sitting on a pile of old blankets. There were more rolls of lead in there too.

As the van careered out of the car park the four saw a man with a dog coming over to them. He had seen and heard the commotion and had dialled 999 to alert the police and give them the van's registration number. All five men were in slight shock, especially Al, who had blacked out for a few seconds after he had been hit.

The dog walker helped them all back inside and within ten minutes the police had arrived to take statements. Soon the officers got a call to say their colleagues had intercepted the van. Al was taken to A&E, by his wife, for a check up and the two rolls of lead put into the hall for safekeeping overnight. The policemen drove away, the hall was locked up and the friends went home to tell of the evening's unexpected events.

Geoff did not sleep well that night. He kept thinking about his wheelbarrow. It had been with him and Madge through nearly fifty years of married life. He could remember bringing it home on the roof of his mini car, weeks into their marriage. Since then he'd used it in building and gardening activities, such as, carrying paving stones, a sandstone trough, bedding plants and latterly a full set of Encyclopaedia Britannica. Nobody needed these anymore and so he stacked them in the boot of his car and drove to the municipal dump.

These innumerable loads and nearly a half century spent standing in the garden, had taken their toll on the wheelbarrow. It was very squeaky, had holes in its base and had lost a rubber hand grip. Yes, it had been in danger of extinction for a few years now, but last night's incident had finished it off completely. The decision to replace it had been made for him.

It would not be like for like. It would have a ball not a wheel and be lighter and easier to manoeuvre. He would miss using the old one, but packed with pots of Madge's favourite flowers, standing in a corner of the garden, he would give it a new lease of life.

A Job to Do

Jan Jenner

It was still dark outside, I yawned picked up the car keys and opening the door stepped into blinding sunshine.

I screwed up my eyes and held on to the door frame, Sunshine?

What was I thinking about, it was 4 am for heaven's sake. It wasn't sunshine, it was my neighbour's security light.

I swore softly under my breath. He was the most thoughtless swine I'd ever had the misfortune to live opposite.

Of Course, he didn't care if the light annoyed everyone else in the road, not if it made him feel safe.

I was about to unlock the car when the security light caught on a patch of white under the hedge at the side of my garden. Was it a cat on the prowl? Or maybe an injured animal? I edged across the drive dreading what I might find. As I got closer I saw it was a bundle of clothes, and the bundle began to squirm tiny mewing sounds coming from inside.

I unwrapped the soft white blanket and saw a small head covered in a blue knitted hat. Curly blonde hair framed his face, and a pair of clear blue eyes look at me curiously.

He was warm, well fed with a clean nappy and a full bottle wrapped up with him, he could afford curiosity. What the hell was he doing on my drive?

Inside the blanket was a scrap of paper, I smoothed it out and put on my glasses to read it.

'I'm sorry to leave him with you, but I've watched you and I know where you work'

My heart sank as I read those words, was this some sort of blackmail attempt?

I continued reading, 'your son is happy and well cared for, so I know you must be a good person. Please look after my baby.'

I relaxed but I couldn't think about it now. I had to go, no way could I be late. I had a job to do, people were relying on me and I relied on the money they paid me.

My car was a rust bucket and Joe needed a new school uniform. He was growing so fast and his clothes cost me an arm and a leg. No job was secure and no job paid as much as people might imagine

Ok, I had to prioritise, nothing I could do now, so I put the small bundle in a box on the back-seat of my car and secured the seat belt around it. He would have to wait until I could hand him over to the proper people.

Thirty minutes later I parked the car outside a small terrace house. I looked over at the back-seat, he was asleep small bubbles coming from his lips on every breath. I felt my heart start to soften, it seems such a short time since Joe was that small, but he'd be thirteen next month.

I shook myself and turned away before I could let myself get too involved. I heard a door slam and saw a man walking along the pavement towards me I checked the photo on my phone, it was him. I opened the car window and placed a small bag of rice over the cill

I took the .357 Magnum from my bag with a flush of satisfaction, it was a perfect piece of engineering. I clicked a silencer on to the barrel, perfect fit. I laid the barrel on the rice to steady it and took aim, I slowly pulled back on the trigger. A sharp putt and I saw him slump to the floor, no fuss no noise. I had no idea who he was, or why he left home at such an ungodly hour. I left the moralising to others. I had orders, I just carried them out.

I checked to make sure the street was still empty before starting the engine and pulling away. Time to go home and get Joe up for school before I went to work. That was my proper job, a three-hour shift at the local hospital. I was only a cleaner, but I enjoyed meeting people and the regular money meant the bills were paid.

When I reached home I carried the box inside the house and put it on the kitchen table while I put the kettle on for tea.

He was awake now looking at me with blue-eyed inquisitiveness and total trust.

"Hey Mum, who's that?" Joe stood in the doorway yawning and rubbing his eyes, his skinny legs poking out of too short pyjamas.

I showed him the note, 'Some poor soul who's having a bad time left him on the drive.'

He grinned and put his arms around me, "She's right Mum I think you're a good person."

"Maybe." I smiled as I poured milk on my son's cornflakes.

Christmas Interrupted

Muriel Claybrook

He woke up with a start and could hear a car engine screeching very loudly. Getting up as quickly as he could he went out through the hall and into the sitting room that was decorated for Christmas. With each step forward, the noise increased, and a smell of exhaust fumes became stronger. As he put a light on he could see that the sitting room window was completely smashed, brickwork around it had collapsed and the bonnet of a Ford Fiesta was embedded in the wall. The Christmas tree was demolished, of course, and pushed a short distance into the room.

Ed grabbed his dressing gown and slippers and opened the front door. Almost at once neighbours were on the scene; Ted from next door, Joan, and Alan from across the road with Josh, who had his mobile phone clamped to his ear. He was speaking to the emergency services. The car door on the passenger side had opened and two dazed looking, young lads had managed to get out. 'Isn't one of them the farmer's son from the end of the lane?' thought Ed. As Joan and Alan reassured the lads, Ted was inspecting the car for petrol leaks before trying to turn off the ignition. All of this seemed to take hours to Ed but in truth only took about five minutes.

Once the sound of the engine running had ceased it felt reassuringly quiet and Ed seemed to be able to think and begin to reassess more effectively, just what had happened to his property. A builder, boarding up, gardening- his mind darted about as blue flashing lights and sirens could be heard approaching. The teenagers, having been assessed were reluctantly taken off for possible scans and x-rays while the fire brigade and police dealt with the car.

Joan had taken Ed inside and given him hot sweet tea. He felt surprisingly lucid in his PJ's and dressing gown as the police started to interview him. He was advised to take photographs, as the police themselves were doing now. The fire brigade had contacted a twenty-four-hour boarding up firm, who were on the way. There was an icy wind blowing through the damaged window, but Ed was only belatedly registering it.

"Dad, are you alright?". The familiar voice of Jan, Ed's daughter, was a huge relief to him, and he began to relax a little as she hugged him. Jan and husband, Mike, had driven the short ten miles from their home, as soon as the neighbours had phoned. Mike had soon turned up the heating and refilled the kettle.

Despite the late hour, three emergency vehicles had attracted five or six, more distant neighbours and passers-by. Once the ambulance had gone and a low loader had arrived the business of removing the embedded car got under way. Within half an hour the job was done, and the boarding up was soon finished too. Blue and white police tape was strung across the front of Ed's lawn and contact information was exchanged before the police left.

Ed, Mike, and Jan retreated to the kitchen where Jan made more tea and they all indulged in chocolate biscuits from the festive Christmas tin. It brought a wry smile to each of them and seemed to inject a gleam of positive thinking to them all. Finishing their tea, they now looked in on the living room.

The wreckage of the felled tree held Ed's attention. Now its baubles lay scattered across the carpet, causing tiny shards of glass from them and the tree lights, to glisten everywhere. What most concerned Ed, though, was the fate of Sue's stars. His beloved wife had died two years ago, and made lace, as a hobby. The beautiful red and silver stars were always hung on the tree. He could see two undamaged ones and thought he might be able to find the others. Jan suggested it was now time to shut the living room door and all try to get some sleep. The bedrooms being at the back of the house were undamaged although a smell of brick dust and car fumes hung in the air.

Next morning, they were all up by seven and had managed to get some sleep. A priority for Ed was to speak to his elder daughter, Mary, who lived in a nearby town with her family. She had a high-powered job and would be at work by 8.30 a.m. Well used to delegating and handing things over to the relevant professionals, Mary was glad to hear her Dad sounding, on the surface at least, calm and positive. Even though Ed was eighty plus, he was still active, and full of endeavour. As the tidy up began Mike and Jan insisted Ed was an on-looker. They totally divested the tree of it's decorations and removed it through the front door to the garden. Tyre tracks and so many heavily booted footsteps had wrecked the lawn, but it was nothing that could not be fixed.

Ed had put the few undamaged tree decorations into a cardboard box. It had been Ed and Sue's habit to collect Christmas tree decorations from holiday trips. Some of these, he was glad to see, had survived as they brought back such happy memories. The Mexican pottery angel and the crib inside a decorated gourd from Peru were undamaged. He had also managed to find a few more stars.

Mike set to work with a dust-pan and brush collecting larger debris while Jan worked with the Dyson, its long arm keeping her well away from the glinting glass. How different the room felt with no natural light coming through the window space. Fortunately, the electric lighting was good, but Ed brought in a couple of spare standard lamps to aid the clearing up process. Once dust and debris had been sucked off the carpet and furniture the room looked much better and after checking that the TV might still work they decided to close the door on the room once more.

The plan was for Mike to contact the household insurance and liaise with the window company. Jan was to help Ed take down all the other Christmas decorations and pack them away, a few days before twelfth night this year. By lunchtime there had been many phone calls from the sympathetic, curious etc. Personal callers included the farmer father of the car driver, the curate, neighbourly friends, the GP that Jan had requested to visit, the local press reporter and a TV crew.

Quite bemused and exhausted by all this, nevertheless, the three of them had survived and were encouraging one another as they ate their lunchtime soup and sandwiches. Ed remembered he needed a few groceries, so Jan and he planned a trip to the supermarket. Mike pondered the wisdom of leaving the house unoccupied and taking Ed to stay with them until the window could be replaced. He tactfully broached the subject now. Ed however had been thinking it through himself and proposed that instead they help him convert the third bedroom into a sitting room.

While they were shopping, Mike had had an hour on his own to re set the TV and check all the other electronic appliances. They could all be easily moved into the proposed sitting room. When Mary came to see her Dad after work Mike, Jan and Ed gave her the story. She suggested Ed's teenage grandchildren come over the next day to give him some distraction and company while Mike and Jan went home.

Two months down the line the new window was in place, the front garden had had a makeover and Ed was looking forward to resuming his normal hobbies, model making and listening to opera. As for the neighbours, several had continued coming to visit, as had the curate. The teenagers responsible for the accident were being dealt with by the courts and their friends were wide eyed and chastened by the mishap.

It had unsettled Ed though, and feeling in that mood he was investigating a possible relocation. Several possibilities were on offer. He saw a smaller bungalow set on a straight road behind a substantial wall, a flat overlooking the river and a retirement flat in a private block. It was the latter that appealed the most. He liked quiet people living around him but liked his own company most. There would be no gardening to do there and this was recently built and on the first floor, overlooking a fairly busy residential road. However, he had noticed, when he went for a viewing, how quiet it was inside, thanks to triple glazing.

He invited his close family over for afternoon tea one Sunday in April and told them of his plans. They were very surprised and shocked at first but quickly appreciated the practicality of his proposed move and were thankful he was still in control. He appreciated that this village he and Sue moved into all those years ago, was about to be transformed by the four new housing estates, for which planning permission had been granted. The prospect of construction vehicles and building supplies rumbling past for years with no new transport infrastructure planned, was something he would be only too glad to be missing out on. One of his maxims was 'there is nothing quite as sure as change' and knowing this he had endowed himself with much needed resilience and this fuelled his own plans.

By the beginning of August, the bungalow had been sold and he was living in the retirement flat. The living room faced south as did the kitchen and his bedroom. They were flooded with midday sun and this always raised his spirits. He had met several fellow residents, got to grips with the self-service laundry and begun exploring the local neighbourhood on foot. There was a small parade of shops and garage with minimarket, though the library had recently closed. A frequent bus service passed the flat and could take him to the main library, railway and bus stations and city centre shops. Overall, he was settling in.

As thoughts and shops turned to Christmas coming, he began to think about decorations for the flat. The box he brought from the bungalow would easily suffice. He had already decided he would not have a real Christmas tree and had never liked the artificial conifers. It was on a visit to a coastal RSPB reserve that he noticed, in the gift shop, an attractive, grey tree fashioned from driftwood. There was little need for lights or many decorations on it and the few he had salvaged from last year would be enough. Glass Baubles? Just don't go there!

The Visit

Jan Jenner

"Oh, my dear boy." Her face opened into a smile when she saw it was him. She took his hand as she led him into the clean and polished living room.

He looked tired. His clothes were worn and none too clean. They were hanging loose on his thin frame. She smiled indulgently, her grandson was a musician. They lived different lives, didn't they?

"Why don't you sit down now while I get some tea, then you can tell me what you been up to," she spoke gently. "It's wonderful to see you, such a lovely surprise."

"it's good to see you as well." He bent down and kissed her cheek then turned his head, eyes stinging with the tears he couldn't let her see.

He looked around the small room, it was just as he remembered. Same ornaments on the mantle, same smell, a mixture of polish and his granddad's pipe. Could he really smell the pipe? His granddad's been dead for two years.

His mouth was dry, and his hands were beginning to shake, he thrust them deep into his pockets. He could hear his grandmother in the kitchen. cups and saucers rattling as she arranged them on a tray, no mugs in his grandmother's house.

"No time for tea Nan." He called.

"Don't be silly dear that is always time for a cup of tea." He had to stop himself shouting, he really loved the old girl, but she wouldn't understand.

He looked around the familiar room, she thought things could always be made better with a cup of tea. Things could, when he was a little boy. Tears flowed down his cheeks as he took the purse from her handbag and left, quietly closing the front door behind him.

The Fence

Anne Marie Phillips & Pat Buckley

Mildred and Herbert Brown lived at the head Vale Crescent, a very nice cul de sac. As well as enjoying the benefits of a well-tended south facing rear garden, their front aspect provided unlimited opportunities for keeping an eye on their neighbours. Indeed, when the weather prevented any work to the garden or walls and paths at the front of the house, their bedroom window gave unparalleled views, over the fences. Not only did this give views of the front doors and gardens, but also excellent view into their next-door neighbours, whose houses slanted round the curve of the road. Mildred always made it her duty to speak to the locals, offering to take in parcels and feed cats whilst owners were away. She enjoyed being helpful but equally relished the insight into how other people lived.

Her long-suffering husband, Herbert, was the chairman of the local Neighbourhood Watch scheme and Mildred liked to feel that she was "doing her bit." Herbert, however, said she was just nosey and her meddling ways would get her into trouble one day. Mildred scoffed at this. She reminded him of the time she had been worried because she hadn't seen Annie going out for her usual bus, even though Mildred knew for certain that Annie was going into town to get new shoes for her son's wedding. Herbert had grumbled but had eventually been persuaded to go round and check on her. He had been shocked to find her laid on the path at the back of her house. She had fallen down the steps and twisted her ankle. It wasn't a serious fall, but Annie had been very cold and frightened. She hadn't been able to make anyone hear her and was so very pleased to see Herbert. She was also thankful for Mildred's nosey ways and had told all the neighbours not to complain about her as they might be glad one day that she knew so much about them. Even Herbert had said that her observational skills might be an asset to Neighbourhood Watch one day.

Emily Smith's house was to the left of the Brown's place. And the raked angle would allow a casual glance into the living room, should one wish to look that way. Mildred had never been sure about Emily. She seemed friendly enough but always managed to keep people at a distance. No-one had anything bad to say about her, but equally no one knew anything about her. Mildred, on the other hand, was the friendly sort. She loved to chat to her neighbours and wanted to know what they were doing.

Emily was very different to the other neighbours; tall, slim, blond, single and definitely more aloof. Mildred called her snooty. She would have loved to see inside Emily's house but no one in the street had ever been invited in. Emily wasn't unfriendly. She did stop and chat occasionally. She just never gave away any personal details and that drove Mildred mad. She had told Emily her life story but got nothing back in return. Rumour had it that Emily did something in the Import and Export business. That raised red flags for Mildred straight away. Didn't James Bond do something like that?

Herbert had laughed when she had told him. "It doesn't mean she is a spy or doing anything illegal dear." He explained patiently. "It's just buying and selling stuff abroad. It could be anything from high end antiques to cheap paper goods. It's probably as boring as anything."

Mildred sniffed. She hated it when Herbert was so sensible. She wished he had a little more imagination. She preferred to think that Emily was involved in something shady. Whatever it was, it certainly paid well judging by the new Mercedes coupe that Emily was driving these days. There wasn't anything Mildred could do, however. She just had to fume in silence.

Things took a different turn on New Year's Eve. Mildred and Herbert were having a quiet evening at home when loud bangs and cracks could be heard from outside. Mildred loved fireworks and suggested they go outside to watch them. Herbert was not keen, feeling that outdoors at midnight in the middle of winter could be seriously cold. In any case he was watching a tele program. Mildred went into the bedroom to watch the fireworks. They were coming from the hotel on the main road and she knew she would get a good view from the window. As she stood in the dark enjoying the display, Mildred saw a flickering light in Emily's house next door. Was that a torch being used? How strange. She knew that Emily went away somewhere warm every Christmas and New Year. As Mildred continued to watch, she was surprised when a beam of light flickered over a face. A face that Mildred thought she recognised but couldn't quite put a name to.

As she watched another light flashed. Must be two of them, she realized, and she heartily wished she had brought the binoculars up with her, if only to gain a much better view of the fireworks. Realizing there could be a robbery in progress at Emily's she shouted to Herbert to call the police.

Herbert shot out of his chair and came upstairs, grabbing the phone as he came past. He was already talking to someone as he came into the bedroom, reporting that they could definitely see torches and knew that the owner was away. Herbert gave his name and the address and was told not to interfere. It could be dangerous. It seemed to take ages for the police to arrive. But before they did, a dark unlit van slipped out of Emily's drive and left Vale Crescent. Eventually, they could see police making their way round to the back of the house and it wasn't long before lights came on and more police arrived.

After about twenty minutes, a detective sergeant was at their door to interview Herbert and Mildred. He asked Mildred to describe exactly what she had seen. She told him about seeing the torchlight as she was watching the fireworks. He smiled at that and told her that the thieves were probably banking on most people being outside to watch them. Mildred couldn't help looking at Herbert when he said that. If they had been outside, then they wouldn't have seen anything going on. When she mentioned that she thought she had recognised one face, the detective seemed a little sceptical. Mildred then had to admit she couldn't remember where she'd seen it before. She added that there was probably another person there, but they were in the background.

After they had described the van but could not give the registration number, the DS Jones closed his notebook. Mildred hated to have to admit that she didn't know exactly where Emily was, but she knew she was away for a few more days. It also annoyed her that she didn't know Emily's mobile number. The detective, however, was quite confident that the police could track that down. When the team had finished searching the house and checking for fingerprints, they would lock up the back door the thieves left open and make the house secure. The mystery was just how they got in and managed to put the burglar alarm out of action. Unlikely as it sounded, they could have had a key as well as enough expertise to disable the alarm.

After their busy night, they both slept in and enjoyed a lazy morning. Herbert was playing golf in the afternoon; something of a New Year tradition. While he was outside packing his clubs into the car, the telephone rang. It was DS Jones telling Mildred that he had spoken to Emily and she was returning to the UK the following afternoon. Mildred replaced the handset just as Herbert came into the kitchen. She gave him a kiss.

"Have a lovely time dear. Say Happy New Year to the boys from me."

"I will, and you, behave yourself. "

"What on earth do you think I could possibly get up to here by myself?"

"I have no idea, but I am sure you could think of something."

Mildred could, but she wasn't about to tell Herbert that. Giving him her best innocent smile, she laughed as she waved him off.

After Herbert had left, Mildred waited a little while to be sure he had not forgotten something and come back before slipping out of the house. Heading next door, she told herself that she was just checking everything was ok. Coming round the back of the house and onto the drive, a small metallic gleam showed in the flower border. Stooping, Mildred soon located a key. It looked very like the sort used to open a house door. She wondered if it was what the thieves had used. With the key in her hand, Mildred knew what she was about to do was very wrong but months of frustration had built up until Mildred was desperate to see inside Emily's house.

Wasting no time, she approached the house back door. Turning the key, and carefully pushing the door inwards, she quickly slipped through the doorway. Standing in the utility room, she waited for her breathing to settle down. Feeling as though she had been running, Mildred reflected that she was definitely not cut out to be a criminal; her heart couldn't take the strain! Taking deep breaths to calm herself, Mildred looked around the house.

Now she was here, she wasn't sure where to begin. Mildred started in the kitchen. Emily's tastes were ultra-modern; shiny white, high gloss appliances with a silvery grey granite top and equally shiny black tiled splash backs. It looked very smart but not exactly homely. Mildred's kitchen wasn't exactly old fashioned, but it certainly had a comfortable, lived in feeling. She opened a few cupboards but found nothing interesting. It didn't look as though Emily did much cooking. She sniffed again when she eventually found the fridge freezer and the dishwasher hiding behind matching cupboard doors. Mildred couldn't see what was wrong with plain white goods. Some rather attractive gold labelled bottles in the fridge caught her eye and she took one out to look at it. Cristal on the label made Mildred reflect that they could afford Cava at best.

Moving into the sitting room, Mildred noted that Emily's Spartan tastes seemed to extend in here as well. Emily certainly favoured a minimalist approach. There was very little on display. As Mildred looked around she realised that there were too many empty spaces. Perhaps quite a few things had been taken after all. There was a white leather sofa, a glass coffee table and fitted shelves along one wall. These were bare except for a few framed photographs. The pictures showed a much younger, smiling Emily flanked by an older couple who were obviously her parents. Anything else that had been on the shelves had apparently been taken by the burglars. The shelves were so clean that it wasn't even obvious where or if items had stood there. Despite her animosity towards Emily, Mildred found herself being impressed.

Idly picking up one of the framed photos, Mildred felt something stuck to the back of it. Closer examination showed it to be a small key. Mildred felt her heart begin to race again. This was getting exciting. She simply had to find out what it opened. A quick look around showed no doors with small locks downstairs, so she hurried upstairs. The fitted wardrobes in the main bedroom revealed nothing more than a range of very smart suits, blouses and dresses for day and evening in the most beautiful materials and designer labels, which left Mildred suffused with total envy. Import export must pay very well she mused.

Eventually, to her delight the key fitted a cupboard door in one of the spare bedrooms. Peering inside, she was a bit disappointed to find just a couple of large cardboard boxes, the sort that removal men brought with them and taped together. Opening the flap of the box on top, Mildred was surprised to find a variety of clocks and ornaments. None of them looked to be the kind of thing that Emily would like, judging by the downstairs decor. Maybe she was just storing them up here. As Mildred looked closer, she counted nine very old looking clocks and several ornaments that looked suspiciously like Sevres. Mildred fancied herself as an amateur antique collector. She watched the Antiques Roadshow every Sunday without fail. She was now convinced that Emily was a bigger mystery than before. Why hide away such lovely things? Was she up to no good? It was at this point that Mildred realised whose face she had seen in the flickering torchlight. Bob Pargeter the owner of the antique shop in town. She felt so stupid not to have made the connection when speaking to the DS.

Leaving everything just as she had found it, Mildred locked the cupboard door again and went downstairs to return the key. First, of course, carefully polishing it in a tissue to ensure her finger prints weren't left behind. Quietly leaving through the backdoor, Mildred replaced the door key in the border, where it had previously rested. She couldn't wait to call the police to tell them what she knew. Then a dreadful thought struck her. She couldn't tell anyone. If she did, she would have to admit to finding the key and poking about in Emily's house. It crossed her mind that the police would certainly be extremely cross with her breaking and entering, and she didn't even like to think what Herbert would say. She would have to keep quiet and be careful to not let slip that she had seen inside Emily's house. For someone who loved to gossip, this was going to be so hard.

Mildred decided to pretend that nothing had happened. She spent the rest of the day decluttering her kitchen and trying to achieve the same look of streamlined efficiency that she had seen in Emily's. Once she had cleared the worktops, she had to admit that it looked quite good. Unfortunately, it meant that her cupboards were now crammed with gadgets, so she didn't hold out much hope that it would stay that way. Herbert noticed when he came home and wondered what on earth was wrong with Mildred. He supposed she had been reading her women's magazines again. She was always getting harebrained ideas that never lasted.

Emily arrived home the next day after lunch. Whilst she did call to thank the Browns for their prompt action, she did not offer any explanation of where she'd been or what had been taken. They were surprised to see a locksmith come the day after Emily got home and change the locks and later more workmen arrived to install a new state of the art burglar alarm. But Herbert decided, on balance, that these were probably sensible precautions.

Mildred and Herbert forgot about the burglary and carried on with their everyday lives. Mildred never saw Emily to talk to again. She only saw her driving away each morning and returning at the end of the day.

So life carried on at its usual slow place. One morning Herbert looked up from the local paper and remarked

"There's been a bad accident on Swinston bank, that steep and winding hill just outside town. A van has gone out of control and crashed into a tree killing the driver. It was Michael Burns, from the market."

"I always knew that it was a difficult and dangerous road," commented Mildred. "I close my eyes when we come down there."

"Not when you are driving, I hope." Herbert loved his little jokes.

Agreeing that they would miss him and his hardware at the market, they returned to their various occupations, without giving him another thought.

Mildred forgot about Emily's burglary until one morning, a paragraph in the local paper caught her attention. A small headline read "Local antique dealer found dead" As Mildred read on, she discovered that it was none other than Bob Pargeter, the man she believed she had seen in Emily's house. He had been found crushed beneath a heavy oak dresser in the back room of his shop. There was speculation that he must have been cleaning the dresser and that it overbalanced on top of him.

"Cleaning, that's a joke" laughed Mildred. "Some of the dust in that place is older than the stuff on sale. Bob never cleaned. So just how did a dresser fall on him?"

"No idea," muttered Herbert. "But I'm sure you will be finding out."

"I most certainly am. I wonder if it had anything to do with his other occupation? "

"What other occupation? "

"Everyone knows, I mean, knew, or at least suspected that Bob was involved with handling stolen goods."

"Mildred, you cannot go around saying things like that about people. It's tantamount to slander. Anyway, if everyone knew, how come he's not locked up? How come he's free?"

"But he isn't, is he? He's dead"

That certainly gave Herbert pause for thought.

At this point Mildred thought it was safe to confess that she believed that Bob had been in Emily's on the night of the burglary. She couldn't understand how she had not realised straight away as his moon face was so well known. It was true. Bob did have a distinctive round face and Mildred did know him very well. She had spent many a happy hour poking around in Bob's shop looking for treasures. That was how she knew about the large cupboard that couldn't possibly have fallen over and about Bob's aversion to cleaning. She couldn't put her finger on it but there was something fishy going on. She wasn't sure how she knew, but she definitely had a feeling about this.

Herbert decided that any suspicions should be reported to the police, hoping that they should at least look into it. They always said that some information is better that none at all. and it could be important. Mildred dialled the number on the card that the detective had left for her. She was glad she had pinned it up on the board. The response was an answer phone, so taking a deep breath, Mildred left her message.

"Good morning detective Jones, this is Mildred Brown from Vale Crescent. I spoke to you last month about the break-in at my neighbour, Emily Smiths house. I have some information that I think might be pertinent. Could you contact me please? "

Herbert congratulated her on leaving such a good message, even though she had omitted her phone number. Concluding that if he could not find out your number, then he wasn't a very good policeman, and he knew where they lived. Mildred smiled fondly at Herbert. Honestly, he could be very funny sometimes.

An hour later, as they were enjoying morning coffee in the sunny conservatory, the doorbell rang. Herbert went to answer it and returned with the detective DS Jones and SPC Alice King. They were interested in Mildred's information.

Initially, Mildred felt that the detective was being a little bit patronising. He seemed to be slightly bored. She began to feel that she might be wasting his time. When she began to talk about Bob Pargeter though, and how she thought he'd been in Emily's house on New Year's Eve, she noticed him sitting forward in his seat and indicating to the WPC to take notes. Reassured that he was taking her seriously, Mildred took a deep breath and admitted to having found the keys and gone into Emily's house and to having looked in the locked cupboard.

DS Jones looked at Herbert who looked as though he was about to explode.

"I'm sorry dear, I really am. I know I shouldn't'' have done it and I suppose I will be in trouble for this. But honestly, that woman makes me so mad. I have tried to be friendly, but she keeps me at arm's length and I was so frustrated; only wanted to have a peek."

Herbert and DS Jones both spoke at once.

"I can see how that might annoy you"

"Mildred, you opened a locked door. That's not peeking"

"Just how did you open that door, Mrs Brown? We left it because nothing seemed to have been disturbed upstairs."

Mildred told them about finding the key taped behind the picture frame. Then went on to describe the items she had seen in the boxes.

"Oh, for heaven's sake Mildred. This just gets worse and worse" Herbert buried his head his head in his hands. "I will have to resign from the Neighbourhood Watch, not to mention the golf club. What will people think of us?"

"Now, now, Mr Brown let's not get too excited. I'll admit that it doesn't look very good for you Mrs Brown, but leaving that aside, I am interested in the items that you said you saw. Describe them again for me so that PC King here can make notes."

Mildred once again described the items in as much detail as she could remember. She had a good memory, especially for pretty things and some of the things in the boxes had been extremely pretty. She couldn't help but notice that DS Jones seemed to be getting very excited and kept exchanging glances with the constable. She wondered if there was something going on between them. They did make a very handsome couple. Later she would ask Herbert what he thought. She caught sight of Herbert's face then and decided that she would probably wait until he had calmed down a little.

"Is there something special about those items?" she asked as innocently as possible.

"No, no, just trying to get as much information as possible. The bigger picture you know."

"What about Bob Pargeter's death? Do you still think it was an accident?"

At this point, a thought struck her, so she added, "Of course his mate Michael Burns died on Swinston Bank a few weeks ago, and that was supposed to be an accident.

"I really cannot comment on that. I will take your observations back to the station and we will continue to investigate. Now can I please ask you to keep away from Ms Smith and under no circumstances should you repeat this conversation to anyone else. Do I make myself clear?"

A very chastened Mildred nodded her agreement. It wasn't likely that she would be talking to Emily anytime soon. Considering the way Herbert was glaring at her, she didn't think she would be out of his sight long enough to talk to anybody. Mildred wasn't afraid of Herbert, but she knew she had seriously overstepped the mark. She probably could have kept quiet about the whole thing but some gut feeling still told her that it was important and she was glad she had told the police.

Meanwhile Herbert was shaking DS Jones' hand and promising to keep her out of trouble. Mildred, of course was a sadly shaken apologetic self and Herbert knew she meant it, until the next time. As the police left the house, Herbert saw them speak to each other and laugh. He couldn't hear what they were saying.

Meanwhile Mildred was sitting quietly in the conservatory nursing her now cold cup of coffee. Herbert was pacing back and forth ranting about how stupid Mildred had been. He didn't care about Emily or what she might have done. She could steal the crown jewels for all he cared. He cared about Mildred and she didn't seem to realise what being found guilty of breaking and entering could entail. In her defence, Mildred pointed out that she had used the keys, she hadn't broken in to anything. Herbert spoke slowly and quietly as though he were talking to a child. He reminded her that she was not supposed to have any keys and certainly not supposed to use them.

Mildred interrupted to tell him how sorry she was. She knew she should not have taken the key or pried into Emily's things. That was very wrong. Mildred stopped, and a faraway look came into her eyes, remembering how interested the police were in those things that she had found. She wondered if they were stolen; if Emily stole them.

Herbert took Mildred by the shoulders and gave her a little shake. He looked at her searchingly. He did not want anything to happen to her. They were supposed to be enjoying their retirement. That couldn't happen if she was in prison or worse, in hospital. He needed her to promise here and now that she would leave this alone and let the police do their jobs. Mildred had never seen Herbert so intense. She finally realised how worried he was. Eventually she promised not talk to anyone about it, nor go around to Emily's ever again. Herbert gave Mildred a relieved hug. As she hugged him back, she uncrossed her fingers and thought "but I didn't say I would stop investigating"

The two police officers were privately askance at Mildred's nerve in taking a key and trying it out. DS Jones shook his head in disbelief but they both found the descriptions she gave to be of great interest. Their only problem was how they could use that information seeing as how they were not supposed to know about any of it.

DS Jones could not think of any link between Emily Smith and Bob Pargeter but asked for check on them to see if anything had been missed. There had to be a link somewhere. They had always suspected that Bob dabbled in stolen goods, just never caught him with any. Arriving at the station, DS Jones stopped with his hand on the car door. He looked thoughtful. Focussing on how to find grounds for a search warrant, he came up with a bit of a long shot, and they headed for the pathology lab.

DS Jones and Alice King arrived at the lab just as the pathologist, David Williams, was leaving for lunch, having just completed the autopsy on Bob Pargeter.

Alan Jones was keen to find if there was anything unusual. He needed to know if his injuries were consistent with what was initially thought to be an accident, pulling the cupboard over on top of himself. He stressed that the answer was important.

David resignedly returned to his office, commenting that he supposed his sandwich could wait a little longer. Alan Jones followed the coroner into his office and watched as he took his notes out of a locked drawer. He watched as he scanned the notes muttering to himself as he did so.

"Mmm, injuries consistent with being crushed by a heavy weight, oh yes, now that was interesting…." David paused and looked over at Alan.

"Anything you want to tell me?"

"No, but I would guess that there is something you want to tell me."

"Your man had an occipital skull fracture. Now, while that can be caused by an accidental fall or hitting his head as he fell, there was nothing at the scene to suggest that he had hit it when he fell. I was going to note that as an anomaly."

"Could he have been hit with something else first?"

"Certainly. There was evidence of minor bleeding around the wound so he didn't live very long after he was hit or hit his head."

"What sort of weapon would you need to cause an injury like that?"

"Judging by the size of the wound, I would say something about six to seven centimetres wide and at least ten to fifteen centimetres long, possibly longer."

"So, a stick, or a piece of timber perhaps."

David shook his head. "No, a piece of timber has sharp, square edges. This was something rounded. If I had to hazard a guess, I would say a baseball bat would do quite well. You wouldn't have to be that strong either. A baseball bat gathers a fair bit of momentum when it is swung. Hit somebody on the head with that and they are not getting up again."

"So, not an accidental death then?"

"Not in my opinion, no. He was struck with something that is no longer at the scene. Looks like you have another murder to deal with, my friend." David looked disgustingly cheerful as he imparted this news.

Alan Jones turned to Alice King who had been standing quietly by, listening. She had never been into the pathology lab before and had been afraid she might see dead bodies. They now needed to find some grounds for a search warrant and let Mrs Brown off the hook. Although not sure she deserved it, her information had been useful.

When they got back to the station, DS Jones told Alice to grab some lunch then check out Emily Smith and Bob Pargeter. He also suggested she follow up with the SOCO's to see what came back from fingerprint evidence. As she went off to do that, he prepared himself to face his DI who was not going to like what he had to tell him.

DI Tom Allenby was not amused.

"She did what?" yelled DI Tom Allenby. "She found keys and had a snoop around. I've a good mind to arrest the woman right now."

He took a deep breath. He trusted Alan Jones' instincts. If he thought there was something in this, then he was most likely right. "Go on then, what did she see?" He sat back and listened.

When Alan had finished describing the items that Mildred had seen in the boxes, he became quite animated. He opened a drawer and took out a file. Inside were photographs of clocks and ornaments that bore a striking resemblance to the ones Mildred had described. The two men went down the list matching photographs to descriptions.

"Well, well, I've been wondering where these little beauties disappeared to. We thought they would surface eventually, but I never thought a nosy neighbour would find them. You know we can't use this information? Not without throwing Mrs Brown to the wolves?"

"I know. I've got Alice King looking into Emily Smith and Bob Pargeter. If we can find any link at all, we might be able to get a search warrant and then we can spare Mrs Brown. I know she was wrong but her instincts were spot on. She could have just saved us months of work."

A knock on the door interrupted him. A very excited Alice King came into room clutching some print outs. Alice put the sheets of paper down on the desk and stood back as the two men read the reports in front of them. Within minutes the men realised they had enough for a search warrant. Congratulating Alice on her work, they agreed to move quickly and organize a search team.

Alice beamed as she gathered up the papers; the ones that showed that Emily Smith had once been Emily Pargeter, wife of the dead Bob Pargeter. They had divorced some five years ago, around the time that Emily had moved into the area. By itself, it wasn't a lot, but coupled with fact that Emily's fingerprints had been found at the scene of the crime it gave them grounds for a search warrant. Now they just had to hope that Emily hadn't been made suspicious and had moved the goods. She hoped Mildred had listened to the DS when he told her to keep away.

Within the hour, a search warrant had been obtained and a team put together. Mildred and Herbert were surprised to see police cars pulling up to Emily's house and men entering the house by force. After what seemed an age, they were rewarded by the sight of men emerging carrying the boxes that Mildred had seen. There was no sign of Emily, however. Mildred was surprised about that, as it was past the time that she usually returned from work. Standing in the window, she saw DS Jones coming up the path. She went to open the door, convinced he was coming to arrest her.

"Don't worry, I haven't come for you, although you are a very lucky lady. My DI did want to arrest you. "

"Am I still in trouble?"

"No, you're not. We found grounds for a search warrant so your part in this need never come out. I don't have to remind you though, that if I hear that you have breathed a word of this, I will be back for you. I need you to be really clear about this. One false word and we could lose our whole case."

Mildred was so relieved. She vowed there and then never to get involved with anything that didn't concern her. She certainly wouldn't be talking about this to anyone. At least, not until it was all over.

"Have you arrested Emily then?" she asked.

"Not yet, I have left someone at the house. We will pick her up when she comes home."

"But she is usually home by now" said Mildred. "She's never later than this."

She was surprised when DS Jones turned and ran down the drive. Shouting to his men as he went, to put out a call to all airports, ferries railway stations and bus stations. He wanted that woman stopped if she tried to leave the country. The rest of his words were lost as he jumped into his car and drove away.

Mildred was left with another mystery. Where had Emily gone?

Revenge is sweet

Maxine Patterson

Arthur's exultation energised him as he swept out of the heavy glass doors of the quiet, secluded country hotel. He'd chosen the venue carefully because it was discreet. An ideal setting for him to complete the deal he'd been planning and working on for nearly nine months. This was the final section of the deal, while he took control of the board and liquidated the assets; complicated but oh so profitable. It had been a stormy meeting, but he was used to that. He wasn't in business to make friends. He didn't need friends, they were an encumbrance. He liked his small tightly knit, handpicked team that were paid just enough to ensure their loyalty. Michael his p.a. and of course Gloria, his wife. He had them exactly where he wanted them, under his control.

Looking across the car park, he could see his Bentley tucked away in the corner. He liked to make a statement about his business power and wealth; but he didn't care to flaunt it too openly. He adjusted the jacket of his Italian silk suit, carefully smoothing down the creases in his jacket where he'd been sitting. The warm glow of success bubbling inside him, he strode back to the car to find that Michael had moved into the driving seat.

It was unusual for Michael to offer to drive, but he was happy to oblige this time. He tried the passenger door handle. But it didn't open. He tried again, pulling vigorously. Bending down, he looked through the car window towards Michael who stared straight ahead, a smile on his face. Arthur suddenly realised he had locked the door.

He rapped imperiously on the on the window and shouted, "For God's sake Michael, open the door! It's bloody freezing out here"

He turned slowly and looked directly into his eyes, but this time there was no smile, no acquiescence, just a hard, cold stare. Michael savoured the moment, the power he now had over Arthur, though he didn't know quite how much, just yet! He enjoyed allowing his utter contempt for him, his so-called business, and his handmade suits and of course, his car to finally show. Those feelings which he had had to disguise for such a long time while he and Gloria worked out the fine details of their "'get even' plan. He stretched his hands and caressed the finest leather that covered the steering wheel; how exquisite. Here he was sitting inside the thing that Arthur loved the most! Yes, his Bentley! Michael revelled in the absolute power of the moment.

Arthur stopped shouting; what on earth was he playing at? His feeling of euphoria slowly evaporating. He needed to be in the car and away. "Michael, open the door!" slightly more urgently now, getting irritated. He couldn't accept that this was happening. He had it all planned. His biggest coup yet and Michael was staring at him. He was his assistant, which involved him doing what he was told and helping him swing deals and charm the gullible saps that he dealt with.

Yet here he was, sitting staring at him! What on earth was going on? He was bewildered. Incredulous, what the hell was going on?

He had allowed himself the luxury of letting his relationship with Michael to develop outside the business. It made sense, he made his life so much easier. He was always there, sorting out his diary, checking his finances, making sure his business deals went smoothly, keeping his wife sweet. And what a charmer, he was able to complement Arthur's brusque directness, business had taken off since Michael had been appointed. He enjoyed his company at work and outside. With Michael beside him, he was able to relax knowing that everything was taken care of.

Arthur instinctively fumbled to get his phone. But he hadn't got his coat with him. Instead the cashmere camel overcoat lay strewn across the expensive leather seats of his car!

Enraged, he rapped vigorously on the window; he tried to manoeuvre round so that he could look at Michael's face through the front windscreen while still rapping on the side window. Leaning against the bodywork of the car, the cold began to seep through his suit jacket. Best Italian silk cashmere looked good, but it was no good in the winter chill.

He didn't move! He just sat, like a statue with a faint smile, or was that a smirk? What was going on?

Desperate now to get out of the cold, he realised that the others from the meeting would be coming out soon. Bloody hell! The meeting! He'd finalised yet another 'deal.' Not his fault if people didn't have enough equity to safeguard their investments. He was just there to manipulate the share price and push things along. Make sure that he got the lion's share of the assets that were left. What he didn't need was for those same people that he'd shafted just a few minutes ago to come out and see him in this situation.

Really furious, he yelled again and kicked the tyre in frustration. He was ignoring him! How dare he!

Michael's enjoyment was clear. Slowly he got his iPhone out of his pocket, distractedly Arthur noticed that Michael's suit was just like his, and the phone, wasn't that the latest model? Looking straight at Arthur he tapped in the home page for HMRC, then turned the phone around to show Arthur through the windscreen.

Stunned, he stopped shouting and just stared. He couldn't understand what was happening. Arthur - The wheeler dealer- was utterly out of his depth.

"No, no! Don't do that! Michael please, don't...." The last thing Arthur needed was HMRC and press nosing around the hotel and finding out about the deal.

Michael fixing Arthur's eyes with a steely glint, closed the screen. Arthur got ready to shout again, but Michael just shook his head. What? What the hell was going on?

"Michael, please. It's freezing out here. Please let me in the car."

Michael enjoyed the pleading and begging – something very new in his dealings with Arthur. But the novelty of the situation couldn't be allowed to hinder the plan.

Oh yes – the plan! It had taken so much time to work out how to unpick Arthur's financial dealings. When he had contacted Gloria he had expected rejection, but Gloria, once she understood what Michael was offering had encouraged him and offered further information about Arthur's monetary dealings. He must have thought he was so clever keeping separate financial accounts with his wife and various businesses.

But, Arthur would never be able to bully and belittle either of them, in fact if they got it right Arthur would not be able to speak to them again. He would be totally out of their lives.

Indulgently he allowed himself to feel just a little sorry for him. Poor Arthur wouldn't know what hit him! Instead he phoned for a taxi. Not for him, but for 'poor' Arthur, I mean it was cold outside and he didn't want him to catch a cold, not physically anyway. The financial cold was going to be quite enough of a shock to his system.

Arthur was by now utterly bewildered, disconcerted and confused. How could Michael behave like this? He was his partner, well not quite, but he knew everything. Unable to process this dramatic event, he just stood. Something bad was happening! He didn't know what and he didn't know why. But not Michael – what was he playing at? Anyway - he wasn't going to think about it now. He just needed to get back in the car.

What was Michael saying? Taxi? Who needed a taxi? Why?

His aggression overwhelmed his caution and stuttering with rage he began to threaten Michael stalking around the front of the car. Just wait until he got into that car- he'd sort this out! Bloody taxi! He'd got the latest model Bentley, what did he need a taxi for?

Michael was holding up the phone again, a call from Gloria? What the hell was his wife calling him for? He banged on the window again – "let me speak to Gloria!"

Michael slowly shook his head again, whilst having an animated conversation with Gloria. What the hell was there for Michael and Gloria to talk about? Michael was smiling and laughing.

Arthur's sixth sense began to twitch. This couldn't be happening. Michael and Gloria? Michael looking at him and laughing! Telling Gloria all about him stuck outside his car – and laughing and laughing.

No, this couldn't be happening! Arthur was incandescent. He couldn't have people laughing at him, especially not his Michael. He was supposed to be his assistant; he was supposed to do as he was told. What the f. was happening?

The hotel door opened, and Arthur's ex business associates began to leave the building. Arthur straightened up; he didn't want anyone to see what was happening. He had a reputation to maintain. He couldn't afford to be seen to be arguing with his secretary through the car window. So, when the taxi drew up behind the Bentley, Arthur moved towards it. He'd sort this out later and Michael would pay! Oh yes! The taxi driver confirmed the destination - the airport! Arthur stood incredulous! Airport? But the taxi driver passed out a folder and sure enough there was his passport and a ticket to Argentina!

Arthur straightened up, he could hear the footsteps getting closer now. That was the last thing he needed to be seen in this situation by the clowns he he'd just 'dealt' with.

The voices were harsh and aggressive; "Another bloody deal to complete then Arthur? Another business to asset strip?" The voices were coming closer.

Arthur overwhelmed, climbed into the taxi. He couldn't face them now! He had to find out what had happened. Why had Michael and Gloria arranged this.

Everything had changed! Before he was in charge, he knew exactly what he was doing! Now bloody Michael was playing silly beggars and as for Argentina – well!

The driver turned and handed Arthur a phone; it was surreal, like something off the telly! Almost immediately it rang. It was Gloria "Hello Arthur, just to let you know there's a case packed in the boot, it's got everything you'll need."

"Gloria! What's going on?" Taking a breath, he began to bluster, "I can't just go to Argentina, I've got the next deal to finalise. How on earth do you think I can go to Argentina?"

"Oh, I think you can. Michael and I have been very busy!"

Stunned Arthur shouted, "What? You and Michael? What do you mean, very busy?"

Gloria's voice had an unusual confidence, "You know Arthur; you're so boring when you keep repeating what people have said! You'll find that what was your business is…"

Blustering Arthur interrupted, "what the hell do you mean was my business? What the hell's going on? Don't be so bloody stupid, I'm coming home; you can't do this to me?"

"I'm so sorry Arthur!" Gloria tried to stifle the giggle.

Arthur, by now apoplectic "Sorry? Sorry? You'll be bloody sorry!" By now the taxi was half way down the hotel drive, followed by Arthur's Bentley purring along behind him.

Gloria's voice had a new depth and power, strength that he had never heard before; "you see Arthur, your business has kind of, been taken over! Michael and I are the new owners. You chose to put the business in my name as a tax avoidance scam, so we just regularised the business. However, while we were checking our investments we've found some irregularities in the accounting system!"

Arthur by now totally overwhelmed by the complete reversal of the evening spluttered. "What? But... ? Taken over....?"

Gloria's voice took on a honeyed tone soothing the final poisonous coup de grace. "Arthur dear, do try to stop being so repetitive, it's not attractive in a man! As I said your business no longer exists. And if you fail to get on that plane to Argentina this evening, Michael and I will be forced, reluctantly of course, to contact the Fraud Squad!"

Arthur's anger and frustration boiled over and he was grabbed by the familiar tightening in his chest as the angina began to stifle his breathing. Unable to speak, he slowly subsided backwards into the taxi seat to be taken on his journey to the airport.

Michael carefully driving the Bentley, watched the taxi turn on to the main road leading towards the airport. With a grin, he steered the car towards Arthur's house to meet with Gloria. The plan had worked!

Body Double

Jan Jenner

Henry put his hand in his pocket for his keys. He was looking forward to sitting down with a cup of tea, a couple of ginger biscuits and the crossword. It was one of the perks of retirement. Instead of the familiar feel of his key ring he felt the rustle of paper.

His heart sank as he read the spidery writing scrawled between the pale blue lines.

He hadn't thought much about it when an old man stumbled and bumped into him while he waited in the queue for his newspaper. He hadn't recognised him.

Nothing happened by chance, not in his world anyway.

The sombre notes of the funeral march sounded from his pocket. Still looking at the note he pulled out a small mobile phone and pressed a key. The dirge stopped as he lifted the phone to his ear and barked yes into the mouthpiece.

The young well-educated, voice greeted him impatiently. Jimmy Meade was always impatient.

"You're needed tonight." He told him.

"Short notice." Henry said.

"Only came in ten minutes ago," Jimmy explained.

"Will it be just the two of us?" Henry asked.

"Yes, of course, always just the two of you. Nothing has changed I take it?" Jimmy asked as an afterthought.

"No," Henry grunted, he listened to further instructions before hanging up.

Morgan had her hand on the door handle of the battered green mini when her phone rang.

Life hadn't been going the way she planned, she was taking a year out to write a novel but after a prolonged bout of writers block she was thinking it might be time to give it up. When she put her phone back in her pocket she was smiling.

When Henry put his phone down he was frowning. He stood for a few minutes looking out of his window at a blackbird scurrying around the garden, his bright yellow beak flamboyant against the dark black feathers.

If only my life was that simple, he thought.

He would like to be a blackbird. No worries about fading pensions and leaking roofs.

He made a cup of tea and looked longingly at his paper, but it was no good he wouldn't be able to concentrate on it not now. He put his empty cup in the sink and left the flat

He caught the bus to a backstreet in Chelsea just off Kings Road.

A bell rang as he pushed open the door to a dark rundown shop.

An old man came slowly out from behind a curtain. His lined face creased in a warm smile as he recognised Henry.

"Hello, my old friend, you have another assignment."

Henry shrugged his shoulders in embarrassment.

"Hello Sampson, I've been meaning to come by but somehow things......." his voice trailed off and he shrugged his shoulders

"Don't worry Henry, don't worry." Sampson came around the counter and shook Henry's hand warmly.

"What is it you want, white tropical suit, dinner jacket? How can I help my old friend?"

Henry sighed and explained what he needed and thirty minutes later left the shop with a parcel under his arm and the laughter of his friend ringing in his ears.

This would be the last time. He promised himself.

She sighed in delight as the gorgeous soft folds of fabric tumbled through her fingers. She adored the expensive feel of silk especially when she wasn't paying for it.

Two hours later she'd tried on six dresses and finally made her choice. She looked in the mirror, her tall slim figure encased in dark green shimmering silk really looked the part, it would be perfect.

At the prospect of the well-paid assignment she called a taxi to take her back to her flat.

She took the dress and hung it up ready for the evening then she picked up her mobile.

"I've arranged the limo to collect you at 9: 30 that gives you time to pick me up about 9:45. It should be a good evening ".

"Depends on what you call good evening I suppose," he grumbled.

"Relax Henry." She laughed. "It'll be good fun."

"Right," he said and ended the call.

Morgan chuckled it was not the role Henry enjoyed playing. They'd first met six months ago when she had joined a body double agency. They'd worked together several times, he was the perfect build for a bodyguard and she bore an uncanny likeness to Bryanna Castillo the opera singer who spent more time on the front page of the tabloids that she did onstage.

She wondered what Bryanna Castillo would be doing this evening. She was standing in for her at a small celebrity party at the Hilton. She loved everything about these parties, mixing with celebrities, flouncing around playing the superstar diva, wearing expensive clothes and she enjoyed the money she would get for doing it.

Henry caught the bus back to his flat he threw his parcel unceremoniously on to the bed and put the kettle on to make tea. He was getting too old for this. He had never enjoyed dressing up in a dinner jacket and acting like some overgrown teenage thug and he hated having to snarl at everybody. But that was the image he was getting paid to portray.

He looked at his watch he had hours yet before he had to leave. It was good money that was the only reason he did it. He took his tea out into the garden and sat down on a wooden bench underneath a magnolia tree. He loved this garden the flat was dark, damp and expensive but it had the garden. it's why he stayed.

He took the piece of paper from his pocket and spread it out on the table while he sipped his tea.

He could have done without this complication.

He finished his tea and leaving the flat took the tube to Hyde Park. He strolled across the grass through the hordes of tourists until he came to the Serpentine then he stopped and sat on the bench facing West. The bench been there many years, what they would do if it was ever moved, he'd no idea.

Eventually a smart young man dressed in a dark suit sat down beside him. He took a packet of sandwiches and a newspaper from his briefcase and began to eat his lunch.

"This weather is due to go on for another two weeks." He said without looking up at Henry.

"Yes, I saw that forecast as well," replied Henry.

The young man turned and smiled at him.

"Good to meet you," he said.

"What's going on?" asked Henry. "I'm supposed to be retired."

"There was no one else we could call that fitted the bill."

"Why on earth not?"

"You work with Morgan Freeman."

"What has Morgan got to do with it?"

In reply the young man smiled. Then he picked up his briefcase and nodded to Henry before walking off across the grass towards Paddington.

Henry picked up the newspaper he'd left and the envelope concealed in it and made his way back to the tube station.

When the doorbell rang at 9:43 Morgan opened the door and Henry greeted her with a low whistle. "Better than the real thing," he said. "You ready?"

"I sure am." She grinned at him. "You look good too."

"Yeah right," he grunted.

They arrived at the Hilton and were shown into a room at the back of the building with doors opening onto the garden lit with thousands of small white lights.

It was the usual collection of celebrities and her reputation as an unapproachable diva kept most of them at arm's length which suited her. Letting someone get too close could lead to mistakes and that could lead to embarrassment. Making idle lightweight chatter and sipping ice-cold champagne was all she had to do. Henry stayed as close as he could, looking like the hard man he was supposed to be. Bryanna Castillo went nowhere without a bodyguard.

Towards midnight she was beginning to tire. She caught Henry's eye and indicated the door. He followed her as she went to look for a restroom to freshen her make up. Instead of going to the restroom set aside for the celebrities she went down a small flight of stairs and found a smaller empty restroom that way she wouldn't have to make conversation. Henry stood outside to wait.

When she came out, Henry was nowhere to be seen. She returned to the main hall, but the door was closed and two security men standing outside.

"Sorry," the tallest of them said. "You can't go in there, there has been an incident."

"Where is everybody?" She asked.

"Everybody's moved to the Nelson suite," the security guard smiled at her reassuringly. "Come on, I'll show you."

He led her down the corridor and up a flight of stairs into a small room where a group of people she didn't recognise were standing around looking disgruntled at having their evening ruined. She scanned the people in the room, but Henry wasn't there.

"Where is my bodyguard?" She asked the security guard as he turned to leave.

He shrugged. "Sorry no idea."

Without the comforting presence of Henry, she found her ability to play the Diva had left her and she stood with her back to the wall feeling out of her depth.

The door opened, and a tall dark-haired man came in she recognised him as Toby Benson a well-known TV producer. He came over to her and smiled reassuringly. "Even the Hilton has its problems."

"Looks like it." She said.

"I never miss one of your concerts." Toby told her.

"Is that right?" she asked sceptically. Everyone said the same thing.

He raised an eyebrow and grinned.

She laughed reluctantly and looked around for Henry hoping he would appear. She didn't like one to one conversations.

"Are you all right?" he asked and when she shook her head he led her to a quiet corner and found a chair for her to sit on.

"Do you know what happened?" she asked.

"Some idiot running around with a gun I think."

"What a gun in the Hilton?"

"Nowhere is off-limits these days. Don't worry, they'll find him"

"Where has everybody else gone?" She asked. "I can't find my bodyguard."

"Most of the other high-profile celebs were ushered away as soon as the alarm when out."

She pulled a face at him. "My fault," she said. "I went walk about."

"Never mind it will get sorted in a while."

She yawned. "I hope so, then we can all go home." She was tired, she'd drunk too much and now she just wanted to go home and go to bed.

A waiter came in with trays of coffee, tea and other refreshments. Toby went over and asked him what was going on.

"No idea Sir. I believe we have an unauthorised person on the premises. Nobody is allowed to leave the building."

"How long are they going to keep us here?"

"I'm sorry sir I don't know, they have police guarding the stairways and the lifts, I can't even access the main kitchen, I had to use the staff restroom to prepare this." he pointed to the trays of tea and coffee.

Toby grabbed two cups of coffee and took them back to Morgan and they sat in silence.

Eventually the door opened and the manager came into the room followed by a police officer.

"I apologise for the inconvenience ladies and gentlemen. The incident has been resolved and you are now free to go home."

"I'll say goodbye." Tony kissed Morgan's hand and gave a small bow. "I should be allowed back into my suite now."

Morgan followed the others out of the room and they were taken down a rear staircase and out into the street where ranks of taxis were waiting patiently.

The next morning, she was woken by the ringing of her mobile phone.

"What happened last night? Are you ok?" came the anxious voice of Jimmy Meade. "The media is buzzing."

"I'm fine, I'm not sure what happened. We weren't told much. Have you heard from Henry? He disappeared."

"No, I haven't," Said Jimmy. "Let me know if you hear from him will you." She promised Jimmy she would and switched on her TV.

The story about a deranged man seen running through the Hilton carrying a handgun with a rifle slung over a shoulder was all over the news.

She was sitting down to coffee and toast when her phone rang again, it was Henry.

"Where did you get to last night?"

"I'm sorry I was ushered away by the police and kept in a small room. He told her apologetically.

"Just as well you weren't my real body guard, or you'd be looking for a new job.' She grumbled.

Having placated Morgan Henry made another call.

"Next time, why not just phone me instead of playing infantile games with bits of paper."

The man on the other end of the line chuckled. "It all adds to the fun of life doesn't it. The great rich tapestry of our existence. Surely you know phones can be compromised but the simple note slipped in a pocket is discrete. I enjoyed the show you put on last night I'm assuming the gunman was your invention. Rather an elaborate ploy just to search a room wasn't it?"

"He has a suite."

"So, tell me what did you find out?"

"Nothing much. He's too clever to leave anything incriminating in a hotel bedroom but I've left a couple of tracking devices that should keep him on radar."

Three days later Morgan had a phone call.

"Are you feeling better now?" asked Toby Benson

"How did you get this number?" She said.

He laughed. "A bit of research, it was obvious you weren't Bryanna Castillo."

"Oh, I thought I was doing a good job."

"You were doing a splendid job, but you don't have quite the degree of arrogance necessary to pull it off."

"I'll take that as a compliment," she said.

"Can we meet for dinner?"

She smiled as she put the phone down, he was picking her up at eight o'clock.

Just after 8 o'clock that evening Henry sat in the front seat of a hired car and watched as Morgan climbed into Toby Benson's car.

His phone rang.

"What's happening?"

"He's just left for an evening out with Morgan."

"How on earth did that happen?"

"I have no idea. I was busy last night if you remember."

"Are you going to follow them?"

"Already am. Nothing will happen tonight."

"Probably not. Does he know it's Morgan and not Bryanna Castillo?"

"Yes of course, he picked her up from Morgan's flat. Who's watching Castillo?"

"We have around-the-clock teams watching her. Nobody will get near her."

Henry followed them discreetly to a small well-known restaurant in Chelsea then sat in the car and waited. He had worked with some very high-profile people over the years but he had never been involved in anything with so much potential for disaster.

Morgan looked around the restaurant gleefully she had never been here before, but she read about it. She recognised several famous faces.

The prices on the menu were eye watering.

"How did you end up in the body double business?" Tony asked her with a smile.

"People kept telling me I looked like Bryanna, so I contacted Premium Stars Agency."

"And the rest is history I suppose." he smiled.

"Yes, that's right. It's good fun and I get to go to interesting places like the Hilton and I get paid for it."

"You do look very like Bryanna, it's uncanny."

"Yes, that's a lucky break."

"How long have you been doing it?" He asked.

"Not long, about six months. I'm a writer. I've taken a year off to write a book. The work from the agency just helps to pay the bills."

"How often do you stand in for Bryanna?"

"Sometimes once a month, sometimes not very often if she is abroad, more's the pity." She grinned.

"Bryanna is appearing in one of my concerts on Saturday." He told her.

"I didn't realise you put on concerts. I thought you were just a TV producer."

"I have a finger in many pies," he told her laughing. "Would you like to come?"

"Yes, I'd love to."

"Rumour has it that she is going to a concert with him."

Henry sat up in bed and rubbed his hand over his face trying to get his brain focused. "Do you always make phone calls this early?" he asked.

"Only when it's important,"

"Ok, tell me all." Henry said,

When Henry put his mobile down his face was serious.

He was going solo on this job.

Morgan woke early on Saturday with a delicious feeling of anticipation. She would spend the morning writing and then after lunch she would go for a manicure and mini make over at elaine's.

"You going anywhere special tonight, then?" asked the young girl washing her hair.

"I'm not sure. It might turn out to be special."

She was looking forward to the concert in the evening. There were going to be a lot of famous people there. Even the president of the United States.

She liked Toby, he was different to the usual no hopers she dated, she knew he was out of her league. She wondered briefly why he'd asked her out.

Never one to worry unduly she relaxed while her hair, nails, and face were pampered.

The doorbell rang prompt on seven o'clock.

"You look spectacular." Tony said as he led her down to waiting car.

They waited while their security passes were checked. She tried not to look star struck as she saw the famous faces in the hospitality lounge. Only a small group of guests would be allowed backstage to meet the President.

The concert went without a hitch. While the 21-piece orchestra was playing the American National Anthem at the end in the Presidents honour, Tony surreptitiously took a message on his phone. She heard him swear softly.

"What's the matter?" she whispered.

"Your look-a-like is playing the diva act."

"What do you mean?"

"Bryanna is refusing to meet the President, says she has a headache and wants to go home. He's only here to meet her. Though why god only knows why." He looked thoughtfully at her. "I don't suppose…No, it would be too much to ask.

"What?"

"I don't suppose you could stand in for her one more time, could you?"

"In front of the President?" she gasped. "He would guess I don't have the makeup or the wig.?"

"My make girls are back stage they can work magic. It would only be for a short while. There are just a select few, all vetted by the US security, she's even got special clearance for her bodyguard. The woman is paranoid. It would really get me out of a hole."

Morgan stood in a line with the other celebrities. Bryanna's body guard was standing behind her trying to look inconspicuous. There was a sudden movement around her and the hum of conversation stopped. He was coming.

The doors opened and out of the corner of her eye she saw Bryanna's body guard move to one side and put his hand inside his jacket.

It was then that all hell broke out.

"I hope Bryanna is ok?" Morgan took a bite out of a piece of toast. She was sitting in a café in King's Road with Henry.

"Probably fine."

"She must have been frightened."

"Well, not much fun being kidnapped."

"Who was the bodyguard?"

"Someone pulled in by Toby Benson."

"I liked him, I thought he liked me."

"You were too good for him Morgan.'

Morgan smiled at him. "What were you doing there anyway? I wouldn't have thought it was quite your cup of tea?"

"My grand daughter's birthday treat."

"I'm glad you were there, I still don't know how you managed to persuade them to let me go home."

"I must have a natural authority." He finished his coffee and stood up. "I must be off."

"Yeah," she grinned at him. "Maybe we'll be working together again once things settle down."

"Think I might be getting too old for it."

Morgan watched him walk out of the café. She liked the old feller. He was such a kind man.

"Is the girl ok?"

"Henry shifted the phone to his other ear and took a sip of coffee. "Yes, she's fine. I met her for coffee earlier."

"Didn't guess?"

"No told her it was my granddaughters birthday treat. How was Bryanna?"

"Ok, not hurt. They bundled her and her bodyguard into a lorry and left it parked in a layby on the M1. Traffic cops found it early this morning. She's talking about suing everyone from the theatre owners to the president."

"And Benson?"

"Ah Benson. He'll be going down for a long time. As well as his friend the bodyguard. You did well."

Choosing a Colour

Muriel Claybrook

Twenty-five years ago they'd had the extension built and furnished the sitting room. They both loved the ten-metre-long room with windows to the front and rear, and only because of fading upholstery colours, wearing sofa arms and thinning carpet pile had they decided it was now the time for a revamp. George wanted to do the decorating himself but also wanted to change the fireplace. Both Lynne and he knew it would take many weeks, but it was summer, and they could always go on holiday and then come back to it later.

The new upholstery had already been ordered and they were excited by their choice – a fawn sofa and one matching armchair and also a floral swivel chair and matching foot stool. The fabric for these last two was very bold: large purple and blue flowers with lime green leaves. Once the new fire place was installed the couple began planning the colour scheme for decorating.

Their taste was verging on minimalist and they had decided all the walls except the chimney breast would be white. In practice choosing "white" was not as straight forward as it seemed. They chose five shades of white and painted thirty cm rectangles of each shade on two walls that caught different amounts of light.

Finally, brilliant white was chosen, and all the walls were painted except the chimney breast. Lime green, of the same hue as in the floral fabric would be stylish for that, but it was time now for the week's holiday and they could possibly ponder this while they were away in Suffolk. The room was tidied up and all the decorating gear moved to the garage and shed

A timbered cottage in Lavenham was their destination. Inside the old property had been tastefully remodelled. The living room ceiling was the full height of the house and the bedroom was on a mezzanine floor over the kitchen. A half spiral wooden staircase led from the kitchen lobby to the bedroom and had been painted a lovely shade of linden green. Lynne's arthritic knee made climbing the stairs painful, especially as for a hand rail there was a length of thick rope, attached to the wall with brass fittings.

The cottage windows were small and to compensate the walls were painted white. The timbers visible outside were also present on the inside walls. Though not cluttered these were hung with prints, faux antique maps, and copper utensils. At the back of the cottage was a private walled garden. Judging from its hard landscaping, choice of planting and design it had been done professionally and was a delightful space.

It was the end of July and most days were hot and sunny. It was a pleasure for Lynne to water the herbs, roses, petunias and geraniums in the mornings. There were two permanent seating areas in different shapes and types of stone.

On an evening, coming back from excursions to the coast, Flatford or Bury St. Edmunds, it was relaxing to sit outside with a glass of wine.

Towards the end of the week, while reading the paper and doing the crossword, Lynne and George were savouring the balmy evening air as they drank their Merlot. There was a bistro next door and convivial voices drifted out through the open windows and across the car park that separated the cottage and the bistro. Lavenham is a tourist magnet and all the pubs, hotels and restaurants had plenty of customers.

Before the light started to fade the couple decided on a constitutional walk up the hill to the square outside the Guildhall. They had followed the same route several times already and each time had discovered new aspects of the mediaeval buildings to enjoy. George loved to find examples of pargeting on the white plasterwork of some of the buildings and Lynne admired the burnt Sienna, rose and even green tints that some of the lopsided buildings had been given.

When they returned to the cottage, it was still warm and there was some light left so the couple gathered up their newspapers and wine from inside and returned to the garden. After twenty minutes or so it was dark enough for outside lights in the bistro car park to be frequently triggered by people crossing it. This seemed to be a good time to go indoors.

They had not locked the side entrance door when they went into the garden but surely, they hadn't left it ajar? They must be relaxing too much they both thought. Once inside it was a different story: two upturned chairs and prints askew on the walls. There had been an intruder. What about their own property? They were tourists and had not brought anything valuable with them. For a sneak thief, though, cameras, phones and electronic tablets would sell fast and raise required cash. These everyday essentials for the 21st century traveller had been left in open view and would have made easy pickings.

They started to move cautiously further into the cottage and when they were near the kitchen they felt a draught blowing down from the bedroom. George now started to shout as a warning to anyone who might be up there. Turning back to the wood burning stove he picked up a poker and cautiously mounted the stairs.

The pristine white surface of the bedspread was splattered with linden green paint. It had been flung from a can that now lay on the floor by the open window. A fire escape, rope ladder, normally kept in a metal box under the window, was now thrown over the window sill and dangled to the ground outside. Lynne smiled to herself. She had wanted to see how this escape route would work yet hoped they would not have to use it herself.

Now to the practicalities. First the police and then the cottage owners were called. There was a land line that could only be used to call the emergency services and the owners' home. The police were on site in ten minutes. While they waited for them to arrive George and Lynne had jotted down details of the property of their own that was missing. It was all electronic hand-held equipment. After about thirty minutes the owners arrived. They realised that two heavy brass candlesticks and a small wooden box, inlaid with fake ivory, were missing.

This burglary, to the police, was a petty crime and apart from testing for finger prints on the tables where the stolen items had been, and bagging up the paint can, no other forensic testing was done. The police left and Bob and Sally, the owners, suggested that their guests pack an overnight bag while they phoned to a pub they knew, on the outskirts of the town, to book them a room for the night. Lynne and George had planned a trip to Sudbury the next day and told the owners they would be back at the cottage by 5.00pm, realising they would also have to buy replacement items for their stolen property while they were in the town.

An hourly bus service, connecting Bury St Edmund's and Sudbury passed through Lavenham. George and Lynne had consulted the timetable for it and planned to use their bus passes for the journey. Fortunately, Lynne's handbag was well out of sight when the robbery occurred, and George's wallet was in his trouser pocket. This saved them the hassle of ordering replacement cash and credit cards. The double decker bus arrived on time and it had struck them on their last journey that this was an incongruous vehicle for small country lanes. The service was well used though, and they relaxed during the journey, enjoying the views from the top deck.

As usual in any unfamiliar town they visited, the first port of call in Sudbury was the tourist information office. The helpful staff recommended a visit to the Gainsborough House museum and after this the couple decided to follow a trail across the ancient water meadows.

After a reviving coffee in the stylish museum garden the couple set off for to reach the start of their meadow walk. Overlooking the river Stour, the trail began by following an old railway track. The trail way markers showed a kingfisher, but this part of the path was very shady with mature trees, on either side, overlapping to form an arch. Hopefully they may see a kingfisher when they reached the open water.

After a mile and a half, they arrived at a stile and climbed over it into the meadows. Then they stood and watched cautiously as a small herd of chestnut cattle were grazing on either side of the path they had to take. Several people passed by near to the cattle, either alone or in small groups, some with a dog on a lead, but the cattle hardly even looked up.

Reassured, Lynne and George started along the path across these ancient meadows. There were many types of wild flowers, but they did not see a kingfisher. They crossed several tributaries of the river and after the last footbridge the Mill Hotel with its mill pool were soon reached. It was past their usual lunch time and choosing an outdoor seat overlooking the meadows they enjoyed beer and sandwiches. If the warm sun and this glorious setting were not blissful enough, the site of a herd of about fifty cattle of varying ages walking purposefully towards the hotel was truly fabulous. They walked in a long column, two or three abreast and were near enough to the pub garden for the patrons to smell them and touch them, if anyone were to be so foolhardy.

Most of the cattle stopped to drink at the edge of the mill pool but fifteen or so strode out into the middle of the pool and three went right over to the far bank. How photogenic, with weeping willows framing the view; BUT they had not had time to buy replacement cameras yet.

Looking around at fellow tourists they noticed a very tall mousey-haired young man of about twenty two or so, with two instamatic cameras. George noticed they were Canons, like theirs. 'Unusual', he thought, 'for someone his age' as most of his peers used their phones for photos. He then began to take in as many details as possible of the young man. The stranger soon became aware, that he was under scrutiny. Smiling and walking nonchalantly, he rounded the corner of the hotel, crossed the busy road, and seemed to be heading to the town centre. All George could do was watch.

Back at the cottage the owners had some news: a neighbour had seen a tall young man run down their path last night, at the time of the robbery. He had been stuffing things into his pockets and was carrying a holdall. This had been reported to the police. George and Lynne shared their observations from Sudbury with the owners, and as their holiday was ending, they decided, philosophically, that they would chalk this episode up to experience.

Homeward bound, the next day, Lynne and George were individually thinking that it would be nice to see the pristine white walls that they had worked so hard on before they left. The sitting room's appearance did not disappoint, but Lynne said, "I think we'll ditch green for the chimney breast and choose a shade of purple instead".

"My thoughts entirely" agreed George.

The Photography Project

Jan Jenner

With his thumb in his mouth and his head on one side he stood there in the park looking at me quizzically. I scrolled the mouse wheel to zoom in on the photograph showing on my computer screen. He was a beautiful, blonde headed child with gorgeous deep green eyes. A couple of years younger than my son Danny, he was about three years old. He looked well fed and well cared for, but who was he?

I'd gone to the park after dropping Danny off at school. I wanted to work on the nature project I'd set for my art students, they were to photograph as many different plants as possible to make a collage. I'd decided to photograph trees.

I looked at the rest of the photographs I'd taken that morning, a silver birch. an oak, beech, rowan, and a majestic elm. Out of fifty photographs, the little boy was in three, each time standing in front of the large mature elm tree.

Trouble was, there wasn't an elm tree in the park. There hadn't been for thirty years, not since I was Danny's age. The last Elm had been lost to Dutch elm disease in 1987.

There hadn't been a little boy in the park either. I'd seen two middle-aged women strolling around the tree-lined paths with their elderly Labradors but once they'd left, I'd had the park to myself.

I turned back to the computer screen and selected the photographs I'd taken that day, I loaded paper into my printer and pressed the print button.

As the photographs churned out of the printer I spread them out on the old kitchen table tucked under the window that I laughingly called my desk.

I'd moved in to the flat just over six months ago after I split up with Danny's father. It was ideal, close to Danny's school and the park. And close to the university where I worked part-time as a lecturer in fine arts. I supplemented this with proofreading for a London agency. It all helped to pay the bills.

I could hear the faint sound of a Mozart symphony coming from the flat downstairs. Joseph was a quiet man, a widower, a lot older than me. He was always friendly and polite. He spent most of his time sitting in his flat listening to music. He was always happy to take in packages for me if I wasn't there.

When the printer finished I picked up the three photographs of the little boy and put them on my magnetic whiteboard. The little boy seemed familiar, a serious little face, he reminded me of someone, but I couldn't think who.

The next morning, I returned to the park and started taking more photographs, trying to remember where I'd stood the previous day. I checked the view finder each time, no elm tree and no little boy.

Back in the flat I took the SD card from the camera and slotted it into my laptop. Over a hundred photographs scrolled up my screen, the same trees, silver birch, oak, beech, rowan and the elm.

The little boy still had his thumb in his mouth, still had the same quizzical look on his face but this time he was clutching the hand of a young woman. Her eyes were sad, they looked straight at the camera and her lips parted as if she wanted to speak to me.

Who was she and what did she want to say? How did she manage to get into my camera?

I googled the area and added a filter to limit the entries to 1987.

Even with the filter I still had several thousand hits. After an hour of scanning the screen for anything that looked relevant, my mind was beginning to drift to the kitchen and coffee. Then I saw a short article from our local paper about a woman and a small boy who disappeared in the summer of 1987, I followed the links and discovered they'd vanished while she was taking him to nursery school, her husband had reported her missing in the evening when he came home from work.

The police launched an extensive search of the area but found nothing. They arrested the husband, but they never found the bodies and eventually the police released him with no charge and turned their attention to other cases. The press moved on to cover the removal of the last elm tree from the area, the one in our park. It took several days and a team of tree surgeons. It attracted a small degree of attention for a while but then the hole had been filled in and the wooden bench was installed there.

Later that evening after Danny was in bed I opened my laptop and printed out the new photographs of the little boy and the woman.

The last one had just finished when there was a knock on the door.

It was Joseph, he smiled and held up a parcel. 'This came while you were out,' he said.

It was work I'd been expecting from my agency. I reached out to take it from him just as the smile on his face froze. He was staring at the photographs on the board with those deep green eyes. I realised then who the boy reminded me of and what his mother had been trying to tell me.

Caring

Maxine Patterson

Emily drew up outside number 32, surprised to see a sleek looking motorbike parked directly outside the gate. She was even more surprised to see the gate open and a young man in black shiny leathers wearing a silver and blue helmet, standing at Mrs. James' door.

Mrs James was standing unsteadily in her doorway, propped up on her zimmer frame. As always, she looked bewildered and muddled. Emily, alarmed, was shocked out of her usual lethargy and ran up the path. "Excuse me! What's going on?"

Mrs James looked up and saw Emily in her uniform fleece racing towards her. "Oh! I'm so glad to see you. I've had such bad news, I didn't know what to do."

The young man turned to face Emily, she could only see his eyes through the narrow visor. He asserted confidently "I've just come to take the lady's card to the bank. It's all been arranged!"

Emily slowed down, momentarily. Then all her protective feelings for Mrs. James surged up "You what?"

Mrs. James added "Yes dear, this nice young man is taking my card, it's all been arranged on the phone. I rang back and checked, just like they said I should!"

Emily, unsure, stopped. Should she interfere? They were always being told to stick to their duties and specified times. But the old Emily Tibbets resurfaced, the stubborn awkward one who always asked why and caused problems. Well, she was going to ask questions now!

Facing the biker "Which bank are you from? He shuffled his scuffed leather boots.

Turning to Mrs. James "Which bank?

"Oh, I'm not sure! You know the one with the purple and pink card, I've got it here!" Mrs. James unsteadily let' go of the zimmer frame to hold up the card. Both Emily and the biker move towards it. Emily's determination won, she shoved him aside and lunged towards Mrs. James in the doorway. Snatching the card, she threw it over the old lady's shoulder along the hallway. Protecting Mrs. James with her body she stood in the doorway, expecting the blow to land on her back any minute. Instead she heard muttered curses and a mobile ringing. Immediately, the boots scrunched on the path and she heard them scuffling down the path.

Emily hugged Mrs. James around the zimmer frame and helped her turn it round in the narrow hallway, guiding her towards her little kitchen. Emily knew she should contact the police immediately, but Mrs. James was in such a state that she was the priority. She helped her sit down and put the kettle on, preparing the extra sweet tea for them both. Emily reflected on the incident, furious, Mrs. James was so vulnerable, such an easy target. As Mrs. James sipped her tea, Emily tried to help her remember what had happened. As she gently talked to the frail old lady, Emily was surprised to realise that she had remembered the registration number of the bike! Quickly writing it down, she phoned the police and gave them the details. They were sympathetic as there had been a spate of these scams locally and said they would follow it up.

Mrs. James settled, finishing her tea and the sandwich that Emily made. Her time allowance had been used up twenty minutes ago so she urgently phoned her duty manager and explained the situation. Jeanette was sympathetic but stressed that Emily really had to move onto her next call. The next old lady was just as vulnerable and really needed her.

Emily's frustration with her situation boiled up. She'd been such a waster at school, awkward and challenging whenever she could. She been obsessed with boys, clothes and music. School had been irrelevant, and she had no qualms about truanting whenever she felt like it. She'd left with no qualifications and no opportunities. It was only later with a young baby to care for and support, that her stupidity came back to haunt her.

For the first time she felt trapped because she wanted to do a good job and really care for someone and she couldn't. She leaned over to Mrs. James and stroked her arm, "You'll be alright lovey! I'm going to phone Olwen, your daughter, she'll come over as soon as she can." Emily didn't feel convinced that Olwen would actually arrive any time soon; but it was important to try and calm Mrs. James down as much as she could.

Another cup of tea and Helen James settled in front of her telly, Emily carefully let herself out of the house, locking it firmly behind her and shutting the gate.

The rest of Emily's visits passed off uneventfully and soon it was time to collect Kate from nursery. She came bounding out telling Emily all about the special picture she had painted. Emily tried to focus on what Kate was saying, "it's a picture of Nanna, look! It's just like her!" Emily agreed, nodding and smiling. That's what older people should be like, with family close to them, able to care for them and protect them, not like Mrs. James.

They wandered home, stopping to play on the swings and look at the ducks. Kate was experimenting with giving them names, but they didn't stay still long enough. Emily realised that she was giving Kate, the same experiences that her mum had given her. She began to understand just how much her own mum had done for her. Her mum had tried so hard to help and guide her. Emily, being Emily, had known better and rejected that guidance. Now she understood and realised how devastated she would be if Kate went off the rails like she had done. But better late than never, Emily was determined to give Kate a good start in life.

After tea, eaten at the table, and some reading practice, it was bath time. Splashy and noisy, time together they both enjoyed. Finally, bedtime and story time. At least three stories, before Kate's eye's drooped and she was soundly asleep.

Now it was Emily's time. She got her old laptop out, the vagaries of the benefits system meant that everything had to be done on line, an expense that Emily found it difficult to manage, but it was the only way to keep checking for different jobs, ones that might offer more of a future. Of course, most of the vacancies were temporary with agencies. They offered no hope at all. She'd tried those, and the hours were ridiculous or shift work, she couldn't afford expensive full day child care.

Finally, she logged onto Facebook, contacting her friends from school and some of her colleagues who she worked with but rarely saw. She explained what had happened to Mrs James, making sure not to mention any names. Suddenly there was an avalanche of comments.

"That's terrible"

"Disgraceful"

"What have you done about it?"

Emily thought – yeh what have I done about it? Not much actually!

"What can I do?" Lots of answers: follow it up with the police; go to the paper; contact local radio, contact Age Concern, make a big deal of it on Facebook to warn older people and their carers.

As Emily worked out what to say and who to contact she realised how important her job was. She began to understand that even at her level what she did was important and that it mattered. Doing her job well, looking after people who couldn't manage on their own, was something to be proud of.

Betrayal

by Pat Buckley

Harold Barnes sat in the corner of the bar, clutching his fourth, or was it fifth, glass of whisky. A casual observer would see a dark-haired man in his early forties; a successful man smartly dressed with good quality polished leather shoes. One look at his haggard face would give the lie to that impression. Elbows on table, shoulders slumped, he hung onto the glass as if it was the only thing saving him from total damnation.

Inside his head, he kept going over the evening. To his shame he'd approached the fellow members of the club he'd been part of for most of his adult life. He'd stood before them and begged and pleaded, abased and humiliated himself. Whatever pride he had, had disappeared. Harold needed this favour more than anything. Gone was the successful business man, pillar of the community. He knew how low he had sunk but he had to bear it, because the alternative was unthinkable. 'How did I get here' he questioned, and his mind went back to an afternoon about six months before. 'Only half a year ago,' his brain screamed 'when I thought I had it made, thriving business, lovely family, and the house we had always wanted to live in.'

He'd missed the first early clues. Perhaps, he should have been more alert when he was approached by Mrs Wilkinson, but the issue seemed so small, it did not seem significant. "Wilko" had been with the family for years; almost part of the furniture. She came in three times each week to clean, cook and child mind Sally and Nicky, when needed. Wilko was loyal, reliable and honest.

On this day, he was working in his home office, totally engrossed in a new project he was putting together; the one he hoped would see the business of Barnes and Williams come to the fore front of regional manufacturers. As the engineering partner, he needed to be sure that the machinery needed could be sourced and installed on the established shop floor. He was not very pleased when there was a knock on the study door and Wilko popped her head round the door.

"Sorry to bother you while you're busy, but as you're at home, I thought I should mention it."
Reluctantly looking up from his pages of calculation, he managed a smile, and assured her that he was always pleased to see her.
"I haven't been paid, again. You see, Mrs Barnes keeps forgetting to leave it out for me, and I have to remind her. Once she even left it for two weeks. As you know, Jimmy and I rely on the income I get from here. I really need the money regularly."

Harold was fully aware of the domestic circumstances of the Wilkinson family, and understood that a loss of this weekly income would have a serious effect. Equally, he was puzzled as to why his wife should be so forgetful. Digging out his wallet, he was relieved to see that he was holding enough to cover what was owed, he passed this over, with an apologetic smile.

"I'll have a word with Jane about this, I can't imagine why she is being so forgetful, but if it should happen again, let me know, and I'll arrange for you to be paid through the bank."

A smiling Mrs Wilkinson gratefully accepted the cash and he half heard her muttering as she closed the door. Later as he sat back with a coffee, it came to him. 'Now why should I inspect the recycling' he mused; 'must have misheard.'

Jane was not at all pleased that Mrs Wilkinson had approached him directly for her wages. When she got over her irritation at the incident, she had to agree that given their busy lifestyles, they needed someone so reliable.

"I'll make sure I give her priority," she promised, with a touch of sarcasm, "but sometimes it's so hard. I have to fit in my work in your office, and in Smithson's at the other side of town. I know that's only three days of the week, but there's time with the girls, and my charity stuff, and the gym as I was getting so unfit."

"Well if it's all getting too much for you, maybe something should give. Do you have to pack all this into a week, and you seem to be gadding out with your girl friends much more in the evening and at weekends. We hardly see you at home, no wonder you forget to pay the home help."

To say that Jane resented this advice, would be a minor understatement, and her face showed her annoyance that he should criticise her hobbies. The discussion was foreshortened when he reminded her that this was the evening for him to go to his club, and unless she had made other arrangements for their daughters, it was her turn to stay at home. After a convivial evening at his club, Harold returned home to find the house in darkness. Jane was doing a good impression of a woman in a deep sleep, spread across the centre of their marital bed, so he decided a night in his dressing room's little single would be a good idea. It was a couple of days before their relationship returned to the habitual relaxed warmth but this state was maintained for a while.

A few weeks later it had been Harold's turn to collect the girls from Oakmoor, their exclusive private school. It was his mother's birthday, and the three of them were taking her to tea in her favourite hotel. As he waited in the entrance hall, he was taken to one side by the school secretary, Miss Smythe, a formidable lady who took no nonsense from girls, staff and parents alike.

"I am sure it's a small matter Mr Barnes," she said, "but the school fees have not been paid this term. You know our terms are very strict, termly in advance. We do have a waiting list so we have to be firm with current pupils as there is a number waiting to take their places."

"There must be some mistake," he responded, "I know I made out the cheque for you when I was sorting out regular payments, Must have been at the beginning of last month."

"Yes, we got that cheque," she persisted," but it was returned from the bank marked 'Insufficient Funds'. We have written to you, but had no reply."

Being a practised negotiator, Harold could cover the embarrassment and confusion he felt. Politely excusing himself he returned to his car, and knowing that his business cheque book was in his brief case, quickly wrote a new cheque on his business account.

"I really don't understand why there has been a problem on the personal account but I have no reason to dispute what you are saying. I have made out a new cheque. This is from my business account, and believe me, there are no problems there."

At this point, his daughters came round the corner into the entrance hall, and he was relieved to be able to offer Miss Smythe a polite farewell and bustle his daughters out of the door.

Miss Smythe stood for a moment watching them leave. She was remembering other families with whom she'd had similar conversations over the years. She knew that when cheques started bouncing it was a sign of greater troubles. He seemed genuinely surprised she thought, and wondering what else was going on in the Barnes household, she returned to the office, stopping only to update the Head Teacher.

He did his best to be happy and relaxed during the family tea party, but more than once he'd caught his mother looking at him quizzically. She was not totally convinced that his excuse for Jane's absence rang true. However, Harold was experienced at not disclosing his thoughts so he managed to head her off and steer conversation into happier areas.

Jane was out when they returned home, so any discussion of bouncing cheques was necessarily delayed. Having seen his daughters into bed, he retired to his study for a detailed online scrutiny of the family finances, and he could clearly see some unusual patterns of large withdrawals and odd deposits. Although his regular contribution to their joint account was shown each month, he noticed that Jane's deposits were often missing. It was the following evening when he was able to sit down with his wife to try to sort out the mess and he tried as quietly and reasonably as possible to explain what he had found.

Jane was defensive and resentful that he should approach her with this minor matter.

"Minor matter", he stormed "it's not a minor matter when our house keeper goes unpaid, and our cheques start bouncing. You're an accountant damn it, you're trained to be precise in money matters. For goodness sake, we are both business people and we know the value of good reputation to a business' success. If we are not careful everything we've worked for will go down the tubes. Please Jane, work with me on this."

Eventually, Jane put up her hands in mock surrender. "Alright, I admit it, I've let things slip. I paid out for some new household things, carpets and the like in the sitting room and I had trouble with my car, and I've been so busy. Christmas is always a hectic time for us with all the socialising we do, not to mention the presents we buy for the family and the gifts for colleagues. With all that I did not give the bank as much attention as I should. Sorry dear, I'll make sure it's sorted." And giving him a hug and snuggling up with him on the settee, peace was restored.

Certainly there were no crises over the next few weeks, and although Jane was out just as much as before she was more pleasant when she was at home. Harold ensured that he regularly checked the bank accounts and collected and opened the post, asking Wilko to collect and place it in his office on days when he had to be away. It was a nuisance but he needed to ensure there were no more nasty shocks.

Easter was early that year so they were able to take a week's break. The family relaxed together in the warmth of Lanzarote. Sally and Nicky spent time in the pool, played tennis and even danced a night or two away at the hotel disco. Harold and Jane were glad of the chance to unwind. Taking time to relax by the pool and catching up with the novels they'd been promising to read but never seemed to have the time.

Harold also enjoyed strolling along the long promenade which stretched from the old lighthouse at one end of the resort to the marina at the other. In the middle of their stay, Harold proposed that they walk to the weekly market held in the marina area. Sally and Nicky were really keen. They loved wandering through the colourful stalls and the chance to buy local craft gifts for Grandma and school friends. In the past, Jane had been happy to join in such trips, but she declined. Indeed, she barely lifted her head out of her ipad to say goodbye.

Indeed, as the days went by, she hardly seemed to leave her ipad for more than a few minutes at a time. Harold's irritation elicited the cold response,
"It's my holiday as well. Why can't I enjoy my hobby? It's very relaxing"

Reflecting that she didn't look very relaxed, and not wishing to start yet another row, he walked away. But he did insist that they all ate together, and during this family time no one could look at phones, ipads or any other distraction. He also consciously spent more time with Sally and Nicky, which he enjoyed, but it was not the cosy reconciliation with Jane he'd envisaged when they had arranged the break.

Life was extremely busy in the weeks after their return. Financial year end demanded extra hours in the office as documents were prepared for the independent auditor. Jane was particularly busy as she worked both for Harold's company partnership and Smithson's. At the same time, Harold had to manage production, as well as courting new clients.

Harold felt good as he stepped out of the taxi at the bottom of his drive. He'd had a full day's business in London, meeting some new clients, building relationships. He was confident this day would pay off in new contracts and some tempting opportunities for joint working. As he turned back from paying the taxi driver who brought him from the station, a large man barged into him. No apology was given, but Harold was left with the distinct impression that the rude man had come out of his gate. Musing on this, he stepped into the house. The pleasure of being in this family home had not changed from the day he first saw it in the estate agent's window. It was not quite the same house, much needed modernisations and improvements had been carried out through the years, but it was the same solid Victorian mansion with extensive grounds that had first caught his eye.

Only the dog, Pip an aging Cairn terrier came to greet him. "Honey I'm home" he called out. This quote from a corny American film he and Jane had seen during their short but happy courtship, had become a joke between them, and was guaranteed to raise a conspiratorial smile. Realising that there was no one on the ground floor, he mounted the stately staircase in search of his errant family. He found his wife in their darkened bedroom, lying back with a cold cloth across her forehead. Jane denied that anyone had been to the house and, shrugging off his concern, assured him that she would be fine very soon. She insisted he didn't need to cancel the dinner with James and Deborah, their close friends since forever. Sally and Nicky were on sleepover with school friends, so it would have been a shame to waste the opportunity to share rare social time together.

These dinners were a regular fixture for the four friends, a chance to relax and chat and sometimes set the world to rights. It was however noticeable Jane seemed to be drinking far more than usual. The cosy atmosphere of the evening was disturbed when Deborah asked Jane if she intended to continue her membership of the Ladies Charity committee and later James made a passing reference to seeing Jane at the new riverside casino. She initially passed it off as a fun night out with the girls. When he persisted and suggested that she was a regular, Jane became quite strident. At this point, Harold decided it was time they went home, and thanking their hosts and promising to meet again soon, he hurried a very drunk Jane out of the door.

They had one of their bitterest rows on the drive home when he made the mistake of tackling her about being what James had said

"You didn't tell me you went to the casino," he opened.

"Can't you trust me to socialise with my girlfriends and do the fun things in life?" she yelled.

Eventually he decided that perhaps this evening was not the time to pursue it and resolved to return to the subject at a later date. But life and work intervened, and they both became busy with work and family and the occasional social event. Harold made a point of having dinner at his club as often as he could, as he needed the sanity of dinner in civilised company. Meanwhile Jane kept up her social round.

It was only a week later that returning late from the factory that he again met the large man. This time he was walking down the drive so there could be no doubt about where he had come from. Banging against Harold, he growled "Just tell her she'll go the same way," and he dashed away through the gateway and off down the road, leaving a shocked Harold staring after him.

Harold was further surprised that Pip did not dash out to greet him when he opened the door. Taking a walk round the ground floor he soon found Sally and Nicky, feet up on the settees in the family room watching a very loud musical film. His greeting was rewarded with a quick wave and smile. They said they'd heard no one at the door, and their attention returned to the screen.

Ascending the staircase, Harold decided that Jane must be at her desk with the dog curled cosily around her feet. However, he did find her in the bedroom, sitting at the dressing table, staring into the mirror. He caught the look of terror in her reflection, but when his wife turned towards him, she had regained some composure. He pulled her to him in a warm hug and as she relaxed in his arms, he asked her what the man had wanted. Although she became noticeably more tense, she maintained it was a casual call; a man looking for gardening work. Although Harold tried to prise more information out of her, Jane was quite adamant that there was no need for him to be concerned. They agreed to have a quiet family supper and an evening in front of the tele.

In the kitchen while they were preparing their supper, Harold suddenly realised that he had not seen Pip since he got home. Again, he searched the house, until Sally remembered that she had let him out through the back door about two hours ago. Like many young people, she'd then gone to watch the film and forgot about him. Leaving the others to sort out their meal and set the table, Harold went out into the back garden. He didn't have to go very far before he found a small furry bundle curled up near the porch It was obvious that Pip was not well so he carefully picked him up and carried him back into the house, and tucked him up in his basket.

Returning into the kitchen would be a challenge. He didn't want to alarm his daughters unduly, and he'd only just got Jane back on an even keel. As he washed his hands in the utility, he debated about the best course of action. Should he tell the family now that their beloved pet was unwell, and deal with further emotional upset, or should he keep quiet? If he left it, and Pip died Sally would never forgive herself that she left him outside while she enjoyed the film, and no one would forgive him for not acting sooner. In the end he telephoned Matthew, the vet, who was a family friend, and arranged to have an emergency visit to the surgery in an hour's time.

A thoughtful Harold went back into the kitchen where supper was ready and his family awaited him. When their meal was over, he quietly explained that Pip was unwell and he was taking him to see vet Matthew. Naturally Sally and Nicky wanted to come with him. Jane looked shocked and started to shake. Harold realised that all his calming efforts had been in vain. Jane managed to hold it together while coats were fetched and Pip and basket were carefully stowed in the car. She declined a visit to the vets but her daughters demanded to go, so Harold set off driving very carefully the short distance to the surgery.

Matthew gave Pip a full examination. Poking, prodding and taking blood and other samples, looking thoughtful throughout. Eventually, he took Harold to one side.

"He shows every sign of being poisoned," he quietly confided, is he able to get anywhere near your household chemicals? Do you keep weed killer any where accessible? You see it's very difficult to treat without knowing the specific poison."

Harold was able to reassure Matthew that all chemicals were securely stowed.

"You forget I am used to handling harmful substances at the factory," he added. "I will check around the garden when I get home, but I am sure he hasn't got into any of our stocks at home."

Matthew accepted this adding, "I can only treat the symptoms and get some liquids into him. I'll pop him into the hospital section for the night so we can keep an eye on him."

After they had patted and fussed their pet, the two girls were ready for home, promising to see him the next day. As soon as his daughters were safely tucked up in bed, Harold again makes a search around the house garage, greenhouse, garden shed, in fact any where a chemical canister could have been carelessly left out for an adventurous dog to chew. He walked the garden perimeter, flashing his torch under trees and bushes. There was nothing and at this point he knew he had to talk with his wife because what kept coming back to him was that gruff, "Just tell her she'll go the same way," and it was all too much of a coincidence.

Harold found Jane in the sitting room, nursing a glass. From the look in her eyes and the level of the vodka remaining in the bottle, he knew that this was not her first drink, nor even her second. Pouring himself large whisky, he sat down beside her. Slowly and carefully he explained what Matthew had said and how he had checked all around their home without finding any possible cause. Taking a deep breath, he turned to look at her full face. He needed to see how she reacted to what he said next. Gradually as he spoke he watched the horror spread across her face, and the panic rise in her eyes. Even with both hands covering her face, she still shook her head; asserted that Pip's death must be an accident. Denied she knew the strange man. Denied he'd been to the house before. Even though he pleaded for the truth; promised he would help her, whatever trouble she was in. Eventually he had to give up. Sadly they retired to bed, where he held her close, hoping that this intimacy would encourage her to tell him what was going on. She maintained her silence and both had a sleepless night.

Matthew phoned at breakfast time saying that Pip had died in the night and asking Harold to call in to the surgery for a full report. Harold agreed. Sally and Nicky were anxious about their pet, but Harold persuaded them that there was no time to visit before school; perhaps teatime would be best. He didn't feel able to tell them about their pet's death, until he knew more about the cause himself. Leaving work early, he listened as Matthew reported on what treatment they had given the very sick dog.

"Our night staff watched over him but he went into convulsions and had been sick. Despite our best treatment, he died shortly afterwards. We did a basic analysis on all bodily fluids. From these we conclude that the dog had been poisoned with a common garden common garden weed killer."

"But I checked", interrupted Harold, "there was nothing around our house and garden that he could have eaten accidentally."

"I don't think it was an accident," continued Matthew, "there were some chunks of meat when he was sick. Our analysis shows that this is what poisoned him. I believe your pet was murdered. Is there anyone who as a grudge against your family? Perhaps you should inform the Police."

Harold couldn't tell him anything. He didn't know enough. He had suspicions, but suspicions were not proof. In the end, he agreed to take Pip's body home so his daughters could say farewell to the pet which had been part of their family for as long as they could remember. They wrapped the dog carefully in his blanket and nestled him in the basket he had arrived in, and Harold took him home, taking time on the drive to compose his thoughts and prepare a story which would be a sufficient explanation for his daughters.

At home, Harold very quietly broke the news to his wife and daughters that vet Matthew had tried everything but Pip had died, adding, "He was quite an old dog you know, at twelve years old it's the same as eighty four human years, even older than grandma."

After the shrieks and sobs had subsided, he explained that they could give Pip a final stroke in the morning, Saturday. They would hold their own special funeral for him, with burial under the pear tree at the end of the garden. No one felt like eating much supper so that they soon gave up the pretence. Sally and Nicky spent the rest of the evening telephoning their Grandma and school friends to share what would be the first major trauma in their short lives.

It was quite late before the girls were settled in their rooms, and this was the first opportunity Harold had to speak privately with his wife. His anger made him quite brutal.

"He didn't die of old age, he was poisoned. Matthew wanted to call the Police", he started. "But I believe it had something to do with that man who was here yesterday."

Jane shook her head. "No it can't be. I don't believe it."

"Well I do and I am convinced you know why. Please Jane, please share with me what you know. There's something bad going on. If you could just tell me, I'm sure we could work it out together."

Jane maintained her silence then, and throughout the evening.

Immediately after breakfast Harold went into the garden and dug a deep hole behind the pear tree. Returning to the house, he was surprised to find his mother drinking coffee in the kitchen.

"The girls were so upset when they rang me," she explained, "I decided you all may appreciate some support this morning."

After giving his mother a quick hug, he gathered the family together and carefully carried Pip, still in his basket, down to the newly dug grave. The girls had worked together to prepare a funeral service. They said fond goodbyes and patted him on the head before allowing Harold to lower him gently into the ground. He was relieved that his mother then announced that she needed another coffee, so the others returned to the house and he was able to refill the hole before carefully placing the miniature gravestone that his daughters had made. Sally and Nicky were allowed to choose their favourite lunch so they all sat round the table sharing pizzas and sharing memories of Pip, his mischief and the times they had shared.

As his mother rose to leave she suggested Harold walk her to her car. "What's wrong between you and Jane?" She asked. "It's obvious you're not comfortable together."

Harold assured her there was nothing major with, "It's just one of those patches most marriages go through."

Reluctantly, his mother accepted this but before she drove off she added, "You know where I am when you need me. I am still a good listener, and there are not too many things in this life that I haven't seen before. It's one of the advantages of old age."

Thanking her for her concern, he kissed her on the cheek and promised he would certainly come to her whenever he needed.

The family spent a quiet afternoon at home. Jane retired to her workroom and the girls said they would do their homework. Harold tried to tackle a mountain of paperwork in his office but found his attention wandering. As he gazed across the garden to the newly dug grave, he felt his anger rising. 'What kind of people would kill an innocent little dog' he wondered. He was still convinced that Jane knew what was behind it and this prevented him from going to the police. Later, deciding he'd prepare supper for them all, he searched Jane out to find whether she had any preferences. He found her in the bedroom, dressed for an outing and applying the last touches of makeup.

"Surely you're not going out," he asked.

"Don't shout at me, I won't have you shouting", she snapped back. "I don't need your permission before I meet my friends."

He tried to be quiet and reasonable. "I just thought that after what's hit us over the past two days, you would like to be here, our daughters are still very upset."

"Don't keep throwing that back at me. You keep saying it's all my fault. I just need to get out and unwind for a while." And with that she picked up her jacket and hand bag and headed for the door.

"Don't wait up," was her final shot.

After a cosy supper Harold, Sally and Nicky settled in to watch films. The girls chose their favourite Frozen. Once he would have complained about having to sit through this yet again but he knew that they needed this small pleasure. He sat back while his daughters, who knew the story word for word, recited, sang and danced throughout. Even though he worked late after the girls had gone to bed, Jane did not return before he turned in himself. He found her asleep beside him the following morning but she was not interested in breakfast. Deciding that he would continue spoiling his daughters for a little while, he offered them burgers for lunch and a ten pin bowling session, a rare treat.

Monday saw the family back into their work routine. As the independent auditor Jonas Yates had finished work at Smithson's, his team were starting work on at the Barnes and Williams factory this week. At 10 am the four of them sat round the conference room table; Harold, Fred Williams his partner, Jane their accountant and Jonas Yates himself. They had gone through this yearly procedure more than once before and so they were all familiar with what was expected. Normally Jonas would be dealing with the Barnes and Williams accounts exclusively but he explained that unusually he had a couple of loose ends to tie up at Smithsons so he hoped they would not mind if the programme overran.

It was in the middle of the following week that Harold went for dinner at his club and ran into Bill Smithson.

"I'm pleased I've met you," Bill began, "it saves me ringing you; better face to face. A problem has shown up in my accounts, I wanted to tell you about it first."

He had Harold's full attention as he continued, "There's a deficiency in the cash. Jonas tells me it's been very cleverly done. Teeming and lading, is the technical term he says. The trouble is, it must have arisen in Jane's area. We've always found her so reliable. Jonas is putting together a full report and it may mean the police are involved. I just hope he's wrong but I thought I'd let you know."

"I can't believe you are trying to tell me my wife may be stealing from your firm. I hope you find that Jonas has made a mistake, but please come back to me when his report is completed, and we'll talk again."

Harold tried to make sense of the idea that Jane could be a thief, but when he remembered the bounced cheques and the transaction in their own bank account, he began to wonder. Keeping this to himself for now, he determined to speak to Jonas directly in the morning and ask him to pay special attention to this area of Barnes and Williams accounts. He did not want to believe there would be a problem, but he needed to know.

It took only a week before Jonas was back with the report. The bad news took some time to accept. Angry and tight lipped, he questioned the auditor. Was he absolutely sure; about the amount, was Jane solely responsible, was the Smithson's deficit similar or larger? The further facts staggered him.

"It's unbelievable," he gasped, "How could she? How could she take so much? What has she been doing with it?"

But at the back of his mind, he knew; the booze, the nights out, the trips to the casino.

Jonas was quite calm. It was not his first such conversation, but his duties were quite precise.

"You do realise, I need to report this in both sets of company accounts and, of course, the police must be informed"

The latter shocked Harold to the core. The implications for the family and his business flooded into his mind, but above all he desperately needed to know the truth from his wife.

"Please delay a few days if you can. Allow me to talk with her. I will come back to you shortly, please give me this chance."

Reluctantly Jonas agreed.

Jane was at home. She'd said that morning that she was unwell. Harold knew the truth. It was sheer panic. Making some coffee, he asked her to sit with him; no insisted. With a calmness and quiet he did not feel, he outlined the events of the past few weeks. None of it would be news to her but he needed her to be sure she knew the extent of his knowledge before they started to explore what he really needed to know; why, how, how much?

"Ok, now please tell me all about it then we can sort out what to do. I know there hasn't been much togetherness recently but unless we can work this out, you are going to jail and I won't be able to stop it."

She thought for a while, turning the coffee mug in her hands, staring into it as if all the mysteries of the universe could be revealed there. Eventually she stirred, and looking at him for the first time, she hesitantly began to tell the story.

"It all began a year ago, maybe longer. I went to the casino with Smithson's office staff. It was a leaving do or some such. I had several drinks, and decided to join the poker table. I'd not played before. It was fascinating. You see it's not just cards but you need to calculate the odds and be able to weigh up the opposition. Different people have facial 'tells' or their body language would show what they were thinking. It was a challenge. I enjoyed it. I was lucky, winning quite often, so I went back regularly, at least once a week."

I was by then established as a player and was invited into the private room, where the high stakes game was played. At first I won, but I lost more often. The drinks were free, and I really got a taste for vodka and coke; nice long drink with a bit of a kick. I've wondered since if there was more of a kick than I expected because as the evening went on I lost more. They gave me credit and more than once I was given an account for thousands which I owed to the cashier. That was when I started to get desperate for cash. You tackled me about paying Wilko and then the school fees remember?"

"But the fact was I was hooked. I even played online. You can gamble that way without any difficulty. I even did it on holiday. Remember my obsession with my ipad? The zing from taking a chance can't be bettered. The low when you lose again and again is like total devastation. So I drank more. Vodka is good for secret drinkers, no smell on the breath, you know. Most days I would sink at least half a bottle, often more."

She looked up and her fingers twitched as she turned towards the drinks cabinet. He rose and brought a glass of coke from the fridge in the kitchen, before adding a sizeable slug of vodka. After moment's thought, he poured a whisky for himself. Saying as he handed over her drink,

"I think we'll need these because I have a feeling that the worst is yet to come."

After a hesitation and disposing of most of the contents of her glass, she continued.

"Then they started putting pressure on me to clear my account and to my horror I learnt the rate of interest being applied. I did my best but poker is a game for calm calculation and the more stressed I was, the less able I was to play. That's when I started borrowing from the companies, yours and Smithson's."

"Why?" he interrupted, "Why couldn't you speak to me? I would have been angry but far less angry than I am now. I thought we loved each other."

"I couldn't bear to tell you what a mess I'd made of things, and how I'd let you down. I was sure I could sort it out"

She studied her hands. Held them together to stop them shaking; couldn't meet his eye. Taking up the tale in a low voice, she continued.

"It just got worse. I couldn't win and I was frightened to give up because then I was denying any chance of making my losses back. Then they started putting more pressure on me; making threats came here."

He gasped. Then his voice rose. "It was that man who came to the house wasn't it? I knew it. That was the man who killed our dog, and you protected that murdering swine, didn't you?"

She nodded and the tears rolled down her cheeks, marking her blouse.

"Ok," he said roughly, "I now know how and perhaps why. The key question is how much?"

The tears streamed faster now and a sob constricted her throat as she tried to speak.

"Sorry, I did not hear that. You'll have to repeat it."

Eventually she managed, "One hundred thousand pounds."

"Bloody Hell, Jane you don't do things by halves. Is that all? Everything?"

She could only nod.

"First let's get you to a doctor, whether you think so or not, you are ill and need some help." Was his best response at this time, he couldn't start to explain what was going round in his head.

Fortunately there was an emergency slot available, Jane was able to get some the help she needed; pills and the promise of an early appointment with a counsellor. Back home, they made lunch together, which neither of them ate. By now, Jane was looking pale, tired and unwell, a combination of the prescribed pills and the realisation of the enormity of the mess she was in. Harold helped her upstairs to lie down and went to his office. He needed to think.

Sitting at his desk, he knew he couldn't let his anger take over. There would be time for that later. Eventually, it came to him, what he needed to do. It would be hard. For a man who was so used to being respected, who was a good manager of his business, this would be very hard. There were personal dangers in what he proposed, but he knew that given the love he and Jane had shared, and for the family, there was no other course of action.

First he had to ring his business partner. If Fred Williams refused to go along with him, there was no point in approaching anyone else. Harold was relying on Fred's understanding that a public scandal would do the firm harm. Reputation once lost, was not easily restored. Fortunately Fred understood what Harold was trying to achieve. It was a difficult conversation, but Harold knew it was merely a rehearsal for the ones to follow. Over the next hour, he also spoke to Bill Smithson, Jonas Yates, Jack Saunders the bank manager and, most importantly David Rogers who was Divisional Police Commander as well as current chairman of the gentleman's club. Harold arranged to meet them at the club that evening.

The men came together in the small meeting room. After thanking them all for being there Harold briefly took them through Jane's story finishing with a list of the favours he needed from each of them to remedy this bad situation.

From Bill Smithson and Fred Williams, he needed their acceptance that he would repay within weeks the deficit in the accounts caused by Jane's frauds. Jonas Yates was asked to verify the repayment and not to include the earlier deficiency in the audit report to the annual accounts, which would become a public document. He needed Jack Saunders to arrange an urgent loan to pay back the two defrauded firms and cover the money she owed to the casino.

Harold assured him that there was enough equity in the house, to secure such an amount but stressed that he needed the cash available soon.

Addressing David Rogers, Harold had three issues to raise. First he thanked the man for being in the meeting and for allowing him to use his club membership to address his private problems. Secondly, he begged that the Policeman would accept his undertaking that every penny would be returned and that no charges would be made against Jane. His final request was that the Police instigate an investigation into the casino and the loan sharks linked with them, emphasising the threats and menaces their collectors used. Before leaving the room to allow them to have a private talk, Harold begged them all to help him through this crisis.

Harold sat in the reading room, pretending to study the local rag, wondering how long it would be before Jane's name was prominent on its pages. The wait was interminable. He kept getting up and staring out of the window. It had rained and the streetlamps cast shiny patches of light on the pavements. There were not many people about and he watched the occasional car drive along the road and the splashes from the puddles broke up the light pools as shiny waves spread across. He realised he was playing a game from his childhood, waiting outside the Head Teacher's door following some small transgression. 'If the door opens before three more cars have passed, it will be OK.' It didn't. He knew he was doomed.

Eventually, they asked him back into the room. The men round the table could not meet his eye. 'Dear Lord,' he thought 'they've turned me down.' David Rogers spoke for them all.

"We've had a good discussion and in the end we've agreed. We will all accede to all your requests. But before you feel too relieved, you have to know there are some quite stringent conditions. Fred has told us that he's been thinking of retiring but he hadn't got round to discussing it with you. He and Bill have talked through the possibility of a takeover or merger and will progress this. The thing is none of this will include you. They will pay you a fair price for your share. The Barnes name will no longer be associated with the business. You may enter the factory once again to clear your desk but after that you will have nothing more to do with it."

Harold looked from Fred to Bill and back. He started to speak, but David held up his hand. "I haven't finished."

Harold sank back in his seat waiting for the next body blow.

"None of us wants the embarrassment of dealing with you or your family again. You will make arrangements to leave this town as soon as decently possible; preferably the country. We expect no later than the beginning of September. That sort of date will allow your girls to be at their new secondary school for the start of term. Obviously after all this distasteful business, you will resign from this club with immediate effect. We don't wish to see you. That's it."

Harold gripped the edge of the table.

"Please, I beg you," he gasped, "please does this have to be so punitive, so harsh?"

"You should have thought of that before you came here pleading for that thief of a wife of yours. What has been said here will remain confidential. I have everyone's assurance on that. You leave here with your reputation intact, so be grateful. The door's behind you."

Harold could barely stand his knees were shaking so much. After an age he managed to find his feet, pulled his shoulders back, and thanking them for their time and assistance, he left. Once outside he headed for the taxi rank in the town centre. On his way he decided to stop for a drink. He needed something to give him the courage to go home and the misery he would share there.

Harold sat in the corner of the bar, holding on to his fourth, or was it fifth, glass of whisky. Elbows on table, shoulders slumped, he hung onto the glass as if it was the only thing saving him from total damnation.

Inside his head, he kept going over the evening. He'd stood before fellow members of the club he'd belonged to for most of his adult life and begged and pleaded, abased and humiliated himself. Whatever pride he had, was now gone. Harold needed this favour more than anything. Gone was the successful business man, pillar of the community. He knew how low he had sunk but he had to bear it, because the alternative was unthinkable.

A hand touched his shoulder, "Come along sir, drink up, I have to close.
" Realising the he could not delay going home for any longer, he staggered out in search of a taxi. Jane was still up when he came home, eager to know the result, anxious that he had been away so long. When she realised he'd been drinking, her anxiety turned to fury.

"Where have you been?" she screeched. "I've been waiting to know what was going on. Waiting and worrying, and you've been out boozing with your mates. Didn't you think I'd want to know as soon as possible?"

It was the noise and the sting in his palm that made him realise he'd hit her. Looking up he saw a red mark on her cheek and a look of total shock on her face. She staggered back into the armchair.

"Shut up," he yelled, "shut up now. I'll tell you what I did and what happened." And after he'd detailed what happened at the club, he went on to tell her what would happen next.

"There'll be a lot of paper work and legal issues to sort out so that has to be my priority. The house has to go on the market. Our beautiful house that we worked so hard for has to go. The girls can stay at Oakmoor until the end of the summer term, they are going to be disrupted enough later. Wilko will have to go, we can't afford her. In any case you will be at home and I expect you to keep things going and ensure that the girls' life goes on as before and we are all fed and the house kept clean. No one else around these parts will employ you and we won't be going out socialising, either together or singly. They don't want us. I will start tomorrow to find another job. I can't hope for the sort of partnership I had here but someone may want my skills. And now my dear I am going to bed. You can have our room. I am quite comfortable in my dressing room. "

With that, he wished her goodnight and headed, unsteadily upstairs.

The following day, being a man of his word, he put in train all the business of detaching himself from his partnership, and putting the house on the market. Harold endured the embarrassment of emptying his desk and saying goodbye to his staff. He called into Fred Williams' office and handed over his keys, passes and company credit card. Trying to hold his head high, headed out of the gate to a taxi home. He would miss his shiny new Audi, but he had to get used to Jane's Mini. They couldn't afford two cars any more.

The next difficult job was to tell his mother. Mrs Barnes sat quietly while it all spilled out. Harold felt so much shame in telling her this awful story and how he was left with little other than his personal reputation intact. As he came to the end of this saga, he started to cry. She handed him tissues, held him close rubbing his back, just like she did when he was a small boy. Eventually, he was all cried out, and she could talk to him calmly, giving him reassurance, saying she would support him whatever he decided to do because that's what mothers do. She knew that she would have difficulty remaining in the town once Harold and his family were gone, but that would be a discussion for another day.

Jane had confessed how much was owed to the casino, and the crippling interest rates being applied. Harold understood that gambling debts were not enforceable in law, nevertheless, he was afraid of the chance of more threats and violence. They may have killed the dog and he was worried at a threat to his children. He was shocked to realise that he was not concerned about any potential of danger to Jane. He determined to approach the casino management, and formed a plan which he hoped would help others in the same trap as she had.

The appointment was made for nine o'clock that evening. Before he went in he wrote a cheque for the most recent amount of Jane's debt and set his mobile to record and stashed it in his coat pocket. Looking more confident than he felt, he entered the casino and made his way to the upper floor and the manager's office. There was one man, Dick Rogers, behind the desk and another, whom he recognised, leaning against the wall. Working hard not to show the disgust and anger he felt at these men and their despicable methods, Harold addressed the boss.

"I've written a cheque for my wife's debt to you", he opened, placing it on the desk.

"Thanks, but that's the wrong amount. It's only for forty two thousand pounds. She owes us forty-eight thousand."

Harold was determined not to give way. Placing both hands on the desk, he leaned forward so he could look straight into Rogers' eyes. "No, that is the last amount you asked for, only last week, so that's what you get, not a penny more. What sort of interest do you think you're charging?"

"I charge whatever I decide. It's my business after all," was the sneering reply.

"Not a penny more," Harold repeated. "Of course, I could take my cheque back and you could always sue me." He allowed that thought to sink in before heading to the door.

The minder stepped forward to bar his way. "You should be careful Mr Barnes." he whispered, "You never know when you could have an accident. Nearly all accidents happen at home, it's a well-known fact."

"Leave him Lenny," Rogers instructed.

Harold turned and as he looked from one to the other he promised that any further harm to his home or family would lead to police action. After a tense face off, the manager signalled that Harold should be allowed to go.

As he left he heard Dick Rogers say, "Just tell dear Jane we miss her and she's welcome any time."

But he continued out of the building without acknowledging the remark, although he was thinking 'over my dead body.' On arriving home he checked whether the conversation had recorded. As it was satisfactory, he attached it to a text and sent it to David Rogers with the hope that it would help lead to further inquiries into the casino's operation.

In the fullness of time all the legal and financial matters were settled. Harold was lucky enough to be appointed Managing Director with a firm in Jersey. It was a little smaller than Barnes and Williams, and of course he was no longer a partner. The whole family, including his mother had visited the island, where they had found a house with a granny annexe to suit them all. Sally and Nicky had visited their new school and while nothing could compare with the joys of Oakmoor, the more extensive playing fields and tennis courts would be some consolation.

To the casual observer and as far as their daughters were concerned Harold and Jane's relationship seemed as normal. He had, however, made it clear that what she did in the future was up to her. If she chose not to come to Jersey, they would manage as his mother would care for the household. If she wished to accompany them, that was equally fine at least until the girls were leaving school, after which he may choose to divorce her. Jane had opted to move to Jersey and Harold thought on balance that this was the right decision. She was still very vulnerable and using medication.

After the house was sold they spent many hours sorting through cupboards and drawers making the hard decisions about what they should take with them. Numerous black sacks of discarded possessions and outgrown clothes and toys were deposited with grateful local charity shops. Everything else was packed up and boxed, ready for the move.

The day of the move eventually arrived. Harold was up early, checking that everything was packed and ready to go. Sally and Nicky were with his mother and they would travel separately to Jersey. The memories came flooding back as he walked round the house and looked across the garden to where poor old Pip had been buried. He realised that there was no sign of Jane. Surely she should be up and moving by now. He'd made some tea so he mounted the stairs carrying one of the mugs intended to be the last things packed and the first things out. She was still in bed. Crossly he shook her.

"Come on Jane," he called, "we haven't time for a lie in this morning. The movers will be here any time soon."

He realised her body was cold and there was no pulse when he searched. There was a note on the pillow beside her.

"Sorry. Please give my love to my girls."

As Harold was leaving the room to call the authorities, he looked around at the packed boxes, the stripped room, the wreckage of his life.

"For heaven's sake Jane, couldn't you have done this six months ago you selfish bitch," he cried and he turned and went to find a telephone.

Consequenses

Starting Again

Maxine Patterson

"How clichéd" she mumbled to herself as she gazed numbly in at the ranks of impossibly perfect roses in the Valentine's display window. Full blown, perfectly petalled dark red roses interspersed with tiny unopened buds; the window dresser's dream display to encourage shoppers walking past to enter and purchase their dream of true love. As if!

She shook her head, shrugged up her coat collar and turning round briskly, marched up the road resolute in her determination not to succumb to misery and self-pity.

She was over the worst now, she thought. After all it had been nearly six months. Well, not quite, but it felt like forever since she'd had to leave. She was coping fine.... well sort of.

She still couldn't quite understand what had happened. They'd been married for fourteen years, she thought she knew him.

Medically unfit! And how!

They'd both tried so hard. The physical arrangements had been embarrassing and irritating. But she foolishly thought once the council had helped them with the changes, a ramp to the front door, the bedroom and wet room on the ground floor it would been fine.

But of course, it hadn't. How could it be? It had been his life in every sense.

He'd left for his last tour, fit and healthy. An exercise junkie. His idea of fun was a ten-mile run with his backpack loaded. Real fun was throwing himself down a mountain on his bike and laughing as he came home covered in mud and scratches. Sky diving or mountaineering his weekend relaxation.

Now! Now Frank sat immobile. Unable, unwilling to move, to talk. His anger and rage encased him in fury and hatred for everyone. Especially her.

He sat in his wheelchair unwilling to do his physiotherapy or follow up on the exercise programme that had been worked out for him. She couldn't blame him, the shock must have been horrendous. She knew he felt betrayed, dumped at home, a double amputee with nothing to look forward to.

She hadn't helped either, trying to hide her dismay and shock at the physical change in him by trying to do too much for him. This was not the man she married. But she knew what her duty was and she doggedly followed the instructions given to her by the medical team and the physiotherapists. She thought she had hidden her feelings, but of course she couldn't.

He knew of course. In the haze of his own anger and confusion he'd become aware of her uncertainty and he'd withdrawn into himself, refusing to continue with the planned rehabilitation programme.

At the Hospital, the focus had all been positive. He'd survived, he was lucky. She had been by his bedside praying that he would live. She hadn't thought about later, she just wanted him with her. Later, as he began the interminably slow and agonisingly painful recuperation process, she began to realise what the reality of his life would be.

But she reckoned without his strength of will, with the other lads around he made the effort. The nurses and physios bullied, cajoled and pushed him into the extra effort so that he could manage to walk on his prosthetics. He began to use the gym to build up the strength in his upper body, he was in the army, he was part of a team and he was valued.

Then he was discharged, from the hospital and from the Army.

But of course, when he got home he was on his own. Yes, there was the doctor and local medical practice, but none of the expertise that had supported him in Birmingham.

They'd warned her at Selly Oak about a possible reaction once he got home. He had lost so much of himself, his physical strength and capability and his mental toughness. The stumps were sore. She didn't have the necessary skill to help and reassure him. She fussed around and irritated him. He reacted by getting angry and resentful, shutting himself away in his downstairs room, letting his demons of rage, resentment and disappointment overwhelm him.

His hospital appointment gave her the opportunity to clean and tidy up his room. The dingy squalor appalled her, the huge stash of crushed empty beer cans under the bed shocked her. Of course she'd handled it all wrong, confronting him when he came back. The argument was fierce and violent. She didn't know what he'd thrown but she woken up in hospital. He'd insisted that she left. He didn't want her back.

So here she was living a new, very different life. She pushed open the door of her one bedroom "compact" apartment; actually small and pokey. But it was hers. She hung her coat in the cupboard, squeezed past the small settee and into the tiny kitchen to heat up her ready meal. She'd treated herself to something slightly different, the M & S meal deal for two, silly really but it meant she got a bottle of wine as well.

The knock on the door surprised her. She ignored it, it would be the pizza delivery boy looking for Flat 16, who lived on takeaways and often forgot to give their flat number. The knock was louder this time. Irritated she went through to the door, opening it just a little to shout through; "it's flat 16 you need!"

"Daisy! Daisy it's me!"

She scrabbled to undo the door chain and opened the door to see a pair of legs and a huge bouquet of red roses. Shaking, she struggled to breathe.

"For God's sake Daisy, I can't move, I've got my arms full of these bloody flowers, Get out of the way!"

"Frank.... Frank! Oh sorry, of course come in. shall I take the flowers?"

Later after they'd eaten the meal for two – why had she bought it? They talked.

After the fight he'd accepted that he needed help. His RSM had known just the right people to contact. Frank was briskly pulled back into life and encouraged to recommence his physio and his active training. It was just what he had needed. It re-awoke his enthusiasm for risk taking and living life to the full.

He'd been given a trial for the Help for Heroes expedition to the South Pole. He'd joined a wheelchair basket ball team. He explained how seriously they took each game, specially adapted wheelchairs which they could throw round the court. He was hoping they'd qualify for the Paralympics.

He was involved in helping other disabled servicemen come to terms with their disabilities. Frank's determination to move forward was etched on his face and the shadows in his eyes made it clear that it would be a difficult journey.

Daisy listened, encouraging and nodding as he talked. The she looked at the huge bouquet of flowers which filled her small bedroom. "Why did you bring flowers? You didn't need to you know."

"Yes, I did. We have to start again, and this is me, starting again."

A Grand Exit

Anne Marie Phillips

Campaign headquarters were in turmoil. The phones were ringing off the hook, computers were being inundated with emails and everyone was tip toeing around, afraid to voice what was in their minds. Things had been a little rocky for the past week or so. Their candidate seemed to have lost his edge. He was no longer enthusiastic. He almost seemed to be avoiding meeting people. When he had no other choice, then he seemed to be uncomfortable. No-one knew quite what was happening. No-one had dared to ask him outright.

Now he had disappeared off the face of the earth and the press were clamouring for an interview. The campaign secretary threw a handful of flyers down on a table.

"Right" he said, "Anyone got any ideas? Anyone got a clue where our illustrious candidate has vanished to?" He glared around the room only to be met by blank looks and shakes of the head.

"Great" he muttered "Just great"

Twenty-four hours earlier;

Simon Carlton, Labour candidate for the marginal seat of Blackwell East was about to do a meet and greet on a local council estate. Confident, handsome and educated at a minor public school, Simon was not your usual Labour candidate. However, despite that, Simon was popular in the constituency. He had a way of modifying his tone of voice that made him seem like 'one of the boys' and people almost forgot about his privileged background.

Today however, was not going the way Simon wanted. He was used to women falling for his boyish charm and for the men to be pleasantly surprised by his knowledge of the local football team. The statistics of which he boned up on before every public engagement.

Today he had been confronted by people who were not interested in football, people who were not swayed by his floppy blond hair and his charming grin. Today he had been harangued by coarse looking men in flat caps who wanted to ask him difficult questions about jobs. He had been accosted by hard brassy women who were angry about rising prices and school closures. It had been a very difficult morning. Eventually the meeting had drawn to a close and the public had filed out of the room. As the door closed behind them, Simon sat back with a sigh.

"Oh my God" he muttered. "Where in the hell did you dredge that shower up from?

"Keep it down Simon" admonished his adviser.

"No, I won't bloody well keep it down"

Simon's frustrations were boiling up. He had tried so hard to be a man of the people, but the effort was killing him.

"Who the Hell do these idiots think they are? Look at them, scruffy, dirty layabouts. I bet none of them have ever done a decent day's work in their lives. Don't they know I'm only trying to help, although God only knows why I'm bothering"

Simon shut up abruptly as the door at the back of the room opened and a few of the people from the earlier meeting drifted back into the room.

"The meeting's finished" said Simon shortly.

"A shower. Dirty, scruffy layabouts. Is that what you think of us?"

Simon looked puzzled for a second then glanced down at the microphone on the table. The blinking green light told him everything he needed to know. His little tirade had been heard by the people outside. More people were pushing into the room now. They were angry, and voices were starting to be raised. With a strangled cry, Simon leapt off the stage and ran out through the back of the hall via the kitchen. That was the last anyone had seen of him.

Naturally the press had got hold of the story. This was gold. A candidate who had, almost, publicly told the electorate what he thought of them. Dynamite. Unfortunately, no-one could reach him to get any answers.

At campaign headquarters, the staff were left with the fallout. Deep down, they knew it was all over. Simon's political career was over. Their jobs were finished. However, they were the ones left to face the music. They looked to the campaign manager for some guidance. He was as lost as the rest of them. He shrugged his shoulders.

"If he had stayed, we could have dealt with this, done some damage limitation. God knows, others have survived worse. But no, he has to do a runner."

He looked around at the expectant faces.

"I'm sorry, folks. It's finished, we're finished. All I can do is tell you to go home."

For a few seconds, nobody moved. Then gradually, folders were put down, computers were switched off and people began to put on coats and pick up belongings. Sadly, they moved to the door. The Campaign manager was the last to leave. He looked around at the room where he had spent so much time over the last six months.

Switching off lights and locking doors, he shook his head sadly.

"What a bloody waste of time."

Life and Death in Beach Huts

Muriel Claybrook

Winter

The thin covering of snow, while adding to the bleakness, left him with a transient sense of wonder. All day the weather presenters had been saying how rare it was for snow to settle on salty sand. White, black, and blue were the predominant colours of the scene around him- snow, beach huts and sky. Meg, by his side, was never reluctant to walk and as he glanced down at her, he smiled ruefully. Yes, his Border Collie shared the colours of the scene around him. On this cold December day there were no tourists on this bit of the Norfolk coast, only a few fellow dog walkers. He was a reliable acquaintance for many of them and by the time he reached home after a walk, he had repeated the same cheery greeting numerous times.

Arthur's days were predictable. He would walk Meg three times daily in most types of weather, drive to town twice a week and call at the pub at weekend lunchtimes. His fairly isolated bungalow, set back from the beach, had been built between the wars and was in need of a facelift. The views it had over the long expanse of shore and out to sea, were what kept him in buoyant mood.

He'd meant to leave home by two but delayed himself by sorting out the post and his footwear. Now he noticed that the light was beginning to fade quickly, and he had not gone so far along the beach as he intended. Should he continue to his usual turning point, he mused. "Why not" he told himself. A few minutes later a young German shepherd dog bounded towards him from between two beach huts. As the dog was barking aggressively Meg cowered as near as she could get to Arthur's legs. In stumbling pursuit, a gangly youth now emerged, following the dog. He started shouting "Rebel, Rebel" in short constricted breaths, as he ploughed through the powdery snow covering the sand.

Rebel's glossy white teeth were flashing within centimetres of Arthur and Meg. Suddenly the youth's legs buckled, and he landed hunched up on the sand. Rebel retreated behind his owner, growling softly. Arthur hurried towards the lad, but cautiously: he'd seen addicts to a variety of chemicals here over the years. On closer inspection this boy's symptoms were familiar and respiratory. Arthur instinctively pulled out his inhaler to offer to the boy. With considerable effort he managed a couple of puffs and then sat quietly gasping for breath. After a few minutes Arthur suggested they try to move up the beach as the tide was coming in fast in the dwindling light.

Leaning on Arthur, the youth shuffled towards the huts at the top of the beach. Meg and Rebel eyed each other suspiciously and stayed close to their owners. Arthur kept a skeleton key that fitted two or three huts, as he acted as a voluntary care taker for some out of town owners. He opened number 23 and the two of them sank on to chairs inside. Meg crouched between them as Rebel kept up an insistent howl for attention. A couple of minutes later a curious passer by shone his torch into the hut startling Rebel who flew in Meg's direction, not with teeth bared but for protection!

Following some brief explanations Arthur and the stranger helped the youth up to the main road and then phoned for a taxi to take him home. Rebel had been fitted with the lead and muzzle her owner was carrying. Left at the edge of the road Arthur and the stranger agreed there had been no major mishaps here on this winter's afternoon. Everyone had survived, thanks to Arthur's swift and brave intervention.

As he walked back up the hill to his home, Arthur pondered that perhaps his reactions to the unexpected were becoming too pessimistic, possibly a reflection of his age. The possibility of his own and Meg's murder, had briefly shot through his head down there on the beach. In future, he decided, he would try to act on what it said on the plaque his late wife had hung in the hall years ago *"The older you get the more important it is not to act your age"*

Spring

Rowan, Ruby and Robyn had gone through the underpass linking school to the harbour area, before taking a short cut to the North beach. Ruby's family had an annual rental on a beach hut on this part of the Welsh coast. The key to the brightly painted orange hut was in her hand now and the three girls were soon inside. It was still five months to the height of the summer season and so the area was virtually deserted. Once inside they fed the meter and switched on a fan heater. Exchanging smug smiles, they had their phones at the ready and then they each set about creating nasty, belittling texts, each to a different class member.

Robyn was the timer, in this practised endeavour, and after two minutes one of her phone alarms went off, signalling that phones were to be passed on to the next writer. There was no need to read the previous message – if the next message was similar it would reinforce this strand of cruelty. If it was going off on a different track it would start torment of another kind. When the phone circulations were complete they simultaneously pressed **Send.**

Smiling at each other they wondered, aloud, how far they could drive the three recipients into black holes of self-loathing.

"The further the better" they all agreed. A change of behaviour, in the victims, was usually a sign that their group messages were working. Targets in the past had become more frequent absentees or dropped out of clubs or become frightened loners. That had let them know their messages were having some effect on their intended targets. These three new victims would probably respond in a similar manner by adopting one or other of these behaviours and becoming very miserable.

Half an hour had gone by in a flash and now the three of them needed to jog back the way they had come before afternoon school recommenced. Exiting the underpass, they were surprised to see blue flashing lights of a paramedic ambulance and police Range Rover, speeding through the school gate. There on the roof of the art block were all three targets. What were they doing? They appeared to be waving and shouting to fifty or so pupils and staff. Now as the three R's approached they could see the "victims" holding their phones up, laughing and indicating there was comedy on them. Then they became quiet and the smallest shouted, "My mum is an IT expert and will be able to track who sent this filth."

The culprits were rooted to the spot: whose downfall had they brought about in the beach hut?

One quick acting pupil had videoed the incident and quickly posted it on social media. It went viral and next day newspapers and TV bulletins referred to it. Hopefully the publicity would prompt second thoughts in some of the multitude of bullies out there, the next time they felt like abusing one of their peers.

Summer

Hot, hot, hot. Laura and Helen were soaking up the rays as they sat on their stripy sunbeds outside the beach hut. Never reliable, even for taking a June break, the weather was doing them proud this time.

"Soon be time for a coffee refill?" asked Laura?

"Mais oui!" agreed Helen, trying to add a continental dimension to the Cornish beach scene in front of them.

The sisters had come here on family holidays, from Yorkshire, many times as they grew up. This time they'd rented a ground floor apartment, with a sea view, in a new development just behind the beach. Helen's job with a city bank paid well and this was her treat for the two of them. She stretched, pulled down her Ray-Bans and asked, kindly

"Black Americano as usual?"

"No" replied Laura, "Make mine a macchiato this time" as she closed her eyes again.

Helen grabbed her bag and set off for the refreshment kiosk. She did not mind the walk from the end of the line of beach huts. Thoughts of yester year's trays of tea popped into her head. There used to be a ceramic pot, milk jug etc and Dad carrying it back triumphantly. Helen meanwhile was appreciating the sea air and solitude. She mused that had this been Spain or the Caribbean, Helen would not have had to walk to get refreshments. Yet, of course, beach vendors were a mixed blessing. She thought of her favourite black scarf, that was beaded and draped so well. She'd bought it at the beach in St Martin. The haggling for it had been fun. Now she wondered whether Helen would like to have it. It had been much admired and looked as if it had cost far more than it in fact did.

Rousing herself from these pleasant thoughts Laura smiled gratefully as the Styrofoam cups were placed on the little plastic table. She needed to wriggle herself to a more upright position and tried not to wince with pain as she did so. The cushions that Helen had brought were so useful.

"If you lean forward I'll put your backrest up a notch" said Helen. From behind Laura's back rest Helen glanced down at her sister's bronzing, but oh so very bony body. Thank goodness, she still has her mane of blonde hair she thought. It had been too late for chemo when the cancer had been discovered.

"That's it", Laura smiled as she leant back. "I'm not lying on my bag and its precious contents." Both girls began sipping their coffee and relaxed in each other's company.

Fifty metres in front of them the tide was beginning to turn. In two hours they would need to be packed up as it would take half an hour to get back to the car park. There was a dozen or so surfers near the centre of the bay so were too distant for the girls to assess their competence. They knew that the wet suited figures would be mostly locals who managed to surf most days and fitted their lives around this hobby.

A young family was making its way down to the water, from a beach hut about six to their left. Another month and the beach would be crowded thought Laura: I'm so glad we have been able to come now. Suddenly whistles were being blown near the water line and a couple of minutes later the unmistakeable booms of maroons from the headland to the west. Helen jumped up quickly and went to fetch the two pairs of binoculars from the hut. Thankfully, after just a few minutes they could see two beach lifeguards and some surfers carrying a body above the waves. Once on the sand expert first aid was applied and soon the prone figure was able to sit up.

It seemed discourteous to watch any longer, so Laura closed her eyes and Helen returned the binoculars to the hut. She started to unpack their picnic and set it out on the formica table in front of Laura's medical pack. Slightly thrown out of her usual equanimity, by the surfing accident, she reflected how transient and unpredictable life is for all of us. Sudden death could strike at any time- we all know that, but for sanity's sake we keep it buried, daily, deep in our consciousness. When one had been given a time to the inevitable, was it so wrong to put your own stamp on it? Once back in Leeds what would Laura's last days be like?

Helen had been given full instructions for the attachment and flow rate adjustment of the morphine pump and soon it would be time to renew supplies. She set the flow rate on the new piece of kit first, so it could be attached more easily and then went out to help Laura into the shade and privacy of the hut. It was cooler inside and after attending to medical matters, comfortably seated in her wheelchair with Helen by her side, Laura started to enjoy her lunch and winked at her sister.

Autumn

This year early October on the Yorkshire coast had been dry, crisp, and bright, so Mummy, optimistically, had reserved the red beach hut on the booking spread sheet of their owners' syndicate. Jo's late October birthday had been celebrated outside on only one of her now five years. When today dawned, Mummy was glad she'd taken the plunge. Five other children, six family members and three other mums would be at the party. All the children had just started full time at the local primary school.

Mummy had worked with beach camps twenty years ago and in the last week had enjoyed organising some games to keep everyone warm. Freddie, Jo's younger brother, Jo herself, Mummy and Daddy were at the hut by 1.30pm to get organised. The guests were invited for 2.00pm.

Not wanting to be late, Granny, Uncle Rob, Nanna, and Grandad were spotted approaching ten minutes too early. Shrieks of "Look what I've got" were heard as, wearing three birthday badges on the dress of her "Frozen" outfit, Jo ran to meet them. A dragon kite was being proudly held aloft. "There's no wind so we will have to fly it another day", she told them.

After a round of hugs and kisses the grownups were offered perching points on two wooden benches that lined the side walls of the hut. Soon the younger guests started to arrive, each giving a present to Jo. She opened them carefully, while the other children looked on expectantly. An Exploding shapes game, Sylvanian figures, a Paws Patrol activity set, and a pirate ship were all received with great excitement.

Sweets were then offered round by Jo's Mum before the gathering went down to the damp sand for games. An egg and spoon race was followed by testing skills weaving in and out between some plastic cones and balancing on logs and crates. Next Daddy and Uncle Rob brought out armfuls of brightly coloured spades from the hut. Jo and the other children began digging a hole and soon a construction of channels and steps had appeared. Grandad had to be restrained from developing the centre of the building site and Daddy relocated him to the outskirts of it. A few spadesful of sand had accidentally landed on grownups but there had been no intentional silliness. Dogs were allowed on the beach at this time of year, but such a relatively large group of noisy people had deterred any from approaching too closely to the diggers.

Nanna noticed the pot of giant chalk sticks that mummy had put out at the edge of the concrete walk way.

She wrote "HAPPY Birthday Jo" in several colours and embellished it with a pink heart. Sea water would lap over it in a few hours, leaving the path graffiti free again. When the children went to look at it Poppy, Jo's friend, decided there were too many capital letters in the message. The grownups grinned with pleasure that the first term at school was not being wasted. Daddy then started to bounce a football and with a cry of "Yes" from Freddie and Tommy, a joyful kick about was soon underway.

Five minutes later Mummy called everyone into the hut. There on the table was a butterfly shaped birthday cake with five long candles alight on the top. Once everyone was seated and Happy Birthday had been sung, Jo blew the candles out. Daddy expertly divided the cake into manageable pieces and individual party food boxes were handed round. Granny gave out drinks. While this was happening, Lucy her eight-month-old, bouncy cockerpoo, mistook Jo's new baby doll, Lily, for her own pink rubber pig. She grabbed Lily by the neck, playfully, but too strongly, so that after a couple of sideways shakes, Lily lay decapitated on the concrete floor.

Eyes wide with horror Mummy reacted in a split second; she collected the two parts of Lily into a handy gift bag, before anyone else noticed, and proceeded to distribute the take home goodie bags. She was not going to let this party be ruined at the last minute by a murder in the beach hut.

The Reading

Jan Jenner

She turned to the cards on the table unable to bear the pain seeping out of his voice.

"I just need to know my son's alive, that's all, just to know he's alive," he said.

The dark curtains at the window had transformed the hard spring light into a warm glow but he'd brought cold into the room with him. His expensive city suit crumpled, his badly shaven face pallid and drawn. His hands trembled slightly as if they weren't connected to him.

Her room was comfortable, outside noises penetrated through the closed window into the soft darkness. Shrill voices and a sharp salvo of laughter. The buzz of traffic. They were all a background to her life. She liked it. It anchored her to the present, it kept her grounded when the knowing threatened to engulf her.

They were all the same, those that came to her small shabby room, with the clichéd velvet covered table and the incense. They tried to keep expectations on a rational level, believing it would be just the one visit.

They were nervous and mostly they talked. The Information dripped out of them. Embarrassed to be here, they had no idea where else to go.

Some, the sceptics, stayed quiet. They held back the emotion because they rationalised there were no answers.

He wasn't a sceptic, he was too frightened not to believe.

"You see he died so suddenly, there was no time to say goodbye." His voice was firm, cultured, his grey hair distinguished, but he was only a spectre of the man he used to be. She winced at the wretchedness in his eyes. Usually at home in the city's boardrooms, confident with the privileged few, he was now defeated, swallowed into his grief

She kept her face closed, sympathetic but not involved. Keeping a distance was essential or they would rifle through her emotions and leave her bankrupt.

He was in his early forties, so his son would probably have been in his mid-twenties. He hadn't mentioned grandchildren. He hadn't mentioned his wife either. Was she still alive?

She went through the ritual of shuffling the cards and laying them on the table. She asked him to select five cards and arranged them in a circle. The ritual gave them value for money, maybe a focus for their thoughts as well. They didn't understand it was there all the time. She didn't need cards, runes or crystals, it was all around her, but not always for the right person and not always the right answer. She sat with her hands on the table, she could hear him breathing, each breath shallow, as if he resented the life it gave him.

She'd had the ability to know things for as long as she could remember. She was not even a seventh child of a seventh child. She was weary now, weary of the pain in their faces, of their loneliness. Weary of their doubt in her and of their fear that there might be nothing after all. It was too easy to read people, they gave you the information. You could use it to convince them, some needed convincing. Not to cheat them, there was no need for that. The knowing was always there, layer after layer, but it was not always what they wanted to know, sometimes they wanted the wrong answers.

"He had plans for the future," she told him. "He was full of energy and life."

"Yes, Yes he was." The man leant forward, an eager smile on his face. For a moment she saw the man he'd been before.

She closed her eyes and sighed, boys in their twenties were always full of energy with dreams and plans filling their heads. She wondered what he would have said if she'd told him his son was a selfish, idle wastrel with no more objective in his life than where to find the next high.

"He was so young, I wish it had been me." His voice was quiet, barely audible. He'd probably said these words many times before. "It should have been me."

"No, no." She told him urgently, "it shouldn't have been you. It was his time, not yours."

"Yes," he smiled dismally, "of course, but I expect every father would feel the same. I want him to know how much I loved him."

"Sometimes," she said, "there is no reason, it can just be an accident. Not contrived, not predetermined, just an accident, an unfortunate, mindless, heart-breaking accident."

That concept was always hardest to get across.

We lived in an unstable world. A world where one mischance could send one person sliding into a life of anguish, as another slips by to languish in a life of contented mediocrity. Anything could happen and often did.

"I do understand it was an accident," he said, did he realise he had tears running down his cheeks? "But I don't understand why, he was my boy."

"Sometimes there is no why, so there is no answer." She told him softly. Of course, she knew the answer, she could see the boy, his eyes bright, shining with whatever it was he'd taken that night. Strong in the conviction of his immortality.

The others were cheering him on. She could sense rather than hear them. The foolish, mindless boys he called his friends. He wouldn't let them down, would he? He knew their expectations. Proud in his daring.

She could feel his elation as he balanced on the edge, the light from the moon had shone across the roof catching his reflection on the wet slate. With a heart tearing suddenness, she felt the rapturous joy as he glided through air. She knew his last thoughts.

'They would respect him now, they would know what he could do.' It was the admiration of his friends he craved, not his father's love. The devastated man was weeping on the other side of her table.

"He knew you loved him," she said, reaching across and touching his hand.

Field of Dreams

Liese Cooper

I packed a couple of small pieces of 12 by 12 cm fine watercolour paper, a jar of water and three tubes of watercolours into a coat pocket and walked a mile to the field. It was a bright early summer's day, with just a few wisps of cloud in a blue sky. My beautiful wife, Rose, was still asleep, our easy love-making that night as always, a beautiful memory. The natural smell of her hair, her neck and arms, were still clear in my mind. She had stretched her hand towards me from the bed, silently begging a last kiss before I left for the day, her blood-red nails lay stark against the white sheets, her sleepy smile inviting and tender. At midday she would join me in the field bringing a basket of bread, cheese and apples and beer and we would lie together in the grass, under the oak tree like the newly-weds we were. This was our honeymoon.

I climbed and reached the top of a small hill at the far edge of the field and sat down, with a view over the dips and hills of the valley below. I could just hear the shallow stream in the distance, trickling across ancient stones. Now and again I glimpsed sparkles of sunlight on the water. Breathing in deeply the nourishing morning air, I sat down and placed my paints and water jar next to me in the grass and prepared to paint. Overhead a skylark sang a warning to me not to go near her nest nearby amongst the tussocks of grass. We shared the tranquillity and of the field. Overhead, the warm, early spring sunlight on my back felt so good. There was as much time before me as I wanted, the day stretched ahead, long and inviting.

In my white bowl I squeezed a dab of each of the primary colours on the points of an imaginary triangle – red on top, yellow below to the right and blue opposite, on the left. I unscrewed the top of my jar of water, selected the large round size 10 brush and mixed a blue for the first wash with plenty of water to dilute the colour, the sky was only at its earliest reflective power of the day. Then I cleaned the brush and, bringing only water to the paper, I wet the top half as much as I dared without soaking it. Quickly picking up a little of the diluted blue I dropped it here and there into the wet paint. Instantly, the sky emerged, the paint running easily into the grooves of the paper, forming rivulets and blooms. I picked up the paper, moved it around to control the flow of the paint until it resembled the streaks of an early morning sky, with the milkiness of early sunlight. With a scrap of fabric from my pocket I dabbed the wetness here and there to resemble soft clouds overhead. There was an alchemy, a magic in water colour painting. Sometimes it worked, sometimes it didn't. Today it did.

I cleaned the brush and mixed the yellow with a little blue to obtain a sappy, fresh green that would capture the colour of the fields and hedgerows in early spring, here and there darkening the shade to give depth and texture. Along the tops of the foliage I dappled the undiluted lemon yellow, to indicate a rising sun.

The sun has moved round behind the great oak to my right and it's feeling cooler. The grass is damp with evening dew and my hands are cold enough to have lost some facility with the brushwork. The stream below reflects a pastel light. It's time to pack up. I throw the chattels of a day's painting into my kit bag. I empty and then leave the jar to fill with rain water for next time.

Just in time, I make my way down the hill when the familiar crash of bamboo sticks against the wooden walls of the hut wakes me. Instantly, the pastel mauve pallet of an early English summer's evening is transformed, without blending, but straight into hot, white, drab greys, where distant scrubland recedes behind the relentless dust of activity in the prisoners' yard. I lift myself up from the bunk and peer out through the gap I made in hut wall. No change. Still the pervasive odour of the sweat of twelve men's bodies during a hot night, still the arid openness of the camp. Even now at five in the morning it is hot and humid. Chalky and Charlie are already down from their bunks. Motes of dust float on the still air in the hut.

"Right, lads, quails in aspic this morning, there's rumours of devilled kidney."

I join in, "Weather's looking good for a sortie into the hills this morning, spot of painting I think," I jump down.

"Aye!", Jimmy laughs, "I'll bring ye that haggis for a spot of lunch, neeps n tatties in a tin. Ye'll be ready for some snap by then. Praps a wee dram too, to finish off and keep ye warm this bitter cold day."

Susho yells from outside "Shattap!" in that persuasive way he has. Our irony is lost on him.

I see their dry, wizened bodies as we are herded to the wash house. Our skin like leather, wrinkled before time like old men's, our ribs and shoulder blades stark in the harsh, white morning sunlight. I think of Rose on our bed, her vermilion nails kneeding the white sheet as I approach the basins.

School's Out

Pat Buckley

After Winnie had been sent to bed, her father's angry voice had risen through the floor from the kitchen, and she'd heard her mother cry. In the morning the house was unusually peaceful. Even the clatter and bustle as the family set off for work had subsided. Then a sound rose, Baby was yelling, "Exercising his lungs" Mam would say. Mam was soothing him. She realised she had been allowed a sleep in and she wasn't even ill.

When she went down to the kitchen, Mam straightaway handed Baby to her to nurse. Winnie bounced him up and down on her knee, while she ate her bread and jam. Jam! This must be a special day; not her birthday either, that was in December and this was March.

Monday was washing day. Baby was put to rest in a pram which had carried too many children and Maisie was tasked with watching over her while Mam loaded the tub with hot water from the range and possing the dirtiest. When the rubbing and scrubbing were done, Mam and Maisie sat and shared a cup of tea before the next stage, which was always hard work. This time, Maisie was able to help by lifting the wet clothes from the sink while Mam turned the big heavy handle on the mangle so the clothes were squeezed between the thick wooden rollers.

The fine day meant the clothes were hung to dry on the line in the back alley. With the steel works at the end of the street, and the surrounding house chimneys, there was ever the hope that not too many smuts would settle to undo the cleansing work. Father was strong on that, especially his best white shirt that he wore to the club on a weekend. Father liked the club. Mam once said that he should take his bed there, but he always came home no matter what the time.

At dinner time, there was another surprise as Mam put some of the cottage pie, made from yesterday's leftovers, onto her plate. This was usually reserved for Father and her older brothers and sisters who went out to work. Mam said she didn't really need much dinner, so she just had some bread and scrape.

As they made up the family's beds, Mam told her about the beautiful linen she had brought with her when she married; the hours spent putting together her bottom drawer; the delicate embroidery, and the hopes for her future. She was working then and had some money to spend on herself and her things, and the time to enjoy them.

The sheets were wearing thin. Mam would later cut and turn them sides to middle to extend their use and later make cot sheets or dusters. She used an old treadle sewing machine which sat in the corner of the parlour. As they worked, Mam stretched and eased her back and, even then, Winnie failed to notice the purpling bruise on her mother's arm.

Mam was going to the shops with Baby in the pram. She raked deep in her purse and found a penny for the child and, freeing her to go and play, also handed over a length of rope, enough for skipping.

Full of joy at these unexpected gifts, Winnie hopped and skipped along the road. She knocked at her friend's door. She wanted Maisie to come and play, and to pick the rare treat of sweets that they would share. No one was home, so she ran on to the sweet shop alone.

Mrs Pearce, who ran the sweet shop, had a permanent frown on her face. "Old acid drop" was what Mam called her. She looked up when Winnie bounced into the shop.

"Not at school, eh?" she demanded, "Not playing hookie, I hope." She fixed Winnie with a steely eye, as if defying her to tell a lie.

"No," said Winnie brightly, "it's day off,"

"Where's everyone else then, funny they are not about?" persisted Mrs Pearce.

"Don't know," said Winnie, "but Mam had me at home and said it was ok to go to the park."

All the while, Winnie was impatiently eyeing the glass jars. Pursing her lips, Mrs Pearce leaned back and let her get on with the serious business of making a choice.

Winnie spent the next five minutes trying to decide how to spend her penny. Liquorice comfits, dolly mixtures, treacle toffee, chocolate; this was a big decision. Eventually, she bought Mam's favourite fruit salads. She watched as Mrs Pearce weighed them out and then even though the correct weight had been reached, pop one more on. Winnie was amazed. She'd not seen that done before. What a day. Wait till she told Mam about that.

Winnie carefully stowed the penny poke in her pocket and skipped to the park expecting to find her school friends but there was no one of Winnie's age, or even anyone she knew. There were only a few of the younger mums with babies and toddlers, and they did not count. So she had her pick of the swings and ran and pushed the teapot lid round and round before jumping on board and spinned until she was dizzy. Having no one to share her sweets with, she sat on a bench, and savoured each one, but she carefully kept a few back, because she knew Mam would enjoy a sweetie treat.

Eventually she realised that it was getting colder. The sun was going down and so she joined the mums and toddlers as they headed home. Along the way, she spotted Maisie, and in great excitement rushed up to her to share the joys of her day. She could not understand why Maisie was not as happy as she.

"But you should have been at school," Maisie spluttered, "It was the scholarship. We've been writing and doing sums all day."

In disbelief, she looked at the others from her class as they told her how hard it had been, how much they'd written, and how they had to add and multiply and divide until their heads ached.

There was nothing but panic inside her. Winnie ran. She ran through the streets, past school friends calling out to her, bumping into anyone who got in her way. Her chest heaving, she arrived in the school yard and, against the rules, ran straight through the main door not stopping until she reached her classroom.

"Please sir," she gasped, "I didn't know it was scholarship day. Could I do it now? I ran all the way as soon as I heard."

Sir was a kind man, and he knew the effect on this bright, clever child of what he had to say.

"I am sorry Winnie. The scholarship is taken on one day only. Everyone has to take it at the same time for it to be fair. There is nothing I can do, you missed it"

In that minute, her whole world crumbled, every hope and dream she had nurtured in her school time just disappeared. She'd had plans. Go to the grammar school, learn enough to matriculate; maybe go to college. She'd dreamed of a good job. Go to work in an office, all dressed up and smart, not like her sisters. They were skivvies, maids or in shops; long hours, hard work, rough hands, little cash. She had expected to do better but now it was gone.

Sir patted her back. "You'd better go home." he said, "They will be wondering where you are"

And, with that final dismissal, she turned and headed back. Not the pell mell hurtle of before but a slow dragging passage. Hardly able to breathe, she choked on her sobs and tears.

Mam was in the kitchen when she returned to the house and she hurtled in still sobbing and weeping. Mam held her close as she listened to the sad tale. As she stroked and soothed her, Mam thought back to the row last night, when Father read the letter from the school. Father was a skilled worker, rough and strong through his work around the blast furnace. He was adamant.

"There's no point in her taking that scholarship", he'd shouted, "Even if she passes, she's not going to the grammar. I'm not keeping her all that time. It's not worth it, for a girl as well. What good's getting her an education? She'll never use it. She'll have to earn her keep until she gets in the family way and has to get married, like you did."

When she'd argued for her child's future, he settled it with his fist as he'd done many times before. As he slammed out of the door he'd turned back.

"Just you remember, for her, school's out"

A New Town

Muriel Claybrook

The sound of laughter drifted up from the street below, making him feel very alone. What would his friends be doing in all their new towns?

He had not got into a Hall of Residence, having scraped into the university through clearing. With his parents' help he had found a small flat above a takeaway. He could move on after the first month, when he'd had time to explore the town and make some acquaintances on his courses.

Well, he wasn't going to sit here any longer. He grabbed his hoody and went downstairs to find a pub in the High Street. That wasn't hard as there were several, and people from the suburbs were congregating here on this Friday night.

Several pubs later, and now in the early hours, he started to walk back home. Trying a short cut down one of the Wynds, he found himself on a well-lit pathway along the river bank. He persisted in what he thought was the right direction.

Next morning, just before lunch, his mum, decided to give him a quick call, on the off chance he would pick up, to see how things were going. Not concerned by the lack of response, she and his dad, enjoyed an outing to visit local friends. Returning in time for tea, alarm bells did not ring immediately when they saw the police car parked in front of their house.

Day or Night

Anne Marie Phillips

I can hear a phone ringing somewhere, but it doesn't sound like my phone. I wonder if I changed the ringtone and forgot about it. Then it stops, and I realise that someone has answered it. I am confused now, as I know that I haven't answered it and Emma must be at school. The confusion increases as I realise that I am in bed, but it is daytime. Why am I in bed during the day? I try to get up but my head hurts. Maybe that is why I am in bed. I lie still for a moment until the pain in my head eases and I try to work out where I am. I open my eyes slowly and the pain increases. I close them again and breathe through the pain. Memories begin to return but they are confused. Daytime becomes night-time, then daytime again. The memories become clearer and I feel my heart rate rising as I remember the last few days.

One week ago:

The call came just as I was thinking about getting ready for bed. I was tempted to ignore it and let the machine pick it up. Then I thought about who it might be and the curious me just couldn't ignore it. As I picked up the phone I felt a tingling sensation that I often felt just before something went wrong or I received bad news. My heart sank. It was my 17-year-old daughter, Emma.

"Hi Mum" she called cheerfully. Alright then, obviously not bad news.

"Hi love, what's the problem?"

"Erm, I'm not exactly sure, but I think I am being followed" The words tumbled out in a rush.

Emma wasn't a nervous person and wasn't given to flights of fancy. If she thought she was being followed, then she probably had very good cause. I immediately began to visualise all sorts of dreadful scenarios. I stopped myself from panicking and thought about the problem. The first thing was to make sure Emma got herself somewhere where she felt safer.

"Where are you right now?" I asked her urgently.

"I'm just coming up to the station. I thought there would be more people around here. It looks a bit quiet though."

She didn't need to tell me she was scared. I could hear it in the slight trembling of her voice.

"That sounds as good as place as any. Get inside and see if there are people around. The café is usually still open now. Go in there and I will be as quick as I can. If you get worried, call the police."

"I will Mum. Thanks for this. I know you don't like driving at night.

"Don't be silly, love. You know I would much rather you call me than get into difficulties. Now get inside."

"Thanks Mum" Emma ended the call but not before I heard the puff that told me she was holding her breath. She always did that when she was worried.

She was right about me not liking driving at night. I never had. For some reason, it always made me nervous. I honestly wasn't sure why. Nothing had ever happened at night and in some ways, it was easier. At least you could see headlights coming before you even saw the car. I was just being silly. I put on my coat, picked up my car keys and stepped outside ......

.... into blinding sunshine!

I blinked several times, unsure of what I was seeing. I opened the front door and stepped back inside, into total darkness. My heart was pounding now, and my breath was coming in short gasps. My first reaction was to want to lock the door and go to bed and ignore what was happening. I couldn't though. I had to go and get Emma. I moved into the living room and peered out between the curtains. It was still night-time out there. I gave myself a mental shake and told myself to stop being stupid. My daughter needed me and whatever was happening, she had to be my priority.

I took another deep breath and stepped outside again. Again, I found myself in bright sunshine. I felt completely confused and disorientated. My brain just couldn't cope with what it was seeing. My watch said 10.00 pm, but this looked more like 10.00am. Resolutely I walked to the car and opened it. At least if this continued, I wouldn't be driving at night after all.

Pulling out of the estate onto the main road was even more confusing. Cars coming towards me had their headlights on. It was after the second car flashed and hooted at me that I realised I hadn't put my lights on. I hadn't thought I needed them, but all these other people obviously thought it was night-time and Dammit, It WAS night-time, of course it was. I put my lights on and continued into town.

It was very quiet on the roads, just as I would have expected for the time of night. If it had been 10.00am, then it would have been considerably busier. My brain and my eyes just refused to communicate with each other. I couldn't wait to see Emma and find out what she saw. I was horribly afraid that it was just me and if it was, then what on earth was happening to me?

As I approached the station, I could see Emma huddled in a doorway watching out for me. When she saw the car, her relief was obvious, and she hurried over to jump in. She threw her arms around me and gave me a huge hug. I hugged her back a little more tightly than usual. I wasn't sure who was the most relieved. After a moment, she sat back and pulled off her hat and gloves.

"Gosh, Mum. Thanks for coming. I really didn't want to get you out at night, but I was so scared. I'm not sure if I was being followed, but I could hear footsteps that got quicker when I did. Anyway, they stopped when I got to the station. There were a few people around and I felt a lot safer. I probably could have got a taxi."

"No love, It's fine. I would much rather pick you up if you are bothered. Now tell me something. It is really night-time isn't it?"

"Yeah Mum, 'course it is." The look she gave me spoke volumes. "Mum, are you sure you are alright?"

"No." I replied gripping the steering wheel harder. "No, I don't think I am."

I took a deep breath, the headache that had been threatening ever since Emma's call suddenly making itself felt. I thought very carefully about what I was going to say next.

Emma sat quietly as I recounted my strange experience. She never interrupted but I could see her looking more and more worried. As I finished, I turned to her, hoping she might say something that would make all of this seem silly and trivial. She didn't. She frowned at me.

"Has this ever happened before?"

"No, of course not. I would have said something."

"Hmm, I wonder. You always try to protect me and make out everything is alright. I don't think you would have told me."

She was probably right. Emma and I had been alone for so long now. I was used to being both Mum and Dad. She had never known her Dad. He had walked out before she was born saying he wasn't ready to be a patent. I wasn't ready myself, but I didn't have much choice. I just carried on and did the best I could. We hadn't done so badly. Emma was a great girl and seemed to have no desire to see her Dad. He had never made contact anyway and we had no idea where he was.

"I'm sorry if I've been over protective. I can't help it. Well, I'm not being that now. I'm scared, and I need your help."

"OK, this is what we are going to do. You are going to drive home, go to bed and in the morning, we are going to see the doctor."

"The doctor? I exclaimed, what is he going to do?"

"I have no idea, Mum, but you need to see someone and he's the only person I can think of."

I thought about this for a moment. I couldn't see any point in seeing a doctor, but at least I would be able to tell someone else. Perhaps he would have a good explanation for this.

We drove home in silence. Emma frowned when I pulled the sun visor down and gave me a look. I ignored her, the sun really was in my eyes.

It was a long night and I didn't sleep very well. The thought kept going through my mind that there was something wrong with me. Then I thought that perhaps the world was going mad. But Emma had convinced me that it really was night time when I picked her up. Of course, it was. She would never have been afraid during the daytime. That meant it had to be me. It was not a very comforting thought. Ideas kept buzzing around my head, so it was little wonder that I didn't get to sleep until the early hours, that and the fact that I have never been able to sleep in the daytime.

I woke up when Emma brought me a cup of tea. It was dark in the room, yet Emma was opening the curtains.

"Come on Mum, it's 9.30 and I have been able to get you an appointment for 10.00."

"At night?"

"Oh Mum, it's daytime. Does it seem dark to you?"

I fell back on the pillows, tears were pricking behind my eyelids. I didn't want to cry in front of my daughter but the fear that rushed over me was overwhelming. Suddenly, Emma had wrapped her arms around me and was holding me tightly. It was a total role reversal, but it was also the comfort I needed. I let myself go and sobbed on my daughter's shoulder.

"It's OK Mum, I'm here. I am staying with you and we will get through whatever this is together. Just like we always do."

I got out of bed and by resolutely refusing to even think about what my eyes were seeing, I was able to get showered and dressed and even managed to eat something before we went out. I hesitated as we went outside and without saying a word, Emma took the car keys from me and got into the driver's seat.

We were lucky at the surgery. Although it was quite busy, for once, everyone seemed to be keeping to time, and before long, I was sitting in front of my doctor wondering just where to begin.

He listened carefully as I recounted the events of the previous evening and this morning. When I finished, he opened the blinds on his window and asked me what I could see outside. I gave him an exasperated look.

"I can't see anything. It's dark outside. But like I told you, that didn't happen last night. It looked dark when I looked through the window, but when I went outside, it was daylight."

"So, things have changed since last night?"

"Yes, I suppose they have." I answered cautiously. Suddenly I was very afraid. Up until now I hadn't thought about it, but things were different to last night. Was this good or bad?

He did a thorough examination. Blood pressure, temperature, eyes, ears, even my balance. Then he asked how I felt myself, physically.

"Alright, I suppose, except for a pounding headache. I didn't sleep very well so that probably accounts for that."

"I am going to make a few phone calls. I need to you to wait in the waiting room and I will see you again in a few minutes."

I returned to Emma who was looking anxious as she waited for me.

"What did he say. Does he know what is wrong?"

"He is making some phone calls and will see me again in a few minutes."

The receptionist was talking on the telephone as I looked over at her. I wouldn't have taken any notice except that she kept looking over at me and then quickly looking away. My suspicions were confirmed when she came over and asked if she could get me a drink or anything.

"Did the doctor call you and ask you to do that?"

"He has asked, you to wait and he wants to be sure you are comfortable while you do."

"Thank you, I am fine and no, I don't want a drink."

She returned to her desk looking a bit hurt.

"Mum, that was rude," exclaimed Emma, shocked at my attitude.

I did feel a little guilty, but right now I as more scared than anything else. I was convinced that something was going on. I was certain that men in white coats were going to come and take me away in a straight jacket. I was just getting ready to get up and run when the doctor stuck his head out of the door and beckoned to me to come back in. So, no men in white coats just yet then. Taking a deep breath, I started towards the door but stopped as Emma got up to follow me.

"It's alright love, you stay here."

"I would like your daughter to come in as well. I need to give her some instructions."

Emma gave my arm a squeeze as we went back into the consulting room. The doctor wasted no time as he began to explain what he had been doing.

"I have called the hospital and spoken to the neurology department. They agree with me that they would like to see you immediately. They have a slot available for an MRI scan in about an hours' time and the neurologist will see you after. We are certain that some sort of pressure is causing your symptoms but without a scan, we cannot begin to guess what is causing it. Don't panic and start thinking the worst. Once we can see what is going on, then we can give you answers."

He turned to Emma. "Can you drive your Mum to the hospital and stay with her?"

"Yes of course I can." Emma voice shook, and I could tell she was as scared as I was.

After that, everything happened very quickly and almost in silence. I couldn't think of anything to say and I was afraid that if I opened my mouth, I would start to scream, and I am not sure I would be able to stop. So, I kept it firmly closed. We arrived at the hospital and made our way to the neurology department. As soon as Emma gave my name to the girl at the desk, I was whisked away, given a gown to wear and within what seemed like seconds I was on a bed, inside a noisy machine being told to keep perfectly still. I did. I felt paralysed, almost too afraid to even breathe. In no time at all, I was in a bed in a small room and a doctor was talking to me. Emma was holding my hand, but I wasn't hearing anything. I heard the word "tumour" and I blanked everything out after that. I was going to die. My beautiful daughter would be on her own. I would never see her grow up, get married or have children.

Then Emma hugged me, and I heard her say "Oh thank God. Mum, did you hear that?"

"What?" I whispered. "What did they say, Am I going to die?"

The doctor leant over and made me look at him.

"Can you hear me?" he said quietly. I nodded slowly.

"The tumour is very small, but the pressure that it is exerting on your brain is what is causing you to experience these delusions. We are reasonably confident that it is benign, but we will know for definite when we remove it."

"When?" I asked. "When will you remove it?" I was anxious now to be rid of this thing in my head. This thing that had me so confused.

"You will go into surgery tomorrow. Hopefully, everything should go back to normal."

I couldn't stop the tears now. They poured down my cheeks and into my hair. I was still afraid I might scream so I put my hand over my mouth. I focused on Emma's soothing voice at my side and soon the panic began to subside. I wasn't going mad. I have something in my head and they are going to remove it. The relief is immense, and I wasn't even afraid of the surgery. I just wanted this thing out of my head.

Now:

As the memories of the last few days come flooding back, I feel a huge sense of relief. I am obviously still alive, and I am fairly sure it is daytime. A nurse appears at my side.

"Well, Hello there," she says cheerfully. "Good to see you properly awake. How do you feel?"

"My head hurts," I whisper.

"It will hurt for a bit, but I can get you some pain relief now you are awake." She starts to move away but I grab her hand.

"Tell me," I croak, "Is it daytime?"

"Why yes, it is. It's the middle of the afternoon. It's a lovely sunny day. Is it too bright? It may hurt your eyes for a day or two. I can close the blinds for you."

"No," I say firmly. "Leave them. I need to see if it is day or night."

She smiles understandingly, pats my hand and goes to get me some pain relief. I breathe a huge sigh of relief. Everything seems back to normal and I know that once my head stops hurting, I am going to be fine. Emma and I are going to be fine. I don't really want to cry, but a tear escapes and runs down my cheek.

"Thank you," I whisper. "If there is anyone up there, Thank you." I close my eyes and relax.

Remembrance Days

By Pat Buckley

Ena James, a small neat dark haired lady in her late thirties, watched the telegram boy cycle up near the house. These boys, once so welcome, had become dreaded bringers of bad news. Ena hoped that he was coming for one of the neighbours but this selfishness she later wished had been true was turned sour when he stepped up and knocked hard on her door. Smoothing down her working pinafore she received the yellow envelope. Her hands shaking so much she could hardly open it. When she opened out the message, she read, "Pte Albert James. Missing in action believed killed."

The dread news shook her body, heavily pregnant with their third child, she fell to the floor. Old Mrs Jones from across the way saw the boy, guessed his purpose and was quickly by her side. Soon neighbours gathered, put her to bed, cared for her and her children, fed them, washed clothes, cleaned the house, while she screeched and wailed in grief and pain until her tiny premature girl child made her way into the world.

The days and weeks following passed in a blur. People came and went. Her sister, whose husband was also a soldier, came to stay for a long while to look after them all. Gradually Ena emerged from the blanket of grief and disbelief, where she had taken refuge, into the reality of her bereavement and her family's condition. She went through the motions of her new existence, signed papers and she knew not what. There was heaviness inside her, which she could not move. Ena feared for her family's future.

The baby, which all the family had looked forward to, filled her with no joy. Nevertheless she grew strong and was called June in honour of her birth month. June could never know her dad. The other two girls had only vague memories of him.

Eighteen months later, a plain white envelope dropped on the mat, the address of carefully formed letters written in a hand she did not recognise.

"Dear Mrs James,

I trust you will forgive my forwardness in writing to you like this.

I was with your Albert in the Pals right through until the end and a good pal he was to me.

If you allow, I could tell you about him and the time away from home.

Your obedient servant

Ernest Williams"

A shock ran through her, not felt since the day the day the telegram came. Ena turned the letter over in her hand. A faint hope had often entered her mind.

Perhaps, she thought, he would tell her Albert was not dead after all; just injured, lost his memory maybe. No matter how badly hurt he was she needed to know. She wanted him back again to touch him, to hold him close, to hear his voice, to stroke his lovely fair hair.

Ena thought long and hard about what she should do. What was best for her and her little family? She vaguely remembered Albert talking about an Ernie. The two men had formed a bond. At last she was convinced. If anyone would know where Albert was, Ernest Williams was the person. Eventually she wrote back inviting him to come to tea.

Ena had set out her best set because his visit was kindly meant and she was desperate for the news he would bring. She had been apprehensive of this visit from the day the letter had arrived and she saw that he too was ill at ease. Ernest sat on the edge of the chair in the tiny parlour and carefully held the cup and saucer as if it would shatter in his large workman's hands. Ena had wanted him to feel he was welcome but she realised too late that instead these trappings made him feel nervous and uncomfortable.

Hesitating at first, Ernest began his tale.

"We joined up together", he told her, "after them in Parliament had decreed that married men with children would be conscripted. Kitchener's army needed us.

I left my Betty behind, with a young one on the way, Albert you and your two. We shared many a good talk about our families while we struggled through our basic training at Ripon.

There were youngsters with us, first time away from home, often unsure and frightened. Albert was good with them. He was an old man at 35 years of age, almost like their fathers. He was a great reader your Albert, not all the lads could. Many nights in barracks he would read out loud, great stories and it gave the lads calm and peace, and a time away from the life of the common soldier."

Ena dabbed an eye, and noticing he paused, until she told him to go on. She needed him to talk, to make Albert alive, to become a person again in her mind.

Ernest continued "We did some more training on Salisbury Plain and had one last home leave before being shipped out."

Ena smiled at remembrance of this. Her mother had taken the children and they had time for each other for the first time since their marriage 9 years before. They had gone to the music hall and laughed and sang. The whole family went together to the park. The girls had played on the swings and chased a ball while Albert had pretended to play football with them. Their squeals of laughter rose in the crisp autumn air; so carefree for a while. The world had seemed so fresh and clean, and far away from the darkness of war. The night before he left, she had clung to him, and he promised to return to her and their little family.

Ernest went on."We were sent to France as reinforcements. My first time at sea, and the little ship bounced and bucketed over the waves. Most of us were ill. Believe me Mrs James; I never wanted to do it again. Over there, we lived in trenches, holes in the ground, muddy, horrible. Us Tommies wondered why we'd spent so much time marching and drilling. Digging and burying would have fitted us better for what we faced.

But there were some good times on relief, away from the front. We found an old piano in the corner of the canteen. It looked like it had been through a few wars itself, but young Fred managed to knock a tune out of it and we sang; old songs, folk songs, stuff we remembered from the music hall. Some of it made us laugh. Much of it made us sad as we remembered where we had heard it before and who was with us; mothers, fathers, brothers, sisters, sweethearts, wives.

And there were letters. Your Albert would help out in reading post for those who could not manage it, and drafting answers for them. I specially remember the day Albert got the letter from you to say there was a new baby on the way. He was so proud."

"Thank you" she whispered as he paused in his tale.

"We returned to the front, we moved and dug, and fired and ducked when they fired back." he continued. Ernest could not share the full horror of the trenches: the dirt, the smells, the blood, the fear, men losing limbs, gangrene, the bodies of the dead, gas attacks, barbed wire, bombs, sometimes going forward, at others pulling back. It would be many years before he could tell that story and address the terrible guilt of being a survivor when so many perished.

"It went on for months until one day we were ordered over the top. We rose up together. I saw him shot and he fell back. I had to go on and never saw him again. I'm sorry missus."

They sat in silence for a while and eventually he made his farewells, leaving her with the certainty that she was on her own, her and the three girls.

Albert's name was listed on the war memorial next to the gates of the park in their home town. Along with many other local people, she attended the unveiling by the Mayor and local dignitaries. The whole town stood with heads bowed in silent respect for the fallen.

As soon as the girls could understand, she would take them there on national Remembrance Day, wearing their poppies with pride. She would tell them about their father how he lived his life, and how he died to protect them all, in the war to end all wars.

Later Ena learnt that the war graves people had commissioned Sir Edwin Lutyens, no less, to create an impressive marble monument to be erected at Arras. All those who had died in that area, without marked graves, would be commemorated there; around 3,500 names including Private Albert James. She knew she would never be able to travel to see it so she kept the newspaper clippings. She thought about all those men, the families they left behind and the many thousands more who died in battles across the world.

Ena never fully knew the privations of Albert's life at war but some understanding of the terror he must have felt came when she cowered shaking and fearing for the safety of her family and friends in the shelter during the Second World War air raids.

The waste and futility of it all overwhelmed her.

The Ticket

Maxine Patterson

She'd made sure she was home early enough to prepare their evening meal. Not something that happened every day and, having made a special effort, she wanted the meal to be enjoyed. His car drew up outside and she waited for him to come in.... Nothing. Exasperated she went out to call him. He was on the phone chatting away. Why couldn't the call wait until after their dinner?

Finally, he bustled in, his expensive suit trousers creased, the jacket suspended by the collar tag; his briefcase slung carelessly onto the hall table. Yet another problem with some delivery or something. She didn't listen, all these urgent work messages blended into one long ongoing list of excuses. The pretence of belief had worn thin. Meetings away, weekends away, money disappearing. It was a pattern that had started early in the relationship, he unable to stay faithful, yet not wanting to abandon the marriage.

Yet still she stayed, inertia is a powerful force. After an earlier affair, she had made plans to leave. He'd been devastated and promised to change. Of course, he hadn't, but until lately he'd been discreet and careful.

They sat down together for the normal evening meal, the usual chat; the short hand conversation. After such a long marriage, they knew each other so well – a companionable ending to their busy day. They worked hard in their totally separate lives and wouldn't countenance weakness. Their individual drive and ambition complemented each other. They discussed work and what they would be doing over the weekend.

She reflected on their, apparently, successful, marriage with all the trappings. His car, the latest, fastest and newest typical executive; hers, an acknowledgement of her mid-life crisis, a post-menopausal Porsche that she scorched around in. The old farmhouse remodelled and lovingly redeveloped to become the family home she had always dreamed of. The walled garden her pride and joy. He enjoyed the house and garden, but it was a backdrop to his real life, his work.

His ambition and drive had propelled him upwards into a post that allowed him huge influence and power. He loved it, he achieved major successes and the subsequent recognition and acknowledgement fed his vanity. She, equally ambitious, had worked hard and been successful, enjoying the challenge as a senior manager in a large secondary school. He discussed latest development plans in the business and she shared the personnel and management issues that she was dealing with. They valued each other's awareness and business acumen.

Yet under the surface, these together - separate people were so different. She was uncertain, watchful, and alert to any hint of who the unknown women might be. He was equally alert, hiding all traces, refusing to admit anything. It suited him. The trophy house, the strong intelligent wife whose successful career he regarded as a positive reflection on his own.

Usually she went upstairs to make a start on the marking or admin work she habitually brought home every evening. He would relax in front of the television, quickly falling asleep. He was satisfied and in control; life as he wanted.

Today, however, she needed to sort out his washing. He'd been away for a week, on business of course. Methodical as always, she sorted out the casual coloured shirts into piles of light and dark. Checking the pockets for tissues, paper clips and odds and ends. That was when she found it.

The ticket.

Pisa Airport – a tear off stub boarding pass. Grubby and creased, but quite clear. Pisa Airport; she checked the date. Yesterday!

Heart beating, such a cliché, but it's true, such a confirmation did make her heart start. She straightened herself, took a breath and went into the lounge. Keeping her voice steady and even; "Did you have a nice time in Italy?"

Shocked and uncertain, he sat up and began blustering. "Don't know what you mean." And continued. "I was at a meeting in Edinburgh."

She marvelled, how can he continue to lie? Why does he continue to lie? What does he hope to achieve? How can this successful high flier be reduced to this level of inadequacy?

Quietly, she stated "I found the ticket. Pisa Airport, boarding pass!"

Utter silence.... The ticket. Clear proof. Suddenly, the importance of such an irrelevant scruffy little piece of paper overwhelmed them both. Their long, long relationship meant that they knew, without saying, what the other would do. He went to the phone. She, as if on automatic pilot, quite numb, continued to sort out the washing for the machine.

That ticket certified the end of the marriage. All the superficial trappings were now meaningless. He knew it and she knew it. It was the impetus that pushed her to make the break and move forward.

He muttered hurriedly that he needed to clear his head and hurriedly packed a few things "to go away for a bit." But he clung on desperately; "I don't want a divorce." His control lost, he stumbled out of the front door and it shut on the marriage quite irrevocably.

She stayed in the kitchen. Stick to the routine. Got to continue, got to carry on. Although she knew what was going to happen, she had no idea how she was going to cope. That night, she did sleep a little, but kept waking up, expecting him to be there.

But the ticket's confirmation was absolute.

Next morning, groggy and now tearful with self-pity and anger, she opened his wardrobe doors. Mechanically she gathered all his suits, shirts, ties, and shoes and carried them down to the dining room. Carefully she piled them up neatly, remembering to close the door so that the cat couldn't get in and cover them with hair. She then cleared out all his drawers and shelves and automatically placed the contents beside the suits and shirts. That done, she got ready for work.

Dressing in her usual uniform, the suit and makeup acted as a kind of prop, a reminder of normality. The drive to work was the usual frenzy and she pushed the car to the limit feeling desperate exhilaration. At work she steeled herself and briefly informed her boss. She froze her emotions and focused on the tasks she had to do. She couldn't remember what she did or how she did it. But she got through. Later in the day, a friend tried to show sympathy, she rebuffed her briskly. No emotions, it was safer.

At home, that evening, she couldn't face food. Instead she focused on the next task. Now cold and determined, she moved his blue relaxer chair into the dining room with all his clothes. She neatly placed his books beside them. The boxed bottle of special port that their son had given them for their thirtieth wedding anniversary was carefully arranged beside the pile. Finally, she went to the kitchen and brought out the huge black pepper grinder that had been a joint holiday buy. She placed it symbolically on top of the pile.

He rang. She knew he would. He wanted to come and talk things over.

"Of course," she replied, mechanically.

They stood awkwardly in the kitchen, both aware that everything had changed. She knew she had lost her friend and angrily told him so. He still wanting to cling on, "I don't want a divorce." He was uncertain and unsteady. Despite everything he couldn't accept that their marriage was finished, that he no longer would have any control and influence over her. "I'll pay you an allowance, I don't want a divorce" he repeated mechanically.

She couldn't think straight, but she knew that nearly thirty-five years of marriage were now dead. No way could she accept an ongoing relationship allowing him any control over her new life; whatever that might involve.

"I want a divorce, and I don't want you back in the house. I need to be sure. Please give me your key." She couldn't really understand what she was saying. But knew she had to feel secure in the house while she tried to work out what was to come. Shocked and pale, he took the key from his key ring and put it on the kitchen worktop.

They moved into the dining room and she showed him the pile of clothes and the chair.

Aghast; he choked. "I can't fit that in the car!"

Quietly determined; she countered, "I'm sure you can." She carefully helped him to pack the car, even managing to squeeze in the favourite blue relaxer chair. They discussed, with such civility, whether he should take the port or the pepper grinder. Quietly adamant, she insisted.

An awkward goodbye and he drove away, she went back into the kitchen.

The ticket was on the kitchen bench. The ticket that signalled the end of one life and the beginning of the next.

Keep on Moving

Muriel Claybrook

'Hurray', thought, Jenny. Now she had lost two and a half stones, and kept the weight off for three months, she felt fairly confident about fulfilling a long-desired ambition, and joining her local Health Club

Early retirement, a year ago, had meant an opportunity to change the focus of her life. During the first four months several people from her village had invited her to join their clubs and organizations. She smiled and gave them all the same answer, "I'm doing my cupboards out before I can feel free. Thanks for the offer though, I'll keep it in mind" She had no intention of taking up any of the offers: "been there, done that, got the t-shirt" she'd thought frequently.

As a young working mum, she had fitted in the job, the child care, community roles, family and social involvements. Granted, she only worked part time while the two boys were growing up. Where were these other village retirees then, she pondered, having rarely seen them involved in village life. Jenny had never felt she needed to work for financial reasons, but she wanted to use her classroom skills, that she knew were good, and she enjoyed being part of the life of a school.

One evening, two or three years before retirement, as she did her lesson preparation at the start of a new school year, she commented to her husband, "I'll be sitting at this work table every night until Christmas." The simple observation seemed to alert her to passing time and the need to move on. She would be involved in education in the future, she was sure, but who knew in what direction. For now, she just wanted to start exercising regularly.

As a school girl, Jenny had enjoyed hockey and some track events, and been a member of some school teams. She was never much good at what was referred to as gym. Climbing ropes and vaulting the wooden horse were not her scene, and truth to tell, even then she was carrying about a stone more than other girls of her build. This new Jenny, though with a respectable BMI and a body that fitted into a size 8 or 10, for the first time ever, was sure she would find something at the Health Club that she could manage.

The Pines complex, was the venue nearest to her home, that had a fitness centre and it seemed sensible to enrol there. Although the buildings were twenty years old, it had been well designed and was in an outstanding location. From the first-floor gym it had a fabulous view across a wooded valley and later in the year she would see a heron fishing in the stream that flowed through it, as she exercised.

Before she was allowed to enrol she was given an appointment with one of the trainers and her fitness was assessed. The manager asked if she would like to be assigned to a trainee trainer during her induction period, and she readily agreed. Carrie met up with her on the same day each week, when she was on placement from college, and Jenny benefited immensely from the staff input. She was careful to adopt the correct position on the resistance machines and build up the frequency and strength of the repetitions in a safe and sustained way.

A couple of months into membership the gym routine had become a very pleasant part of her life. Three times a week she would beat the school traffic and arrive at 8.15am to start her programme. A fifty-minute workout, followed by a swim, the steam room and the sauna were the perfect start to her day, leaving plenty of time for other things. By now she knew many members by sight and was on chatting terms with quite a few.

It was time to try out some classes and there was a wide range on offer. She had been wanting to try yoga since the 1960's when it first came to her attention and thought she would try Pilates too, when someone had explained to her what it involved. Jenny was delighted that she could do most of the things asked of the yoga class and was surprised at how supple she was.

The focus on breathing in each class, and the variety of patterns of it that they practised, intrigued her and she found some very useful. If she ever felt too stressed she would practice alternate nostril breathing to restore her calm. While sitting on the floor they would sometimes do an exercise to lengthen the time of an exhalation and encourage deeper breathing. The visual prompt was to imagine a little white feather rising from the floor and the task was, with head slightly bowed, to breath out through the mouth gently and for as long as possible, exhaling downwards, to stop the feather rising upwards.

Every class finished with relaxation and she found this tranquil time soothing, remembering some of the teacher's techniques to use regularly at home when her active mind made sleep elusive. Morven, her teacher would sometimes read a short section from "The Prophet" by Kahlil Gibran when their bodies were relaxed.

For Jennie this was an introduction to Eastern mysticism. The yoga postures had Sanskrit names, that didn't exactly trip off the tongue, but it reminded her how ancient yoga practice is, having been used down the centuries as an aid to health and well-being. Although the classes were in the morning, during relaxation, it would have been easy to be less mindful of one's body and drift off to sleep. Jenny had never actually done this, but occasional snoring sounds suggested other class members had.

After a few years The Pines closed as the owner had lucrative offers for the extensive land it was on, from various building firms. A good transfer deal for members was available. This was to a branch of a national Health Club chain, in a nearby new town. Many made the switch and settled down to newer equipment, a bigger pool and different classes. Jenny only tried yoga there once, as the class was much more intensive than she had been used to and she was quite concerned about the trembling in her legs when she held the poses for the expected time.

Some Pine's members had moved to other gyms. Jenny was delighted to meet up, at a Spanish class, with Sonia, who was one of these. They had developed an acquaintance while pounding adjacent treadmills during their morning workouts. Jenny knew that Sonia and her husband owned a flat in London. The emphasis in the Spanish class was on speaking in everyday situations and through role plays and descriptions, the students soon became familiar with each other's daily life and family. Jenny was the new comer to the group and realised that Sonia was often teased by the rest of the group about being a lady of leisure and having a cleaning lady. It seemed an unlikely lifestyle for her, though one should never judge by accent nor appearance.

Jenny imagined that Sonia's husband was a high flying, business man as she realised he often worked away from home. He was actually a leading guitarist in a rock band, of a certain age, and spent 6 to 9 months a year on tour. When Jenny asked her son about the band she realised that knowing Sonia had given her some street cred with the younger generation!

Long ago Jenny knew why she had taken to the Health Club with such relish. Firstly, most of the people she met there had a positive outlook on life, attending to improve or maintain their fitness. It was also a place to broaden the range of your acquaintances and lastly, apart from class attendance, there was no fixed time or duration for attendance. This was perfect for someone like herself that was annoyed by the need for punctuality.

Life moved on in other ways too. Through a contact she had met as an examiner, Jenny became a writer for a digital media company in London, that specialised in educational software. She found it exciting working with young professionals again. The company was so successful that it was taken over by a big American group, that swiftly asset stripped it and closed it down. This left the bright young things in the London office, immediately jobless. One conscientious young editor that she had worked with found a job with a big publishing company. It was because of her recommendation that Jenny came to be involved in writing a series of textbooks.

Now, nearly twenty years since retiring, Jenny was still a Health Club member. The frequency of her attendance had been reduced to 2 days a week and she arrived later in the morning. She was kind to herself on the apparatus and enjoyed Pilates classes. She had been keen to continue her yoga practice and had found a good teacher whose classes were in a local village hall.

Last summer Jenny's family spent a long weekend at Centre Parcs, celebrating her husband's 75th birthday. They had been many times before but this time the 3 and 4-year-old grandchildren were there too. Evie rode in a seat at the back of Mummy's bike, while Joseph rode his own bike very well with Daddy riding close behind him.

Jenny had always loved the cycling at CP but was surprised to find she had become more timid and cautious since the last time they were there. She was wary of hurting herself if she fell off. The same was true in the pool complex. It was two days into the holiday before Jenny descended the white-water rapids for the first time. Her sons were a little bemused by this unfamiliar attitude she was showing. She realised that the experience of accidents and joint problems that her friends had suffered must have contributed to this cautious approach.

As they packed up to go home she thought, 'Well I'm leaving happy but unscathed. I've always relied on the phrase "adapt or die" and I still want to enjoy the benefits and pleasure of exercising for as long as possible'.

Twenty years down the line from retirement she knew that losing two and a half stones had been the best gift she had ever given herself. It had increased her enjoyment of life immeasurably.

Vicious Gardening

Anne Marie Phillips

If anyone had ever told her that gardening could be this much fun, she would never have believed them. She was a city girl and had never had a garden to take care of before. Mind you, 'taking care' wasn't exactly what she was doing right now. It was still fun though. She let her mind wander back to the day nearly a year ago now when he had brought her to this house and enthused over the garden. She had kept trying to tell him that she didn't know anything about gardening, she had never had a garden, having been brought up in Manhattan and having always lived in apartments and never on the ground floor. He had brushed her worries aside and said it was only a matter of cutting the grass and doing a bit of weeding. She hadn't thought that it sounded too bad at the time. He had promised her a fancy ride on mower and she thought that sounded fun. She had quite looked forward to spending time in the garden centre choosing plants and shrubs.

Reality had been a little bit different though. He was always at work and expected a meal ready when he got home, even though he never actually came home at the same time each evening. He also expected her to be waiting for him looking neat and groomed. He was a little put out some evenings to find her in grubby jeans with her hair tied up in a scrunchy having just come in from the garden. He would turn his nose up in distaste at her dirty fingernails and would turn away from her.

It wasn't just the garden either, he thought she should cook and clean as well, after all, she wasn't being expected to go out to work. She tried to suggest that she should go back to her job. After all, they could get a cleaner and a gardener. He wouldn't hear of it. No wife of his was going to work. He liked the thought of her pottering in the garden and filling the house with fresh cut flowers. Unfortunately, he had no idea how much work was involved in developing a garden from scratch. There had only been an expanse of lawn when they moved in. She was beginning to wish that she had just left it as lawn. At least it would only need cutting in summer. The ride on lawn mower had never materialised. Just a great brute of a petrol driven beast that was a nightmare to start and practically dragged her around the garden once she had got it going. He had laughed when she had complained and said it would save her going to the gym.

After several months, she couldn't lie to herself any more. She was nothing more than a glorified housekeeper, cook and gardener. He never showed any interest in the garden except to complain that nothing seemed to be growing. Reminding him that it was now November didn't seem to make any difference. She gave up on the garden for a while and concentrated on the house. He wanted to hold a party, so she spent weeks tidying up and dressing the house to impress his colleagues. She knew he would want to show her off and boast about how clever she was. She would much rather be an intellectual equal which she knew she was, but he would have been horrified if she had begun to discuss business with his colleagues, so she kept quiet.

As Spring approached, she had a brainwave. Instead of planting small shrubs and waiting for them to grow, she went along to the garden centre and ordered more mature bushes and trees. With help from a local gardener, all these were planted, and the garden started to look much better. The roses were starting to grow and looked very promising. There were some beautiful shrubs that she had been promised would carry attractive flowers in late spring. Even the lawn had responded to some careful feeding and was looking green and healthy. All in all, she was feeling very positive.

At least she was until he came storming in one evening brandishing his bank statement. He wanted to know what on earth she had spent so much money on. She pointed him towards the garden.

"All this on plants? I thought you just needed to grow some seeds."

"Plants from seeds take years to mature. You wanted things now, so I bought mature bushes."

"But all this much for plants. They surely can't be this expensive."

"Of course, they are. They have taken years to get to this size. Someone had to take care of them."

"Right well that's it. From now on, you stay away from that garden centre. You can take care of the garden yourself."

She had said nothing. There was an awful lot she had wanted to say, but she was afraid that if she once started, she wouldn't be able to stop. She had remembered something that her father had once said, "Revenge is a dish best served cold" She hadn't understood what he meant at the time, but now she did. Getting heated and angry wasn't going to serve any useful purpose. If she was going to teach him a lesson, she needed to be cool and calculating.

She had walked to the window and looked out at her garden. The garden that she had spent so many hours in. She realised that she didn't even like it that much. It was just something else that she had to take care of. As she looked out, a plan began to form in her head. She smiled.

A few weeks later, he had to go away on business. He would only be away for a week, but that would be all she needed. As soon as he had left, she had booked a flight home, business class of course, 'phoned her parents and arranged for them to meet her at the airport. She had quickly packed her belongings into a couple of suitcases. Next, she had gathered the things she needed from the garden shed.

Now, two days later, she surveyed what was left of the garden. The roses were mere stumps, with the blooms scattered across the soil. The mature bushes that had caused so much friction were hacked to pieces and branches lay strewn about the grass. It hadn't been so difficult. The long arm shears that she had bought were so easy to use and made short work of even the most stubborn branches. She hadn't been all that sure about the trees, but a local hire company had supplied a chain saw that had proved to be ridiculously easy to use. The trees now lay on their sides like fallen soldiers. She thought about cutting them up but couldn't be bothered. He could sort that out.

Now she had about another two hours before her taxi arrived. Picking up the watering can into which she had mixed a very strong solution of weed killer, she started to walk up and down the lawn. As she poured, she wondered how long it would be before he opened the bedroom curtains and read her message in the vandalised lawn. It was probably more than a little childish, but she really didn't care anymore. She only wished she could see his face when he read the words. They were words she would have loved to say to his face but could not risk the anger. This was the next best thing.

Now she just had time to get herself cleaned up and then her taxi would be here to take her to the airport. He would be arriving home tonight in the dark, so he probably wouldn't see the damage until the morning. He would wonder where she was, but the message in the grass would leave him with no illusions. Suddenly she felt a lot happier. Gardening really could be quite good fun.

The Conversation at Splendid Bay View

Liese Cooper

Footsteps, more than one person's, approach the conservatory where we sit, staring out to the sea below and beyond. Weak sunlight floods the room with the glow of late summer. It has been a hot day but now it is time someone came to close the windows, I reach round for a shawl on the back of my chair. The guests enter the room and with them, through the open door, there is a strong smell of food from the corridors.

I see three of them. The first one is a middle-aged woman. She looks around and says to one of us:

"Hello Mother," and then addresses her companions, both younger men, speaking very quietly.

"Well, I think this is lovely, ideal. She's perfectly happy, look at her. She loves the sea, likes looking out for birds."

The young men reply.

"Yes, it's beautiful, but she's only been in for respite, is she ready for this, permanent I mean?"

"But the food looks good and the place doesn't smell of. you know, toilet-wise. Like some."

The group have come into the centre of the room and are looking out at the wonderful view. The woman speaks, more softly in case she is heard, I suppose.

"The kitchen was spotless and the meal for tonight looked delicious, sausages, creamy mashed potatoes, cauli and the lemon meringue pie, it's all home-made. She'd never have that on her own. And honestly, we just can't see to her every day, can we."

"How much are we talking?" says one of the young men, "can we, she afford it?"

"I've done the sums, just quickly, you know, roughly and. Of course, she can afford it, she has a good pension and there's the house. But. the more she pays the less there is later, for … you know. Think about it."

The woman put her hand on the back of the plastic chair on which I am sitting, as if to steady herself. She says in a voice of mild panic:

"Actually, I'm afraid cost wise, we're going to have to look elsewhere. I'll have a chat with Mother, you go, I'll follow."

The young men turn to leave, and as she withdraws her hand from the chair, the woman catches my hair, pulling it painfully which makes me scream; she turns and says loudly, as if I'm deaf: "Sorry, dear! Now then, Mother. what a lovely view! It's a bit cold in here, isn't it!? I haven't seen any staff yet. Are you all right?"

I feel cold and wrap my shawl tightly and say to the strange, noisy woman who caught my hair: "Hello, dear. Who are you? I don't think I know you?"

The Book

Maxine Patterson

Edwin Ingram carefully turned the dusty old book over and over in his hand. The dull faded green cover was scuffed and threadbare. The thin brown pages were creased and worn where they had been repeatedly flicked through. What would his life have been like if it had been given to his older brother, David, instead?

David had smiled smugly as the solicitor read out the will confirming that he and his wife Cressida were to receive the house, farm and lands. Edwin knew that was what had been agreed and was relieved that there would not be any further veiled hints and unpleasant suggestions as to David's superior claim to the farm and the estate.

David had been irritated that his father had insisted that his books should go to Edwin. Michael had resisted David and Cressida's constant criticisms about the arrangements knowing that David wasn't really interested in the books, only the possible monetary value. However, one quick look at the dusty book jackets and faded bindings convinced David that they weren't worth much and after the funeral Edwin had grudgingly been given the boxes of books from his father's study.

More importantly, Edwin had to find a new job and somewhere to make a new home. David and the pushy Cressida had made it abundantly clear that he was welcome at Christmas and at no other time. There had been suppressed tension and anger during the time of Michael's last illness as they waited impatiently to take full possession of what they considered to be rightfully theirs. David urgently wanted to introduce the more efficient farming techniques that he had learned about at University. Cressida had thoroughly researched what was necessary to create and market an organic range of local produce as part of the new farm plan. Their farm would reflect their modernising personalities and complete focus on profit.

Edwin, much more of a traditionalist, hadn't appreciated how much he had loved the old farmhouse, until he had tried to establish himself somewhere else. His new flat was small and cramped. But it was all he could realistically afford, and it gave him security and a sense of independence; that was something he vainly tried to convince himself of, as he tripped over furniture and boxes whilst settling in.

Establishing himself in the new job had also been challenging. Working as an estate agent in a small country town had been cosy and comfortable. In Manchester it was cut throat and competitive, Edwin had had to grow a thick skin very quickly and learn to stand up for himself.

So, it wasn't until eighteen months later that he finally felt able to consider his father's bequest. The boxes had been tucked out of the way, stacked in the spare bedroom. Six boxes. But why had his father been so insistent that he had to have them? He carefully opened the boxes, one at a time. They contained early editions of well-known books, but nothing valuable or important. Why had his father thought they were important enough to specifically mention them in his will?

Edwin went through the boxes carefully, looking at each book and its dust jacket, replacing it afterwards. He really didn't have the room to display all the books and he wanted to keep them safe until he had decided what he was going to do with them all.

He was still mulling over the vexed question of why his father had wanted him to have the books when the letter fell out. The actual book wasn't anything special to look at. The shabby, nondescript cover certainly was not an indication of the contents.

He carefully picked up the letter and opened it out. Four pages of ornate copperplate handwriting. The florid signature of Herbert James Esq. personal assistant to Andrew Carnegie scrolled across the bottom of the fourth page. Edwin shook his head, this could not be real.

But it was.

The letter was an acknowledgement of an earlier letter from Edwin's grandfather. The correspondence obviously had been going on for some time and concerned the co-ownership of farmland and mines in America and Canada. He was astounded, he'd never heard any mention of lands in America. Grandfather had spent his whole life in the north of England and focused on establishing the farm that David now ran.

Intrigued Edwin carefully re-examined all the books checking for any further letters and documents. Had his father known about them? He must have done, but why hadn't he researched them himself? He found a total of six letters which he carefully filed, then repacked all the books. He needed time to consider what he had found and even more time to research.

What he did decide immediately was to keep his find quiet. David was not to know about the letters until Edwin was sure they were genuine and understood what the farms and lands referred to. He knew only too well how David and Cressida would help with the research and assume ownership of the resulting information.

Edwin steeled himself to attend the family Christmas and rebuffed Cressida's intrusive enquiries as to his continued single status. His secret knowledge of the letters and their possible import gave him a warm self-satisfied glow that helped negate David's smug lectures on effective farm management. He left for Manchester and his flat as soon as he politely could. There was no way that the farm represented home for him anymore; that part of his life was over and done.

Back in his flat in January he began the research. Andrew Carnegie was easy, in fact, there was too much information. He tried to narrow it down by adding in the name of the assistant, that led nowhere. Instead he googled his grandfather, again nothing! This project was going to be long and difficult.

He decided to organise his ideas into a structured plan and began the project. Over the next few weeks his notes grew. He visited the central Manchester Library and even managed several visits to the British Library. Much more detail emerged about Carnegie, his philanthropy and his keen eye for business. However, he couldn't find a link between Carnegie and his grandfather. This was looking like a dead end, there would be no romantic family goldmine in the Colorado hills.

Rereading his notes, he began to appreciate the depth and detail in his grandfather's letters, which helped him appreciate where the farms and mines could have been and what they could have produced. This made him even more frustrated at his inability to find anything concrete to support the correspondence.

Further visits to the Manchester City Library began to fix an idea in his mind. He had the background, the people and the storyline. This was going to be his project, a book.

And so, it became. He wrote in the evenings and at the weekends. He recreated his grandfather, created a link with a Carnegie like character. Introduced several farms and mines in America where the young protagonist fought to establish himself. It was a brutal, realistic, raw adventure.

To ground the novel, he introduced his own character as the anti-hero trying to trace what had happened. He particularly enjoyed that aspect of the writing, choosing his own character traits and flaws.

Finally, the adventure was finished, and he began the soul-destroying process of trying to get it published. Dozens of rejections almost overwhelmed him. His Christmas visit to David and Cressida was difficult as he had to make sure he made no mention of his writing.

Out of the blue a small publisher accepted his book which was published and became moderately successful. It appealed to a wide readership and social media helped publicise it. Suddenly he was asked to attend literary festivals. He enjoyed speaking at those, the audiences were eager and interested and he appreciated the feedback about his writing. He managed to fit those in around his work so little changed in his life. The publicity machine suggested that he opened a Facebook and twitter account so that his readers could see what he was commenting upon and respond. At first Edwin declined, that was step too far. But eventually he was persuaded into opening his own website, Facebook and twitter account. But more importantly he had begun the sequel. With the second book grandfather's fictional character had become established and famous.

When the film rights were taken up and Daniel Craig was cast to play his grandfather's character; that was when David and Cressida got in touch. The envy oozed out of the phone while they tried hard to be so civilized. They had seen him on television and were so pleased for him! Where did he get the idea from? Would he like to visit to meet up with old friends? Edwin had to be very persuasive and convince them that he was still the same boring younger brother that he had always been, and they reluctantly accepted his refusal to visit. Edwin was adamant, they had made it very clear that he was no longer part of life on the farm; they certainly were not going to be part of his new life as an author.

Occasionally he wondered about his father's decision to bequeath the books. Had he known what Edwin might do? Had he hoped that there would be an actual farm or mine?

No. The letters were a door into another world; one that he thought was physically closed but which had allowed his imagination to open. The gift of the books and letters showed his father's deep understanding of Edwin's character and perseverance, that had been the real bequest.

So, when the email query from a Robert Ingram in Colorado arrived some eighteen months after the film's release he was unsure how to respond. Could the information be genuine? Yes, the family name was the same, but it was very common and could easily have been gathered from the social media page. His reply was careful and restrained, merely acknowledging receipt. However, he knew he could not ignore a possible connection to the letters that he had spent so long researching. He joined a prominent family history website and soon discovered the information that had eluded him and was annoyed with himself that he had not followed this possible line of enquiry earlier. It had not been his grandfather that had travelled to America and settled in Colorado, but a brother. Edwin was astounded as no mention had ever been made of grandfather's brother James Herbert Ingram in the family.

He returned to the letters and began to understand the significance of the references to the farms and the mine in Colorado. Great uncle James Ingram had emigrated to America and been able to part buy some land using money loaned by grandfather. He'd been successful and gradually extended his land to include a small mine on the edge of the Rockies and repaid the original loan. The letters that Edwin had found referred to grandfather's agreement to act as referee for the original part lease. Carnegie had also owned farms and land in the area, hence the ongoing correspondence.

Researching his great uncle's family in America was relatively straightforward, now he knew what he was looking for. Edwin was able to confirm the names of his email contact and acknowledge him as a distant cousin. His typically English hesitant email did not discourage his newly found American family. His inbox was flooded with family trees, family photos and pictures of their ranch and livestock. Their delight at having found their English relatives made clear by their enthusiastic emails, followed by letters and more packets of photos. Edwin was at first overwhelmed, he couldn't but help compare his brother, David's reticence and suspicion with his distant American family's warmth and joy at having found their English roots.

One special package arrived, carefully boxed and secured. Edwin opened it wondering what was so important that it couldn't be sent by email. The box contained a framed copy of an original black and white portrait of two very young men standing stiffly in their Sunday best suits. Edwin was easily able to recognise his grandfather and there beside him was great uncle James. He imagined the photo had been taken before James left for America and wondered why there was not a copy at the family farm.

With the photograph was an invitation to visit the ranch and meet all the family.

How could he refuse. Despite being an infrequent traveller, he booked tickets for New York and on to Denver after making sure he could get time off work. Unsure about airport regulations he packed a small suitcase ensuring that he took copies of all his research and the letters, he knew the American Ingram clan would be desperate to see it all.

In his head he imagined the dusty old pickup truck that would be waiting for him at the airport and a few of his distant relatives. What he hadn't anticipated was the huge crowd of family waiting for him as he walked out carrying his small suitcase. They all wanted to speak to him, hug him and tell him their names. By now, very jet lagged and stunned he was over whelmed and could only smile and repeat "pleased to meet you." Robert's wife took pity on him and ushered him outside to the waiting vehicle – a huge gleaming black monster. The four-hour drive although long, was comfortable with Sarah and Robert filling in the background to the American family history.

Edwin's imagined ranch was very wide of the mark. The actual ranch was huge, many thousands of acres spread over hundreds of miles. Robert and his three sons and their families helped run it, hence the large family reception at the airport. The family gathering continued over the two weeks of his stay. He shared all his research and gave Robert the copies of the original letters. The warmth and love he experienced with his newly found family reminded him of his home when he was growing up. So very different now with David and Cressida running the farm.

Robert was eager to speak to David, so Edwin phoned. As always Cressida's greeting was brusque and business like. "You're where?"

It had taken quite some time for David to accept where Edwin was and the existence of the American side of the family. The disbelief and scepticism clear in his voice. But importantly David agreed somewhat reluctantly that they would be pleased to welcome Robert and Sarah; if they chose to visit the UK.

Edwin had an inner giggle, entirely inappropriate for a middle-aged estate agent and author, David and Cressida really didn't have any conception of the family invasion that was to follow. The arrangements had already been made and finalised. Manchester was to be their base so that they could be close to Edwin and then visit the family farm. They wanted to see and experience just a little of the life that grandfather had lived; the life that Edwin had described so vividly in his books.

Through the letters, the two disparate branches of the family had been reunited.

Reflections

Pat Buckley

Jimmy Williams aged 79, born and brought up in Middlesbrough, was making his last visit to his home area. Jimmy expected the old places to change. The tiny street house near the town centre where he'd spent his youth, as well as the factory where he'd first worked, were all gone. Now he realised that there was no longer anyone here who remembered or even recognised him. He didn't think he'd changed so much. Maybe a little greyer and perhaps carrying a few more pounds around his middle, but he was still the fine upstanding tall, kindly man he had always been. Nevertheless, as the area had changed, so had he. Nothing stayed the same.

Jimmy had previously enjoyed his visits and he'd made sure to see the sights and cherish the memories. On this trip, the weather was fine and dry, so he had been walking the footpaths bordering the Tees. It was tiring. Taking a rest, he settled himself onto a bench on Stockton riverside and took out his flask of coffee. Easing back, he surveyed the water. A light wind ruffled surface which sparkled in the sun. As he watched, a pair of swans, followed by three fluffy grey cygnets, swam down the river. 'Quite a novelty', he thought, 'swans on the River Tees; can't believe it's changed so much.'

In his youth no one would swim or paddle in the river. The joke was that if you fell in you were more likely to be poisoned than drowned. In those days there was heavy industry all around the river. Chemical and steel works, tanneries and, of course, the drains and sewers from the houses, all discharged their waste, so the river could take it away to the sea. Around low tide, the evidence of these pollutants was clearly seen. Thick black dirt coated the banks. Tree trunks, branches and a multitude of flotsam and jetsam were deposited. Above high water mark, the contrast was clear with cleaner buildings and greenery.

He'd read about the big plan which meant that this pollution no longer hit the river. Industries and councils had had to change their ways to create a big clean up. This was all to the good but equally over time the factories had disappeared, leaving vast devastated areas of industrial wasteland and blighted streets. For many years and for numerous families this had meant unemployment and hardship. Many like him had left the area to seek work elsewhere. He'd moved to the Midlands and made a good life for him and Joan, his wife.

Not far from where he rested was the barrage, a modern dam across the river. As an engineer, Jimmy had been fascinated to inspect the system of tilting plates which controlled the water flow, wondering at the same time if enough local skills still existed to build such a structure. Linked with the cleanup work, it created a clean water area upstream, which could be enjoyed by everyone. The white water canoe slalom course, which he was told was international standard, was another marvel.

For the first and only time in his life, Jimmy had tried canoeing; in Yarm with the youth club. It was fun, and they had laughed a lot, mainly at their lack of skill and progress, but he didn't like being so close to, or even swimming in water, and decided it wasn't for him. The fish ladder fascinated him. The idea that salmon was swimming in the Tees and that man would create a means to help them into the clean water zone. 'Funny thing', he mused, 'when I was a kid, the only salmon we ever saw came from a tin.'

He'd wandered the paths at each side of the downstream river. The nature park was a joy with varieties of plants and birdlife he hadn't expected to see so close to major roads and commerce. One day he walked in Dinosaur Park, a vast green space on the riverside, adorned with large dinosaur statues. Jimmy remembered the long gone steel works, which had been on the site. Pausing for a moment, he decided, 'My generation are all dinosaurs now.'

A trip on the Transporter had been high on his wish list. Jimmy was initially surprised at how much the crossing charge had increased but realising that everything cost more than thirty years ago, settled to enjoy the return trip. Declining the shelter offered for foot passengers, he'd gazed out over to the river mouth. Catching sight of the massive structures of defunct North Sea oil rigs, he reflected that they don't build them now, just take them apart; same skills but very different work.

In his youth, men like his dad had crossed the Transporter Bridge in their hundreds going over to the shipyards in Haverton Hill. They rode bikes in those days not like the flash cars he saw today. The platform crossing the grey dirty river would sway in the wind. When the weather was really bad, the platform was unsafe and would not run. No man could afford to give up a day's work, or even give the bosses an excuse to give them their cards. For every man in work, there was at least one or maybe two standing behind him, ready to take his place. 'Pulling a sickie' belonged to a much later generation. Some would go the longer route around across the Newport Bridge, but others picked up their bikes and climbed the structure of the Transporter and took the perilous journey over the top and down onto the river's far bank. You had to be fit to do that he realised. A picture flashed into his memory of his dad returning from work on one such day; wet, dirty, spent.

A young Jimmy had enjoyed travelling with his mother on two buses to Stockton. The market stalls filled both sides of the High Street. They sold meat and fish, fruit and vegetables, dress and curtain materials, clothes, plants from local nurseries, and hardware. In fact, just about anything you would want to buy. His mother had bought not only food but lengths of materials, which she would carefully transform into dresses or skirts. The noise was intense as market traders shouted their wares, offering bargains, trying to entice the public wandering through to part with their hard earned cash. In the early dark of winter afternoons, each stall was lit with a large oil lantern, which flickered and hissed and created dark shadows between each one. Jimmy's favourite at this time of year was the roast chestnut seller's barrow. The nuts were spread on a metal sheet over glowing coals and crackled as the shells split open exposing the creamy kernels, ready to eat. He'd buy a packet and after holding it close to warm his hands and chilled body would shell the nuts and savour the flesh. His mum was not fond of them so he was secretly pleased not to have to share his special treat.

One evening they were heading home. As the bus approached Victoria Bridge he'd seen a wonderful site. A cloud of starlings had risen in the sky; an iridescent, swirling, swooping dance of shapes and loops and bows. The noise had been overwhelming as the birds shrieked out in their joy to be free and part of a magnificent family ritual .The bus moved on and the boy looked back until the road's bend meant he could see no more. Excited, he'd told his teacher at school next day, breathlessly describing the colours, the acrobatics, and the sheer magic of it all. Teacher told him that a group of starlings was called a murmuration because of the noise the birds made. Jimmy knew that the birds were not murmuring but shouting to each other and sharing the exhilaration of their flight.

On an earlier visit, he'd taken Joan on a river trip from Stockton to Yarm and they had passed under that bridge. The noise from the starlings was deafening. Hundreds if not thousands of them were roosted in the steel supports of the structure, and they did not appreciate the intrusion. He now knew from where they emerged to dance in the sunset and return. Joan had been confused during the river trip. "Where are we now?" she kept saying. Jimmy would explain that it was still Thornaby or Eaglescliffe. He understood that the bends in the river meant they kept seeing the same places from different angles. At the time he had thought that Joan's confusion was because of the river's meandering but later realised it was an early symptom of the disease that would destroy her. He'd met Joan at the dance at the works social club. Fair haired and barely reaching his shoulder, she had been light on her feet, and they had soon made it more than a dancing partnership. To him, Joan would always be that happy dancing girl.

Before he set off for home, Jimmy visited the new Infinity Bridge. The silver curves were impressive on their own but the reflection that evening, when it was lit, was quite magical and completed the infinity sign. This, he decided, was a very clever concept and design. Perhaps, he thought although the people, the houses and workplaces on the river banks would change over time, the river itself was infinite.

The Vision

Jan Jenner

Jacqueline Seymour yawned. She'd had busy week. It had been meetings every evening and the strain was beginning to tell. She half closed her eyes against a sudden rush of oncoming headlights.

"Not far now", she muttered as she joined the queue of traffic snaking its way to the M27.

"Take second exit at the roundabout", said the metallic voice of the sat-nav. The car clock showed 10.20 pm. With luck she'd be home by 10:45 and Tom would be waiting with a cup of tea.

She smiled. He was a good man. She would never have managed these last few months without his support. She knew she'd been overdoing it lately because he'd started to make a few comments, checking up to see where she was and when she was due back. He was usually so patient.

They were taking a holiday next week. She'd promised to keep the time free. Tomorrow she had no appointments, so they could relax and plan some long relaxing walks.

She brought her mind back to the road, just up ahead of her was a battered Mini tootling along at about thirty-five mph. "I don't understand some people," she grumbled. "If they want to drive that slowly, they should keep off motorways." She looked in her mirror, the road was clear, so she flicked on the signals and steered into the middle lane to overtake.

As she straightened the wheel, a lorry appeared from nowhere without warning blocking her rear-view mirror. She only had time to briefly wonder where he'd come from when the horrendous screeching of brakes filled the car. She closed her eyes and braced herself. In her mind she watched it happen in slow motion. The shuddering impact as the lorry hit the car. She watched horrified as her cherished car was shunned along the road like a black plastic toy. The crash of splintering glass echoed in her head as the windscreen imploded. the heat of tearing metal burnt through her clothes as the weight of the lorry pushed the car into the asphalt, crushing the breath from her body. From a long way away she heard Tom's voice, "Why did you agree to go?" he sounded so reproachful. "You should have said no."

The cold empty pain of loss filled her head as the noise slowly subsided.

Kind faithful Tom, her childhood sweetheart, she wouldn't hurt him, not for the world. They were everything to each other.

After what seemed like an age, the ear-piercing sound of metal on metal faded and was replaced by the rhythmic beat of the windscreen wipers. She opened her eyes.

There had been no impact. The road was empty. She could see the battered Mini retreating in her mirror. Apart from veering slightly towards the right, her car was travelling along the road in the centre lane. She could only have shut her eyes for a second.

Jacqueline pulled across on to the hard shoulder and turned off the engine. She reached to unclip her seatbelt fumbling with trembling fingers. Closing her eyes, she took deep breaths holding tightly on to the steering wheel and waited for her mind to clear and the panic to subside.

The sickening crunch of metal on metal still rang in her ears. Tom was looking at her shaking his head sadly, dear Tom. She climbed out of the car and looked up and down the road. It was clear. No wreckage, no broken glass strewn across the road, no black skid marks, no lorry. Nothing. Just the battered Mini. it has driven past now still traveling sedately along at thirty-five miles per hour.

She returned to the car, her fingers still trembling and clumsy as she turned the key to start the engine. She gingerly pulled back into the road and drove to the nearest exit, coming off the motorway to take the longer but quieter route through the empty suburban streets.

She reached home just after eleven o'clock thankfully pulling into the drive of their small bungalow, with a sigh of relief.

The light in the hall came on and Tom opened the door his face creased in a smile.

"Hello love, how did it go?" He came to the car and took the case from her. "You look tired, come and sit down, the kettles just boiled."

She followed him indoors and dropped into a chair. When Tom came in from the kitchen she told him what had happened.

"It was so real Tom, I'm still shaking." She held her hand up for him to see.

"Maybe it was just a warning, someone telling you to take time-out. You have been doing rather a lot lately."

She shook her head. "It was one of my visions Tom, they're always right."

"There's no sense in worrying, love. It might not have been your car, there are loads of black cars on the road. Come on let's take our tea up to bed."

In bed, after Tom had gone to sleep, Jacqueline lay awake thinking about what she'd seen. It was her car, she was sure of that. But something had been wrong with the vision, but what?

She was a psychic. She'd been having visions of one sort or another since she was a child and knew enough to trust them. When she was younger she'd tried to ignore them, but her grandmother had taught her to open her heart and not to be frightened. Eventually she'd come to trust the visions even if she didn't really understand them.

Now, it was how she made a living. She drove round the country giving psychic readings. Mostly she worked with small groups but lately, she'd been called upon to do a lot of platform work. At first, she had found it rather daunting, standing up in front of a hundred or more people but now she enjoyed it. She gained a great deal of satisfaction from her work. She was gratified at the comfort she managed to give people but seeing the many lonely people she couldn't help left her tired and drained.

Maybe Tom was right. She had been over doing it these last few months.

She turned over and closed her eyes. "What's meant, will be," she muttered softly to herself and drifted off to sleep.

The next day after breakfast she sat down with Tom and they began to plan their walks for the week.

"How about driving over to the New Forest. We haven't done that for a while?" Tom suggested.

"Yes, that's a wonderful idea." She stood up as the phone rang. "Maybe we should switch this thing off as well, we might get some real peace then." She answered the call, still smiling.

"Jac, it's Lisa, are you busy tonight, "

Jacqueline's heart sank. Lisa was an old friend. They'd been friends for years and she'd helped Jacqueline when she'd first turned professional.

"Please Jac, I've been let me down, I wouldn't ask if I wasn't desperate and it's near to you." Lisa sounded desperate.

Jacqueline sighed, hardly daring to look at Tom and said, "What time do you want me to be there?"

"About eight o'clock, can you make it?"

"All right, if I leave at seven thirty, I should be there just before eight."

"Jac, I love you, thank you darling."

Tom stared at her as she put the phone down. "I can hardly believe you did that," he said

"I"m sorry Tom, it's only one evening."

"Why didn't you just tell her we were on holiday?" Tom stood up pushing the chair back from the table.

"You know how difficult it is to say no to Lisa."

"Difficult for you maybe. I'd have said no if I had taken the call," Tom said crossly.

"I am sorry, we have the rest of the week. Lisa's stuck, she didn't want to let them down."

"No, and she never does let them down, she always gets you to fill in. Jacqueline, she does it on purpose, she takes advantage." He sounded so dejected she was tempted to call Lisa and tell her she couldn't go. He was right. She was a dear and it was hard to say no to her but she used people. She lived alone and sometime didn't seem to understand Jacqueline had commitments to Tom.

"Never mind," Tom shrugged his shoulders and began to fold the map up. "We have the rest of the week."

"How will you get there?" Tom asked, as she was getting ready, later that day.

"Up on the M27. Why?" She asked absently. She was holding two cotton shirts in front the mirror trying to decide which one to wear.

"What about your vision?" Tom sat on the bed, chewing his bottom lip absently.

"Oh, I'll be all right, it was probably tiredness like you said, it hasn't come back."

"I think you should take my car, in case."

"What difference will that make? If I'm going to have an accident, I'm going to have an accident. There's not much I can do about it."

"In the vision you were driving your black car, my car is white."

She smiled knowing how much he prized his car he must really be worried. He never let anyone drive it.

She laughed, "Ok, dear, if it makes you feel better Ill take your car. I promise I'll drive very carefully." She hugged him.

She arrived at the venue with ten minutes to spare to find the hall knee deep in water.

"I'm sorry, we did try to call but the contact number's not answering," The middle-aged woman told her as she ineffectually tried to tackle the water with a sweeping brush. "The mains pipe in the kitchen has sprung a leak. I arrived here this evening to find all this." She pointed to the water dismally. "I've call the plumber, but he has a long way to come."

Jacqueline left the woman pushing water around the hall and walked back to the car. She tried to call Lisa but there was no reply, so she texted a short message before setting off home.

There was more traffic on the road this time of the evening. She thought again about her vision. She was being extra careful, and she was driving a white car. She wouldn't call Tom, it would be a surprise when she arrived home early.

First, she wanted to call on Lisa, it wasn't far out of her way and she was worried about her. Lisa always answered her mobile.

Jacqueline drove steadily past the junction she usually used to get home. Lisa lived in a village a few miles further north. She was about to pull out into the middle lane to pass a string of slower vehicles when she heard the squeal of brakes. In her rear-view mirror, she saw the lorry begin to fishtail out of control. She watched mesmerised as it skidded across the road, through the crash barrier and into a black car, coming in the other direction.

That's what was wrong, she had watched it all happen in the rear-view mirror, but the black car had been going in the wrong direction. It had been travelling towards the lorry.

From a long way away she heard Tom's voice, "Why did you agree to go," he sounded so reproachful. "You should have said no."

The cold empty pain of loss filled her head.

Kind Tom, her childhood sweetheart, he would never hurt her, not for the world. They were everything to each other.

At his funeral Lisa tried to explain. "You were spending so much time away he was lonely.

At first, he came around just for company. We didn't want to hurt you. When I received your text, he left immediately to rush home."

The Story

Anne Marie Phillips

Mo walked home from her creative writing class with ideas buzzing around in her head like flies. They were going to enter a competition, a short story competition. This was her chance to shine. She knew she could write. All she had to do was knock out a story and she would show those clever people in the class. They all thought they were so wonderful and were so patronizing of Mo's attempts.

"That's nice dear" they used to say when Mo read out the piece she had slaved over all week.

"Nice" she wanted to scream. "Nice, it's better than nice. It's a masterpiece" But somehow she knew it wasn't a masterpiece. It was adequate.

Mo had always loved writing. Even as a child, she used to write pages and pages of stories. Her Mum and Dad always read them and told her that she would be a famous writer one day. Even at school, her English teacher used to encourage her and said she wouldn't be surprised to see Mo's name on the cover of a best seller. Somehow Mo had always thought she would write. What on earth had gone wrong? Why was she struggling with a weekly creative writing class at the age of fifty-three? Where had the years gone? Where was the eighteen-year-old with the head full of stories? She knew what had happened. She had let life take her over and she had just drifted along with it. She had married David when she was twenty. Had to marry David would be more accurate. She remembered her parents' disappointment when she told them she was pregnant. They had been kind and had stood by her. They even said she didn't have to get married. What had they known, even then? She had thought she was in love. Thought everything would be great. She knew now that they were just playing houses, just in a more grown- up way. They had been happy at first. David was thrilled when Daniel was born and even happier when Sally was born just two years later. Mo thought her life was complete. At twenty-two she had a husband, a house and two wonderful babies. Could life get any better?

Apparently, hers couldn't, but David's could. Ten years ago, at forty-five, David had left her for a twenty-five-year-old secretary at his accountant's firm. He had said that Mo was boring. She never wanted to go out or do anything, which was grossly unfair as she was working full time as a teaching assistant and Sally was just about to go off to university. They had agreed that they would pay her fees and living accommodation costs. They didn't want her to start out with huge student loans. Mo had even been helping at summer schools to try to make a bit more cash. David didn't seem to notice that on top of working full time, she was also taking care of the house, the garden, two young adults and him. He, on the other hand, came home, got changed, poured himself a drink and waited for his dinner, all the time telling everyone how tired he was. Mo knew that a lot of that was her fault. She shouldn't have been so eager to do everything herself when they were first married, but it had been such fun, looking after a beautiful baby, cooking lovely meals and greeting her husband when he came home in the evening. She had always tried to look good for him and to have the house tidy. He could never complain that he came home to a frazzled wife and screaming child.

Still, thought Mo as she arrived back home, that's all in the past now. Somehow being alone hadn't been so bad. Sally had gone off to university, Daniel had gone with friends to Australia and apart from a fleeting visit home a few years ago, hadn't been back. He was having a great time and had a good job. He was married to an Australian girl and they had a little boy called Sam, neither of whom Mo had ever met. Mo now worked part time in the local primary school and helped out in one of the charity shops. She didn't have a lot of free time, but she made the most of the time she did have.

That evening, as Mo cooked dinner and tidied away, she felt herself beginning to get excited about the competition. She felt that she was just bursting with ideas and couldn't wait to get started. As soon as she could, she went into her little study and switched the computer on. Mo had always been a keen reader and would read all sorts of stories. She loved biographies, but she could also lose herself in a romantic fiction or an historical novel. Sometimes even a good "bodice ripper". Some of the stories she had read hadn't even been that well written, in fact, some of them were downright terrible. How hard could it be? Mo knew that in no time at all, she would have a fantastic story written, she would win the competition and she might even be published. She stopped and took a deep breath. Perhaps she was getting just a little bit ahead of herself. Really, all she wanted to do was to show those snooty women at the class that she could write just as well as them.

That would do for now.

An hour later, Mo had created a header and footer for her page. She had made a cup of tea and had re-arranged the books on her bookshelves. What she hadn't done was written a single word. She couldn't even think of a subject to write about. Mo loved writing letters. She sent long newsy, chatty letters to Daniel and his wife, telling them all about things that were going on in England. She didn't get a reply, but that wasn't the point. She sent postcards when she went on holiday and had to write very small in order to fit in everything that she wanted to say. She didn't even have any problem in class when they were given a word to write about. She thought she came out with some amazing things. So why was she sitting here staring at a computer screen with not a single sensible thought in her head?

Just as she thought she must go mad, the telephone rang. She knew as soon as she picked it up, that it would be Sally. No doubt, there was another crisis and she would be called in for babysitting duty.

"Mum" said Sally softly. "Are you busy tomorrow evening?"

Oh great, thought Mo. No "How are you Mum? Have you had a good day? Are you well?" Just straight down to it. Honestly Sally seemed to think she had nothing better to do.

"Hello dear" said Mo. "Actually, I was going to get started on my short story."

"Oh you can do that any time. I have a slight dilemma. Richard is hosting a conference in the city for a few days and I thought it might be nice to surprise him one night. He's always moaning about how boring the evenings are, so I thought I would go and spend the evening, and night, with him. Obviously having Jack around won't help me much.

Mo knew that Sally was concerned about her marriage. She thought Richard was losing interest. Obviously, she had thought of a way of reviving his interest. "Good for her," she thought

"Alright," she found herself saying. "Bring him over tomorrow and I'll bring him back to you the following evening."

"Thanks Mum" said Sally. "I knew I could count on you."

Mo sat back down at her computer and started to type. She was really writing down her thoughts about Sally and Richard's marriage. She thought it might be the basis for a story. She changed the names but after a paragraph or two, she stopped and re-read what she had written.

"Oh crikey." She said. "Sally will know exactly who I'm talking about. That's no good"

She quickly deleted the words and breathed a sigh of relief as they disappeared. Not for the world did she want to hurt her daughter or alienate her son-in-law and that would certainly have done both those things. With a sigh, Mo switched the computer off. If she was looking after Jack for a couple of days, she was going to need an early night. Two days out of her week and she still had no idea for a story. She was supposed to have an outline for class next week. Goodness knows when she was going to get anything done.

The next morning Sally arrived with Jack just as Mo was clearing away the breakfast things.

"Crikey" you're off to a flying start this morning.

"I have so much to get done today. I have a hair appointment, nails, waxing, you name it, and I'm having it done." muttered Sally.

"You really are going to town, aren't you? Richard will think Christmas has come."

"Mum" Sally blushed slightly but smiled as well. Mo could see she was already beginning to think about just how much fun she could have tonight. She took hold of Jack's hand as they went down the path to wave goodbye to Mummy. Jack wasn't at all bothered about being left. He was a very easy-going child and loved spending time with his Grandma. She gave him her full attention and he made the most of it.

Mo and Jack had a great day. They went to the shops bought stuff for dinner. Then they went to the park and played on all the rides. They fed the ducks and even managed a game of football before Jack started to slow down. Mo took him home, fed him, bathed him and curled up on the spare bed to read him a story. This was always her favorite time of the day. He didn't have the energy to wriggle and was quite content to curl up sleepily and listen. She read one or two of his favorite books then she started to talk about the day and what they had done. Jack was content to nod every now and then but would remind her if she forgot something. As he began to fall asleep, she gently kissed him, crept out of the room and tip-toed downstairs. She knew he would be soon so deeply asleep, she could probably vacuum in the bedroom without disturbing him. Just for a few minutes though, she needed to be quiet.

With Jack sound asleep, Mo had another go at her story. She tried a sexy romance but deleted it when she realized it sounded farcical. She tried a mystery but couldn't remember who was supposed to have done what. It seemed so easy in the books she read. She gave her collection a baleful look.

"I think some of you need to be binned or re-cycled"

Just as Mo was getting ready to go to bed, she heard a car pull up into the drive. She went to the bedroom window and peeped out. It was Sally's car and she was still sitting in the driver's seat. With a sick feeling, Mo went downstairs and opened the front door. As she approached the car, she could see Sally hunched over the wheel, obviously crying. Mo opened the car door and slipped into passenger seat.

"Oh love," she said, sliding her arm around her daughters heaving shoulders. She held Sally tightly. Mo couldn't begin to imagine what had brought Sally to this state, but she would put money on it having something to do with Richard. Eventually Sally's sobs began to ease and she pulled away from Mo.

"Where's Jack?" she asked.

"Fast asleep in bed. Shall we go and have a peep?"

Sally nodded and climbed out of the car. Mo followed her into the house. While Sally went to take a look at her sleeping son, Mo busied herself in the kitchen making a cup of tea. No matter what happened in life, a cup of tea always seemed to help. When Sally came back down, she seemed to be a little more composed. Mo didn't want to press her. She knew she would talk when she was ready. Sally sat warming her hands on the mug of tea. She stared into its depths for a long time before giving a huge sigh and turning to face her mother.

"Tonight, wasn't a great success then, I take it?" said Mo.

Sally laughed mirthlessly. "You could say that"

"What happened?"

"I got to the hotel at about six o'clock just as I had planned. I knew the number, so I didn't go through the front desk. If I had then I wouldn't have known."

"Known what?" pressed Mo

"I wanted to surprise Richard. Well, I certainly did that. I knocked on the door and heard him shout something about room service. I thought it was strange, but when he opened the door in his bath robe and saw me, I saw the look of absolute horror on his face, I knew it was bad. Part of me wanted to turn and run away, but instead I walked past him into room and said "Surprise." He stood looking at me like a goldfish. He tried to get me to go back down to the bar and wait for him and that's when I knew for certain. I simply sat down and waited. He didn't know what to do or what to say to me. It was quite funny in a sad sort of way. Like a car crash that you know is going to happen but you can't stop it. I just sat and waited for the crash.

"He had someone with him, didn't he?"

"Oh yes, he certainly had someone with him."

"Who was she? One of his secretaries?

"Oh no. It was much better than that. It was his partner.

"His partner? Mo repeated feeling confused. She knew Richard had started his business with his old school friend, Graham.

"Yes, his partner. I must say I wouldn't have felt quite so stupid if a blond bimbo had walked out of the bathroom. When Graham walked out still drying himself with a tiny towel, I wanted to fall through the floor. Mind you it was nothing to how they must have felt. Graham just looked at me, turned round and walked back into the bathroom. Richard sat on the bed and just said "Oh God" over and over again.

"What did you say to him? What did you do?" queried Mo who was now totally confused. '*Richards not gay?*' she kept thinking.

"Do? Say? Nothing. What could I say? The look on Richard's face said it all. It had obviously been going on for some time. I thought of all the late meetings that he had had with Graham over the years. Obviously, because it was Graham I never thought of an affair. He was his business partner. It was completely normal. I suddenly realised it had been going on under my nose for years. No wonder he didn't desire me anymore. He never has."

Sally looked at her Mother in despair.

"So that's it" she said. "My marriage is over. I'm not sure if I even had a marriage at all."

Sally seemed very calm now that she had got it all off her chest. She took herself off to bed. She would use the other bed in Jack's room. He would have a lovely surprise when he woke up in the morning. Mo suddenly didn't feel sleepy. She would not have been surprised to hear about an affair with a secretary but to hear that Richard was gay had completely floored Mo. She had never had any suspicion, nor had Sally. Mo began to feel just a little bit sorry for Richard. He must have felt wretched, believing that he had to live a pretend life. Then she felt angry because he had hurt Sally and somewhere down the line, this would have to be explained to Jack.

"Crikey, whoever said real life is boring?" Mine certainly isn't.

As Mo went upstairs to go to bed, she went in to her study to turn off the computer. Before she did she sat down and started to type. She was doing what she had done earlier, writing about her family. Somehow, this time, it felt less contrived, less like her family. Words flowed from Mo like a river and she made a lot of typos trying to get the words down before she forgot them. She wasn't worried about that. Mistakes could be corrected. Mo only knew that she had the germ of an idea and she needed to get it down.

As she typed, she knew it was good. She was using her own feelings of sadness and confusion to help her to understand how a gay man might live another life in order to hide from public view. She knew that in this supposedly PC world that it shouldn't matter, but the truth was very different. The world in which Richard and Graham lived and worked was very conservative and "coming out" as a couple would most likely open them up to ridicule and abuse from the business world. No wonder Richard had hidden it. This was the story that Mo was telling. It wasn't about her daughter or about Richard. It was about any one of a number of men who still feel they have to hide their true selves.

Mo wrote long into the night. By the time the first light of dawn was touching the sky, she knew she had a good story. Perhaps even a wonderful story. As she was finishing off, she heard Sally moving about on the landing. The door opened slowly.

"Have you been in here all night? "

"I have. I had an idea and couldn't wait to get it down on paper. "

"Can I read it? "

Mo hesitated. This was all a bit fresh for Sally and she might not understand. Still, she would read it one day. She took a deep breath and handed over the sheaf of papers. She waited quietly as Sally read. She didn't even dare look at her.

Sally put the manuscript down. Most could see tears slowly rolling down her face.

"Oh sweetheart," she whispered. "I'm not trying to hurt you, I just couldn't help myself last night. It was as though the words just poured out of me ... "

"Mum, stop. It's alright. In fact it's better than alright. This is amazing. I had no idea you could write like this. "

"You're not cross because it's your story are you."

"No, funnily enough, I'm not."

Sally looked very thoughtful for a moment. Mo waited.

"In fact, in a strange way this helps."

"It does?" squeaked Mo. "I mean, it does," she tried again in what she hoped was her normal voice. "Just how does it help?"

Sally looked at her Mum for several minutes, then let out her breath in a rush.

"Last night, all I could think about was me. How I felt. I was angry, let down, confused. I kept thinking, how could he do this to me? Now I realize that it isn't just about me. Richard must be going through hell. I know he loves me in his way and he adores Jack. It's the end of our marriage , but I don't want it to be the end of our friendship. I love him too much for that. "

Sally wiped her tears and looked at her Mum. Mo knew she wanted her to understand. She reached out and took Sally's hands in hers. Rubbing them gently, she began to speak.

"Sally, love, every word I wrote in that story is true. It is exactly how I feel. My heart goes out to Richard, and to Graham. I am so relieved that you have stopped being angry. I think we have a good chance of staying a family."

Sally picked up the manuscript and waved it at her Mum.

"This story is amazing. You definitely have to read it to your group. It will certainly make them sit up and take notice." Now, I am going to call Richard and arrange to talk to him. We have a lot to sort out. "

Mo watched her daughter leave the room and felt a surge of pride. Sally had certainly grown up overnight. She looked at the manuscript in her hands and couldn't stop a little bubble of excitement from rising. She would read her story next week and she was prepared to justify her opinions if necessary. She was going to enter it in the competition as well. She probably wouldn't win anything, but that wasn't the point. She wanted as many people as possible to read it. 'Somehow', she thought, 'that was more important'.

The Pink Envelope

Muriel Claybrook

'What a joy to be out in the Spring sunshine, this Sunday morning' thought Jill, as she ran down to Broomhill. This was the intended start of her jog up through the parks to the moors. The Yorkshire stone and millstone grit houses always brought a little surge of appreciation to her heart, and there were so many old, but well-maintained boundary walls in this leafy part of the city. Descending the rather steep hill, she noticed a pink object near the foot of one wall.

It merited a second glance and she noticed it was a pretty envelope. Curious, she stopped, picked it up and saw "Mum" written on it. Inside were about ten, brightly coloured, metallic-like pieces of confetti, in the shape of champagne flutes. She stooped down to replace the envelope where she had found it.

She was nearly at the park gates now and passing the "Bistro on the Park", a stylish venue that hosted family celebrations. Had the envelope been part of a birthday, wedding, or engagement celebration? Of course, she would never know but the discovery had set her relaxed mind off on thoughts of her own mum, Sheila, who, now in her late seventies, was enjoying a wonderful and most unexpected relationship in her life.

Sheila had been a very conventional mother: family oriented and nurturing. Although she was a keen sports woman, it was only after her family had flown the nest that she could indulge herself as much as she liked in sporting activities. It was her proficiency on the golf course and sociable manner, that made her so popular in the club house. Jill's dad had died after a short illness nearly twenty years ago, and though Sheila had plenty of friends there was no one special for her until Barry.

Barry's wife had died of cancer eight months before he and Sheila got together as a couple. Only a few months into the relationship, Barry sold up his home and moved in with Sheila. He had many lifelong friends from his career in the army, and readily made new ones. His zest for life shone out from all he did and he was soon integrated into Sheila's family. How marvellous that Jill's mum now had this wonderful man to share life's ups and downs with. Only last summer Jill's brother and his family had hosted Sheila and Barry for a holiday at their villa in Majorca. Barry's diving off a chartered boat and swimming blissfully in the warm Med, for twenty minutes, had already become legendary in the family. He was nearly eighty. Yes, they were all delighted at mum's happy times.

Jill was a mum too and her daughter, thirty-year-old Hannah, was in a happy relationship with a colleague at the school where they both taught. A little packet for Jill had arrived in the post during the last week. It had a "do not open till" instruction on it. Today was the day, and anticipating the action spurred Jill on during the homeward leg of the run. She had wanted to share the opening with her husband. . Over their coffee in the kitchen she found a photo frame inside the packet. It contained an ultra sound, scan image of their first grandchild to be.

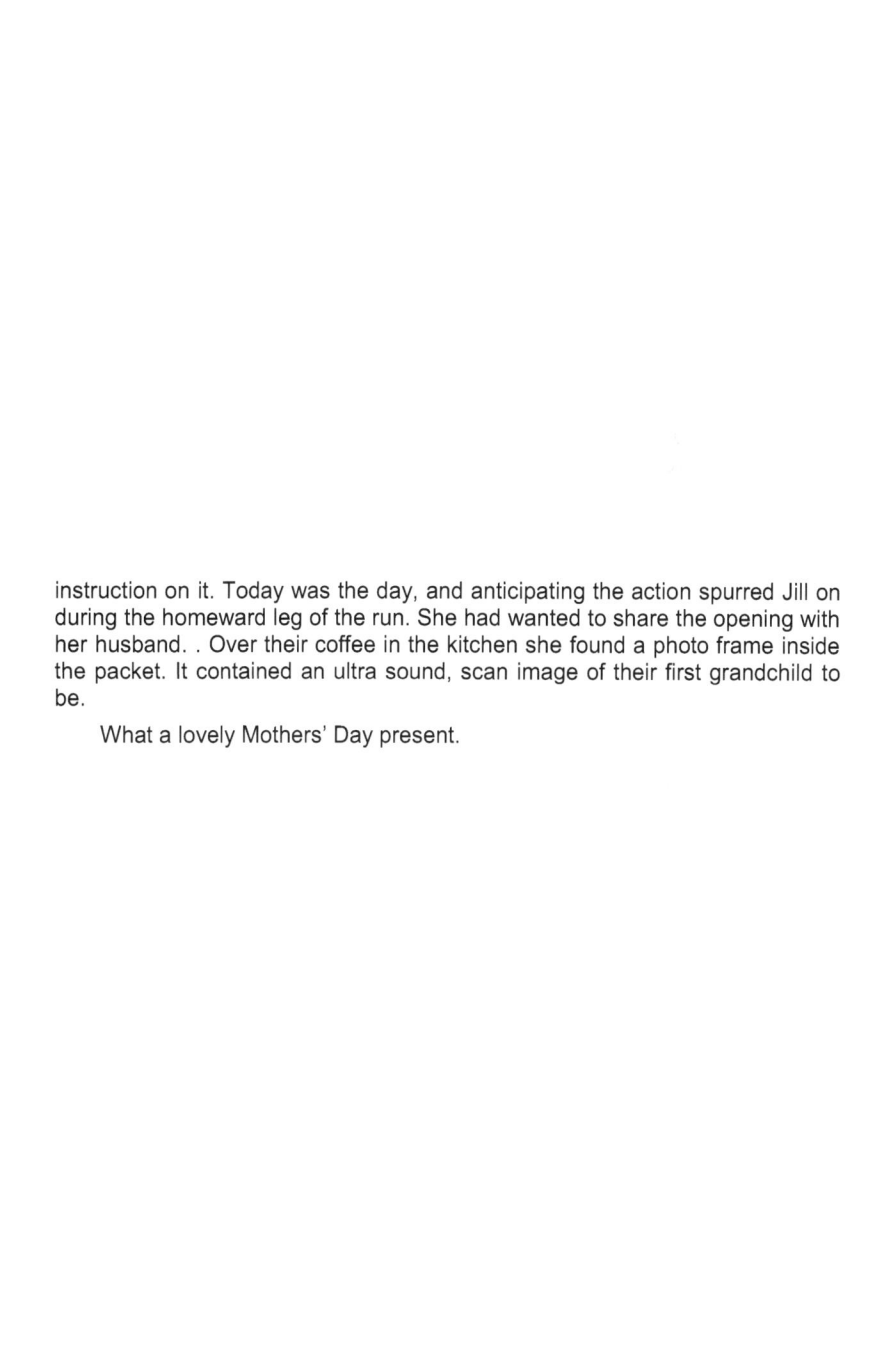

What a lovely Mothers' Day present.

The Bookshop

Maxine Patterson

I had wandered for nearly an hour, up and down the narrow pedestrianised streets being barged aside by careless students. And attacked, by pavement panzers, those double buggies designed to cause as much damage as possible to anyone foolish enough to get in their way.

It was the quirky window display that attracted me; it featured the latest releases attractively displayed with hand written comments underneath. The theme was, of course, The Booker Prize Longlist. My chance to find out about the books and writers and choose a couple. I needed to organise the book group programme and it's so much easier when browsing through the actual books rather than just reading the reviews on the internet.

The smell of coffee wafted towards me as I opened the door and walked in, mmm! A leisurely browse with a cup of coffee – what could be better?

I had to manoeuvre my way carefully between the small crowded tables, two loaded buggies and the stacked display tables managing to reach the counter without mishap. Feeling some measure of success, I was faced with another dilemma.

"Hello love, what would you like?" Asked the plumpish, blue haired student serving behind the counter.

"Umm, coffee please…"

"Just coffee?" She queried, gesturing to the list behind her head.

The coffee menu was daunting, at least six different types of coffee with umpteen types of syrups that could be added; even more types of tea. Flummoxed, I opted for an Americano with milk.

"Where are you sitting?"

I turned and managed to see a small table tucked right in the corner where I could sit and drink and browse, I pointed "over there."

"Ok love, I'll bring it over." And she busied herself dealing with the knobs and dials of the gleaming machine on the counter behind.

I squeezed between two stylish buggies, two larger tables and managed to pull out the small one so that I could sit down, facing into the shop. In my head yet another grumble: what was the point of having tables – if you couldn't sit down?

Unhooking my bag and untangling my scarf; I couldn't help overhearing.

"I'd be furious. I mean it's not what you expect is it?"

I was so close, I was almost part of the conversation.

"So, what did Anthea do then?"

"She threatened to cancel his golf club membership."

I angled my body so that I didn't appear to be listening. But, my mind grappled with possibilities.

"I'm not surprised, she's always determined to have things her own way."

"What did he do then?

"Well, he apologized and promised it would never happen again."

"Yeah right! As if that'll make any difference!"

The blue hair expertly wove her way through the tables; "here's your coffee love. Just come over if there's anything else you need."

"Anthea told Greg he had to be more responsive and understanding"

"Oh yes, thanks." Smiling in thanks, I positioned the coffee pretending to stir thoughtfully. Drat, responsive to what? I made a show of stirring my coffee again and looking over towards the bookshelves; responsive – what?

"But that would be so difficult, considering what has happened."

"I know."

The slim, long legged blonde leaned forward towards her companion, her smooth long hair curtaining the low-voiced exchange that followed. "Really!" Her companion nodded appreciatively.

"I'm not surprised, I mean he was always different."

I was on tenterhooks, but I couldn't sit and pretend not to be listening, I needed something on the table to disguise my avid interest. I manoeuvred my way back through the tables and grabbed three of the Booker Prize long listed books. Back at the table the conversation had moved on. "So... what did her mother say?"

Immaculately manicured nails picked up their coffees and sipped delicately, then the polished blonde heads met in the middle of the table; "Well, she didn't like it, she was worried about the neighbours finding out."

I was lost in the possibilities that could arise from the difference and the lack of responsiveness.

I picked up a book and turning to the back, tried vainly to focus on the blurb and the reviews. *'Life and death issues, powerful imaginative exploration of essential themes'*....

"Well you would worry, wouldn't you," followed by a snort of laughter and a carefully modulated shake of the artfully straightened hair.

Could I ask them about his responses or lack of them? No, of course not! Coffee! Drink the blessed coffee! Stir, slurp, focus on the cup.

"I mean he does look good when he's all done up, but."

"I know, it's so embarrassing. She makes him leave by the side door."

I was utterly hooked. No Booker story could be as riveting or as intriguing as the story I had become an impromptu and unplanned part of.

The latest model phone trilled on the table and the conversation was abandoned. The two yummy mummies collected up their bags and packages, loaded them onto their trendily expensive buggies and assertively pushed their way through the tables to the door, throwing casual goodbyes over their shoulders.

My planned leisurely browse and coffee break had been hijacked by someone's real life experience. Except I would never know what happened at the end. What kind of denouement could there possibly be? Could there be a happy ever after ending? It seemed very unlikely that there could be.

Being made to leave by the side door away from neighbours' prying eyes implied dramatic change, perhaps exacerbated by the lack of responsiveness.

My brain was filled with the words that I had overheard. How could the much-hyped long listed Booker Prize entry concerning those *"life and death issues"* compare to the tantalising snippet of real life that I had just allowed myself to become a part of?

I hadn't managed to choose an appropriate book for the book group. Instead I had been entertained and given a little peak into someone else's "life issues". Hopefully they wouldn't develop any further. And what a wonderful tale to recount to the Book Group.

Autumn

Pat Buckley

Brown scrunchy leaves were thick on the ground as they walked the woodland path. It was a track they had followed many times before. The trees are magnificent at this time of year.

Looking at the distant hillside, she reflected on the vision of those early woodland designers, who had selected the trees to provide luscious greens in the spring and summer and a glorious contrast of reds, browns and oranges in the autumn. Did they know that long after they were dead, others would be marvelling on their creation?

This walk, so familiar, encouraged a reflective mood and thoughts of walks in years past.

When they were friends, not yet lovers, newly discovering the thrill of shared pleasures, she'd brought him here. They ran, carefree through the trees and he too had seen it through her eyes. Later when they married and moved away, a regular visit to the old family homes was an essential part of autumn, as was their woodland pilgrimage.

They brought their children there, in all seasons, but they were most delighted in the way they'd run through the trees kicking leaves to see how high they could make them fly, playing hide and seek, building mounds of orange, brown and red. There was a lively family discussion on the way home about whether the mound could be an autumn man, not snow of course because of the colour. Eventually all agreed, it was their own Vesuvius. Later, on a family trip to Pompeii, they remembered the colourful mound in the woods, and it gave a visual prompt to the molten lava that cascaded over the town.

As the years passed, and although their parents were long gone, they still took time to travel and come to this spot in the autumn to walk and talk and reflect. Their own children grew up, left home to pursue their own lives and start their own families, but Vesuvius both Italian and woodland, was often featured in their "Remember when" chats.

After retirement, they had returned to their home area and so again could walk the woods throughout the seasons and with joy, introduce the grandchildren to the woods, and watch as they too played hide and seek in the spring and summer greens, kicked the autumn leaves and built their own Vesuvius.

It was important to them to keep up this ritual; there was so much of them and their family happiness here. This year he struggled to do it, leaning heavily on his stick, slow, breathless and weak. A visit to the specialist days before had confirmed what they both knew but dare not express, his autumn had arrived;

not in a blaze of colour but in a pale despair, with no hope of the reawakening spring.

They knew that next year she would need to walk alone.

But the trees would still be there, and later generations would again share fun, build memories and marvel at the majesty of colour in this little area.

Pressure

Jan Jenner

Outside the surgery Michael leant heavily against the iron railings. Despite the warm April sunshine, he felt cold. The roar of the London traffic was deadened by the words pounding in his head. "Heart attack'. His throat and chest felt tight making it difficult to breathe. A shadow of panic spread through his limbs. His hands felt damp, and he thrust them deep into his jacket pockets throwing it out of shape. His broad shoulders slumped. His face was pallid behind the neatly clipped beard. The sudden realisation of the doctor's words hit him in one blow. Up until now he had ignored the implications. He knew he'd had a heart attack, but somehow it didn't mean for him, what it inevitably meant for others.

"You need rest now Michael. Medical science has done its best, the rest is up to you." The doctor had spoken gently. His words had echoed around the sombre wood panelling in the office. "A year to live at most, unless you make some critical changes to your life style. You've had a mild attack this time Michael. It was a warning. The next one could well kill you.'

Michael had heard the words. He'd watched them, followed them around the room, but the words had never really attached themselves to him, until now. The doctor must have said those same words a thousand times to a thousand different people. There was no doubting them. You couldn't question words from a specialist of Jeremy Paxtel's standing. He was one of the top people in his field. He was being paid for by Michael's company. They'd insisted he had a complete medical before he returned to work.

Michael levered himself off the railings and pushed the feeling of panic away, he began to walk towards the park. The doctor had offer to call Michael a taxi, but Michael had refused, preferring the exercise, maybe he should have accepted the offer, maybe the exercise would be too much.

"Come on man, don't be stupid." Michael forced himself to take a deep breath. He'd walked to the surgery that morning. Nothing had changed since then. He straightened himself up, aware that several people in a bus queue were looking at him curiously, not really interested enough to ask if he was all right, he was just a diversion until the no. 38 arrived.

Rest the doctor had said, not immobilisation, he walked slowly past the queue. They'd lost interest now their bus had arrived, they were more intent on the usual pushing and shoving to keep their place.

Michael found an empty park bench opposite the lake and sat down. It seemed much longer than two weeks since he'd been taken ill. He'd thought the pain had been indigestion at first; Until he'd collapsed in the office. His secretary had gone with him in the ambulance. He could still hear the sirens as they raced across London.

How could he change his life style, his life style was his work? He was a senior sales manager with one of the biggest computer software developer in Europe. He'd think nothing of flying halfway across the world for a three-hour meeting and back again in time for dinner. Without his work, he had nothing; he was nothing. It was easy for the doctor to say. But it meant giving up everything he'd worked for, for the last twenty-five years.

As he watched the children sailing boats on the lake and heard the cheerful giggles, he felt a sudden surge of regret, and wished, just for a moment that he'd married and had his own family. It was too late now. He'd been too busy making a career for himself, not that he had ever been short of female companionship, he hadn't, but he had never met anyone he couldn't live with out. He made his way careful to the gate and waited there until he saw a taxi.

He spent the rest of the week at home locked away in his flat, thinking. Much as he loved his work he loved living more.

Monday morning, he travelled into the office and handed in his resignation. They wouldn't accept it at first. David Schofield the sales director and Paul Richards the M.D. had taken him out to lunch. They told him how the company couldn't survive without him.

"Take some time off Mike, take as much as you need," said David, "You'll soon be back to your old self. The company needs you, just think it over, if you want to ease the pressure I'm sure we can work something out.'

"You shouldn't rush decisions now, old chap said Paul "You might regret it.'

Michael took a taxi home feeling very tired and empty. He didn't need to think it, over his mind was made up. He was at a turning point in his life. The old one was finished. If what the doctor had said was true and he had no reason to doubt it. To return to his old life now would be suicidal. His new life started right now.

Michael had never realised how small his flat was, he'd never spent much time in it. Why not make a complete change, move away somewhere quiet? He had always wanted to go to Wales. He had had several short holidays there as a boy, fishing and scrambling over the hills. He could paint, all his adult life he had wanted to paint, but apart from the occasional weekend break with a sketchbook, he'd never really had the time.

The emptiness stayed with him all day, but a small light had also started to glimmer. He began to see how thin the city sunshine was, and he began to smell the stale air. The clean, fresh air of Wales was becoming increasingly attractive.

Two days later Michael went into the town and called on several estate agents for details of a property in Wales. He liked the idea of the peace and the tranquillity. He could paint and walk, do the things he never had the time to do. He had some money invested. With careful management, it should fund a modest lifestyle. He found himself almost looking forward to it.

Within weeks, he had put his house on the market and leased, unseen, apart from photographs, a small cottage in north Wales. The village sat in the shadow of Snowdon. A quiet place, about a dozen or so houses, a shop and a church and a pub. A small river meandered through the village complete with ducks and swans. It was truly idyllic

When he arrived at the cottage he almost had a change of heart. It was early evening and the surrounding country was sleeping, hidden beneath a fine white mist. It seeped through his clothes and trickled down his neck.

Snowdon was unseen, and the cottage defied description. It was dirty and damp and badly needed painting. It had a hole in one end of the roof just over the kitchen, and two of the panes of glass in the front window were cracked.

"Exchange one sort of stress for another." Michael muttered to himself as he unloaded his possessions from the rented van. "There must be at least six months' worth of work needed just to make it habitable.'

But by the end of May the painters, decorators and sundry workmen had all finished and gone home. Every paintable surface had been painted in brilliant white gloss and Michael was ready to start his new life.

He took a trip into the nearby town and bought everything he needed, brushes canvases paint pencils, sketchpads and an easel. He spent the afternoon arranging everything neatly on the bench in the large front room he had allocated for a studio. The next day he woke with a feeling of excitement and anticipation. After breakfast, he went into the studio and arranged a canvas on his easel. He was all set, but where did he get his inspiration. The bright sunshine streaming through the window gave him his answer. He would go out and look for it. He would find inspiration in nature.

He put a sketchbook and a small watercolour box in a canvas bag and set off. He followed a track away from Snowdon. He walked up through the bracken-covered hills the warm smells and soft, vibrant colours were a million miles away from London.

He found a small group of white painted cottages lurking next to three tall, dark poplar's. Pleased with the contrast they afforded he settled down to work. After one or two false start he began painting in earnest, by the time the light was fading he had made two passable watercolour sketches. Slowly he walked home tired but satisfied. Tomorrow he would go into the village, he wanted to try his hand at painting the church.

Throughout the summer Michael spent the days working, gradually falling into a routine of walking and sketching in the mornings and working in the studio in the afternoon. In the evening he caught up on the reading he had been putting off for years. As the weeks, went by his confidence grew. He was relaxed and fit. He began to think that getting a heart attack was not such a bad thing after all. He was enjoying his life. He'd made friends with several of the villagers and occasionally went for a lunch time drink and a game of darts in the pub. He'd found a peace and contentment he had never thought possible.

The summer months brought tourists to the great mountain. Some would stop and talk as he worked. One couple became quite friendly and at the end of their stay they asked if they could buy one of his painting as a reminder of their holiday, he was delighted and gladly gave it to them.

Over the next few weeks, he was asked to sell more which he willingly did, and he grew to appreciate the recognition. Late one afternoon he called into the pub for a drink before going home. Mrs Mason the manager suggested he hang some of his work on the wall.

"They'll sell here with the tourist trade, you should do well. You might even become famous." She smiled at him.

"I'm not sure I want to become famous," Michael said. But he let her hang some of his painting on the wall and sure enough they did sell, almost as fast as he could paint them.

About the end of September, Mrs Mason had some visitors. They showed a very keen interest in the paintings on the wall and asked for Michael's address.

A couple of weeks later Michael received a letter offering him some space in a London gallery. An exhibition was duly planned for three weeks after Christmas. He was flattered and mentioned it at the pub that lunchtime.

"Good for you Michael, you deserve it," said Mrs Mason and gave him a drink on the house.

A week later he received a letter of confirmation. He had some paintings ready, so there wasn't much work involved. He would only need two or three extra canvasses.

Michael travelled up to London for the occasion. The show was a moderate success, and he agreed to show his work in a larger one being planned for the autumn. Michael also found himself accepting several commissions.

He didn't get to the pub very often these days he didn't do much walking either, he found it quicker to paint from photographs in his studio, usually he worked well into the night.

One morning in the early spring Michael climbed out of bed feeling just as tired as when he had laid down the night before. He collected his post and opened a letter from London. It was from his agents asking how his work was progressing. They had had several inquiries about his work, and they were pleased to say he was starting to get quite an enthusiastic following. Maybe it would be possible to travel up to London sometime soon to talk about the arrangements for the show. He thrust the letter down on the table. How could he be expected to find time to paint if he was travelling up to London every five minutes? He made a cup of coffee and took it into the studio. He had no time for breakfast, he had to get on with his work. As he picked up his paintbrush, he felt a sharp pain in his chest.

Michael fell backwards, and the paintbrush dropped from his fingers leaving a bright viridian green smudge of paint on the floor.

Single Track

by Pat Buckley

"It's my holiday! You expect me to spend it in a drafty old hut near a railway line. I might have done this years ago, but now I am 53 years old, I don't do camping" was one of her gentler responses. "I need rest and relaxation, sea, sand, scenery and having someone preparing meals for me. Not self-catering and looking at trains. I'll organise my own break, thank you".

These were the final words of the morning's discussions. 'Discussions' he called them, but in reality they were quite spirited. Indeed, it would be fair to say that she had put on a better display of fireworks than on the village green the previous November.

Three months previously, Henry Baxter had seen his dream trip advertised in the local paper, and decided there and then that he would book. He'd told his wife Sheila that he was organising a surprise holiday. Over the following weeks he had answered her carefully crafted questions with equally carefully crafted answers.

"Yes, it was for a week. No, she would not need her passport; or a bikini. Yes, an anorak should be brought. No, it was not full board, although there would be some meals out."

The crunch had come when he had suggested they go shopping for the basics for their breakfasts and some snacks. At this point, the demands for the where and how became quite insistent. After Henry had joyfully shared his surprise, he had been taken aback at Sheila's reaction. It had then become obvious to Henry that Sheila shared neither his excitement, nor his enthusiasm for this trip of a lifetime.

Having done his necessary shopping, Henry returned to find Sheila, credit card in hand, searching for a late deal to somewhere warm. A very confused Henry spent a frosty evening, followed by a lonely night in the spare room. Henry and Sheila rarely argued these days, and he was quite hurt that she did not want to share his dream. And with mixed feelings he set off on his solitary quest.

He had been pleased to find the well-furnished train carriage, climb aboard and deposit his large suit case and a bag of provisions. The holiday railway coach was fitted with all mod cons was perfectly placed in a rural siding, in a sunlit valley.

'This will do,' he thought, and set about sorting his belongings and making himself comfortable. Henry was achieving one of his ambitions; he'd wanted to do this for many years. Having already visited the tourist information site for the area, he had a list of places to visit; enough to keep him stimulated for most of the week. But the joy, the purpose of the stay in this precise location, was not just the pleasure of staying in a converted old LNER railway carriage but the events programme on Sunday.

The railway museum (due to be visited on Tuesday) and a group of enthusiasts had organised a cavalcade of steam, bringing a number of the engine classics from the days of yesteryear out onto the tracks again. He'd looked them all up in the train spotters hand book, which he'd owned since he was a boy, and a small frisson of excitement passed through him as he checked it out.

But the pinnacle of his almost 50 years as a train spotter was that they would all be passing within yards of his holiday home on both the outward and return journeys. As Henry sat at the window of his carriage, and watched the parade, his delight knew no bounds. His sandwiches and flask of tea at hand ensured he did not miss a minute. More than once he wondered if Sheila was regretting not sharing it with him.

Sheila meantime was sitting on her balcony in a hotel in Majorca. Nursing a large glass of Sangria, she surveyed the scene. The hotel pool below her sparkled blue in the sun. All around were couples and families, playing in the water, lying on sun beds and just enjoying the warmth and light. She lay back in the lounger and started again to read her novel; a latest best seller she had picked up at the airport.

'This is the life', she thought. 'Bit difficult to put sun cream on my back but otherwise, things are great, much better than watching trains in dreary wet Yorkshire.' At this, her anger flared up again, at Henry and his assumption that she would enjoy a week of his darned trains.

Leaning back, she enjoyed a few more sips of her wine, and relaxed again. She sighed contentedly and it was not too long before her eyelids closed and she settled into a gentle snooze. Waking later, she realised that the pool was almost empty and the clatter of plates and cutlery rose up from below. Dinner beckoned.

Showered, smartly dressed and made up, she headed to dining room, where she was shown to a single table, from where she was able to view her fellow residents. 'Families and couples,' she reflected, 'Still, I didn't come to share, but to please myself'.

Sheila had prepared by taking a book with her and found it a useful shield from the outside world. She returned to the novel she was enjoying the luxury of reading without the domestic demands and duties, and ate her dinner in peace.

Sheila spent the next few days in restful solitude and did not stray from the hotel. On the fourth evening her solitary dinner was interrupted.

"Excuse me, I can see you are deep in your book, but your shawl has fallen on the floor," and looking up she caught the face of a grey haired lady, who smiled as she returned the item to her chair back. After thanking her, she picked up the story again.

The following day, Sheila decided to explore the resort. The stone buildings and tiled roofs added a charm to the place. Knowing it was in one of the quieter areas, she felt quite safe in wandering alone. The sandy beach was filled with parasols and sun beds as holiday makers soaked up the sun, dashing into the sea to cool off. There was a little cafe where she enjoyed a coffee and watched the world go by. For the first time, Sheila wondered what Henry was doing, if his trip which he'd planned with so much excitement was living up to expectations. She also realised, she was no longer angry, and actually missed him. Many people thought accountants to be boring, but that was to misunderstand the nature of the work and the need for precision. Henry was a gentle and considerate person, which just added to her confusion over his holiday planning.

From the little information booth, on the main street, Sheila selected leaflets. It was market day in Soller, the next town; she boarded a rickety old tram which rattled its way to the town centre. The journey was short but pretty, the market disappointing; the usual collection of tourist tat and designer fakes. And soon she was heading back to her hotel. One thing she did discover was that there was a heritage railway service to the capital, and she planned to take a day trip there.

That evening, as she sat in the lounge with her after dinner coffee, the same lady approached her and asked if she minded her taking the empty seat beside her. Looking round, she realised that the lounge was, indeed, quite full, and she nodded her assent.

"My family have gone off to one off the evening shows, so I've been abandoned," she explained.

Feeling that to continue to read would be just plain bad manners Sheila smiled and asked about the family. After describing her daughter, son in law and the two grandchildren, with great affection and pride, the companion then asked about her. Reluctantly Sheila explained that her husband Henry was enjoying a train enthusiast's holiday, so she'd decided to take in some sun.

"No children?" she asked.

The thought opened a part of her, she had buried for too long. "No," she hesitated, "it was just not possible."

"A sadness, I think," was the quiet reply.

Sheila realised that it was a deep, deep sadness; how they had tried and cried at the failures and the eventual recognition that it would only ever be just the two of them. They had come to realise that there would never be anyone else for them to share with or plan for; they were the family with only each other to rely on. Just nodding, because she could not express to this stranger the deeply personal thoughts and emotions the question had opened up, Sheila started to tell her about her day out. Her new friend smiled and shared tales of earlier holidays, when her husband was alive, and they had regularly come to this area.

After they parted Sheila realised that her time for quiet and solitude was coming to an end. It was pleasant to share your reflections with someone as life passed you by. She also saw that in their comfortable relationship, she and Henry had stopped talking about what was important to them. They were taking each other for granted. Sheila did not know when this had started, perhaps so gradually that neither had realised what was happening to them.

The planned trip to Palma next day was a great success. The vintage electric train, with its hard wooden slatted seats wound up the valley through orange and lemon groves, surrounded by colourful hills. And the viaduct, although not very long, was stone built and well preserved. 'Henry would love this.' The ironic thought came unbidden to her mind, together with the acceptance for all his ways and boring hobbies, she really did miss him.

Palma itself was fun. Sheila strolled the narrow streets of the old town, marvelled at the magnificent cathedral, and walked the fort area. There were plenty of quality shops to browse, and cafes to rest in. On her return to Soller, Sheila bought a little model of the train to take home for Henry.

When Henry returned home after his week's railway indulgence, he was concerned to find the house in cold darkness. Letting himself in, he searched for any note or clue to where Sheila might be and when she would return. Her suitcase was gone, but most of the rest of her stuff was still in the house in its usual place, so he expected she would be returning home. He hoped it would not be too long. Having eaten a miserable supper, Henry retired again to the solitary bed in the spare room.

The following day dragged by as he caught up with the jobs around the house and garden. Henry was, as always, amazed at how much the grass could grow in just one week, and the weeds had used the time to invade the borders.

His afternoon tea was interrupted by the sound of slamming of car doors. Peering out of the front window, he spotted a man carrying a suitcase, walking up the path. Throwing the front door open, his planned, "Who are you?" Or "I don't buy at the door," were made unnecessary by a bronzed Sheila appearing beside the man. She paid her taxi driver and taking the suitcase from him, marching past an amazed Henry into the house. Putting down her case in the hall, she looked around, reflecting that whilst the house looked just the same, it felt different. In truth it was she who had changed through not being there.

Henry on the other hand was delighted to see her and enveloped her into big hug.

"Welcome home my dear," he gasped. "I was so afraid you would not come back."

"I nearly didn't," she confessed, "but then I realised, that we are a pair. For years it's been us against the world, and we should not give that up."

Happily they sat and ate together and afterwards shared the news of their adventures. To show her how much he'd missed her, Henry had bought a whole box of the handmade chocolates she loved so much, and Sheila produced the little model train. The little gifts showed that they had indeed missed each other.

Their evening ended with an understanding that although they may wish to do different things sometimes, they would always need to be together as a couple. There was also a promise that Henry would return with her to sunny Majorca and ride on the little train, whilst she would share the occasional specialist train enthusiast's days.

That night, there was no cold spare bedroom for Henry, but they snuggled together in the room they had shared for thirty years.

"Welcome home, my dear," said Henry sleepily, as he turned off the lamp.

Ready to Chill

Muriel Claybrook

"I'm home" he calls as he comes into the hall.

"Kitchen as usual!", she replies jauntily.

As he comes through to meet her, he jumps with shock, then stares at her in disbelief.

"What have you done and when?" he asks, puzzled.

"Did you forget I've had a free half day? I spent it well don't you agree?"

"Well it's a colour we haven't had before" he says, smiling now.

He slips an arm around her waist for a moment and then slowly turns her round.

"An impressive brunette!" he tells her. "When I'm looking for you tomorrow, in the airport, for instance, it won't be helpful. I'll be scanning around for a gorgeous blonde" he says frowning slightly and then sees the funny side of it.

"Well I'll have to wear something distinctive, like a bright red top, that will go with these dark tresses" she flirts.

Phil briefly kisses the back of her neck and then retreats to read his post.

"I'll throw a few things in my case while you finish cooking" he tells Emma.

These partners are due to fly to Malta tomorrow, for two week's R&R. Phil must make time this evening to chat with fourteen-year-old Ethan, who misses his dad not living at home any longer.

'Why not now?' he decides and organises a Skype call.

"Thought you'd be online now." Phil beams with pleasure, as Ethan comes into view. "How did the camping trip go?"

"Cool, dad. All the gear got soaking wet, but we stayed for the full three days" Nathan smiled broadly. "Pete's mum picked us up at the station. You won't have to worry about rain. I checked Malta's temperature for yesterday and it was over thirty."

"Yes. The hotel has a rooftop pool with shade and that's most likely, where I'll be every day"

"Won't you get bored suddenly being so inactive? Remember how you were the best at beach games"

"Yeah, you two were always so competitive. Is Dave still at Grannies?"

"Yep, back tomorrow though", comes the reply.

Emma calls upstairs, "Tea will be on the table in ten."

"Lucky you, Dad" Ethan smiles, as he hears the call too. "It's pizza for us but not for an hour and a half. Enjoy your hols and send me a photo to my tablet. Talk to you later"

"Go steady, Ethan, and look after Mum. Love you loads", Phil smiles sincerely and breaks off the connection.

Packing for a hot destination is so easy for Phil and he seems to have all he needs in ten minutes flat.

Emma has prepared a veggie lasagne, salad and warm bread, one of his favourites. "How much luggage allowance have we got?" she queries, as they eat their supper.

"Only eighteen kilos-that should be plenty"

"Oh yes, we can always do some washing together" she says, raising her eyebrows. Resigned to it already, he now regrets not paying for extra kilos. He looks at Emma appreciatively and mentally tries to compare yesterday's blonde image with today's brunette model.

"We're both ready for our hols, aren't we?" she smiles."

"You've certainly got them off to a good start", he confirms with a kiss.

The Adventure

Maxine Patterson

Hugh been planning the itinerary all year. It was thorough and detailed, and the paperwork was interminable. Every detail of every planned railway journey; every maharajah's palace, every garden and even the short beach holiday. A precise timetable had been produced and checked. Everything would go according to plan! Hugh's plan! Nothing, but nothing had been left to chance.

Every one of us in the group had been given meticulous instructions on what travel insurance was needed. How to organise our visas and what medical preparations we needed to make. Nothing was to be left to chance! It was a U3A visit par excellence!

Having day dreamed about seeing India for such a long time, the safety net of the structured tour had encouraged me to sign up. I particularly wanted to visit Varanasi; the ancient cultural city on the banks of the Ganga. In the brochure the hotel looked splendid, clean and modern and shiny and so very western. Western rooms, western food and supposed western service. From home, in the cold drear winter weather anything white and shiny had looked inviting and I'd nervously agreed that this would be a comfortable way to visit India.

Our check lists had been handed out at the third pre-visit meeting. It was never ending as Hugh laboriously checked his master spread sheet and carefully and deliberately ticked each item as it had been covered.

I knew then it was a terrible mistake, but of course, I'd paid, and all the paperwork had been done and it was impossible to back out. I was trapped in a nightmare of Hugh's pre-planned organised bureaucracy! Now I was absolutely dreading the holiday. I had wanted an adventure, but I was trapped.

At the airport the group was shepherded into a separate seating area. I did consider making a break for it and wandering off to get a coffee – but my insurrection was forestalled because we were swiftly organised into the queue for the check in and then taken straight through to the departures lounge. Just like a school trip, but for crinklies determined to have a good time.

The only saving grace was that he didn't have a whistle. Mind you with some of them, a whistle, or even a foghorn might have been an advantage. After he had been asked to repeat all the instructions three times I began to see why he had to be so precise and exact otherwise he'd have already lost some of the old dears.

Hugh visibly relaxed once we were all on the plane as not too much could happen, apart from the queues to the toilets and the complaints about the food. There was a momentary panic as a couple of the forgetful members of the group realised that they had forgotten their itinerary and maps. However, Mr.

Resourceful had of course prepared spare packs – I had to admire his organisational skills; but I was so very glad that I didn't have to live with him.

We arrived in Delhi, which was predictably hot. Not just ordinary hot, but really hot, stifling. Hugh had arranged the visit for the cooler season trying to avoid the monsoon, but even so it was a huge shock to the system and many found it overwhelming. So, it was a meek and obedient group that made its way to the transport that would take us to the hotel. The air conditioning hit us as we entered the hotel foyer and most of us visibly relaxed.

We were given time to unpack and acclimatise; but there was of course the obligatory group meeting in the bar before the evening meal. I dutifully obeyed and arrived in the bar to see Hugh shepherding all the unruly group members into an area so that he could ensure everyone knew what we would be doing tomorrow! No possible chance of an adventure with Hugh in charge. I went to bed with a heavy heart; why had I agreed to this?

Having rested a little, my mind was made up. I had joined this group visit because I had wanted an adventure. So, I decided I would have one.

I was going to visit Varanasi and see the Ganga Learning Centre and the children and teachers that I'd been skyping with for the last four years. During that contact with the children and the teacher I had begun to understand how important Varanasi was in the religious life to many Indians. But my lovely children didn't participate in the wealth and splendour of the many tourists, they were extremely poor and existing on the margins. My weekly skype sessions was a way of helping them improve their English, which was after all the official language of India.

I got up early and went down to the desk to ask about transport from Delhi to Varanasi.

The surprised hotel receptionist was taken aback. He suggested that I could hire a car! No way – I'd seen the driving on the way from the airport. The next suggestion was that I could go by train – but it would mean five changes. Arghh! – too much hassle and opportunity to get lost. Finally, the receptionist offered the possibility of going by bus. I could see that he didn't think this was a good idea as usually the hotel clients wouldn't mix with the locals in this way. However, it was the ideal answer for me. I enthusiastically agreed, much to his surprise. Direct, long and tedious, but I would see the countryside and I couldn't get lost! Reception reluctantly arranged for a tuk tuk to take me to the bus station and wrote down everything I needed to ask to make sure that I got onto the correct bus. The list of instructions was comprehensive as the poor receptionist was terrified that both he and I would be in terrible trouble.

Back in my room I carefully packed my rucksack and bag with as much as I needed for three or four days, plus the bags of toothbrushes, felt tip pens and crayons that I'd bought for the children. I made sure I left long before the others were up. I left an apologetic message with the desk for Hugh – he'd have a fit. I was so glad that I wouldn't be around to hear and feel the full force his displeasure at my disobedience.

When I got to the bus depot I nearly fainted. I'd imagined a National Express Coach, a bit dusty and drab – but this was so, so different.

Brightly painted and decorated and packed with people and luggage. Not just full; but crammed and over flowing. Nearly every seat was occupied – thank goodness, I'd got there early enough to secure a place and only packed enough luggage that I could keep on my lap.

Suitcases, boxes, crates and large plastic bags were tied precariously on to the roof racks. Beside which were passengers perilously perched, smiling, laughing and chatting amongst themselves. I stood wondering. Was this really was a good move? But I had wanted an adventure – so I got on the bus

They were going to Varanasi on a pilgrimage, just like me in a way. They were going to venerate and celebrate the dead, and I was going to celebrate life with the wonderful children at the Ganga Learning Centre. I had been skyping with the children for more than four years, reading to them, encouraging them to widen their vocabulary, pushing them to use proper sentences. Even helping the teachers to extend their own English skills

I'd connected with the centre through the Granny Cloud, an amazing international organization that connected interested "grannies" of either sex who were prepared to give of their time connecting with children in many different countries and on different continents.

I managed to contact GLC and let them know I was coming. They were over joyed and quickly offered to book me accommodation in the local guest house that most foreign visitors used. The warmth and enthusiasm of their response reinforced my decision to break away from the rigidity of the pre-arranged tour and have my own adventure.

Situations Vacant

Pat Buckley

Emma carefully scanned the jobs column in the local free paper. She was getting desperate, she really needed some cash. Her dad died suddenly when she was half way through the first year of her degree course. Her mum insisted that she continue knowing how much she loved her studies, and that her job prospects would be greatly enhanced with a good qualification. There was not now enough cash left in the household to pay Emma's living expenses. Initially she had used her savings from being a Saturday girl at home, but that had run out.

Halfway through the second year of her course, Emma was facing the stark economic reality. Both her student loan and credit card were maxed out. She had not eaten properly for days and the rent was due. She needed a job, cash in hand and quickly. She'd walked round all the bars, but their jobs were already taken with students in similar situations. Some bar managers had taken her mobile number "just in case" but she was not too hopeful. Shop work had proved difficult as the hours were fixed and she needed space in the day for the lectures, tutorials and lab time, which were all essential parts of the physics degree she was striving so hard to achieve.

Emma was in despair, and tossing the paper aside, decided to go down to the corner shop. They sometimes had reduced items close to their sell by date. The shop also had a notice board where hopefuls offered for sale their unwanted goods. She'd often wondered about the stories behind these little cards. The one she remembered with sadness was, 'white lace wedding dress size 12, unworn' and she'd wondered about the girl, her story.

Today out of habit, she'd read them all again. It was then she spotted the small, beautifully typed card stating starkly. 'Cleaner wanted, 9 hours per week. Hours flexible'

Emma read it twice. After a short internal debate, she convinced herself she knew enough about pushing a vacuum cleaner and wielding a duster, and could even extend to polishing the bath taps. Pulling her phone out, she was relieved to see she still had some credit left, and she rang the number. A very cultured male voice answered, and, after a short inquisition, current occupation, why she wanted the job, age, etc she was invited for interview that evening. Emma was so elated; she bought a bar of chocolate to go with the bean burgers, which were the only reduced items in the cooler.

Having eaten, and buoyed up with the chocolate sugar rush, she got ready for her interview. What to wear? Viewing the contents of the large wardrobe where her few clothes seemed to cover in a dark corner, ashamed to display their poor and worn pedigrees, provided little inspiration. Not too smart, but her only dress had been worn and washed too many times to retain its original shape and finish, too casual and she may not present herself as a potentially good housekeeper. Eventually, she decided to go as she was, clean but worn top, jeans and trainers.

The address was in an area of town Emma had not previously had any reason to visit. Large brick and stone built houses set back from the road, ornate gate pillars and wrought iron gates, gardens spacious enough for established trees to flourish. Eventually she located her destination. A long drive led to an impressive double fronted Georgian house, and with some trepidation, she rang the bell.

The door was opened by a grey haired man of medium height, who smiled, ushered her inside and led her into a large and tastefully appointed sitting room. Having sunk into a beautifully cushioned chair, she composed herself and prepared to answer questions. He introduced himself as James Berkley, a business man who led a busy life and who needed his home to be clean and tidy for whenever he was there.

"I appreciate you have only basic knowledge of cleaning tasks, but I have already spoken to some of my contacts at the university so you come with excellent references for hard work and dedication. I am happy to give you a trial, if you want to come three days each week. Is £25 per 3 hour session satisfactory?"

That's a whole £75 per week, cash, thought Emma, hoping that the joy and amazement did not show too well on her face and she waited to take a deep breath before she could answer properly.

Sensing her hesitation, James continued. "To help you get established, my PA has prepared a schedule of the jobs you should be doing, and their frequency. Within reason, you can fit them in around your university work, but I do not expect that you will be here after 5pm, so I may come home to the tranquillity I need after my business day."

As they shook hands on her acceptance, he paused. "One condition I have not yet mentioned. You must not under any circumstances enter my office; it should be locked anyway but I keep confidential papers from business in there. I need to be able to trust you, as well as having the work done."

Emma's subsequent meeting with the PA was brief and to the point. She handed over a folder explaining.

"This contains an itemised job schedule, weekly time sheets, which you will complete and leave on the hall table, the alarm code, contact numbers for the office and emergency contractors."

After a quick tour of the house, identifying the rooms and where cleaning materials and equipment was kept she left, having also handing over a set of keys, and reminding Emma to fill in time sheets.

Emma found the work not too challenging, and she was able to fit in all her studies, never missing a deadline. She loved the house, and enjoyed being allowed to be in such luxury, even if it was for 9 hours weekly. She often wondered about why the study was so sacrosanct but on the one day she found the door slightly ajar, she peeped through the gap, glimpsed the beautiful polished wood desk and leather chairs, but did not step inside. She was also scrupulously careful to provide receipts for any materials she bought and was reimbursed on her next visit. Equally, when she found his wallet on the floor beside a chair in the sitting room, she stowed it away in a drawer and phoned the PA to tell her where it was.

One morning, she had overslept, having allowed herself a rare night out with her fellow students. There was no power and after searching her purse, she could not find any coins to feed the meter. She left the flat without shower or breakfast. When tidying the kitchen, which was always her first task, she spied a half slice of toast abandoned on a side plate. Coming from a household where no food was allowed to go to waste, almost without thought, she picked it up and ate it. She also found some lukewarm coffee in the cafeteria, which she thoroughly enjoyed, savouring the rich aroma as much as the taste.

Emma had always admired the main bathroom, chrome taps, which shone and reflected in the mirror wall. She felt immense satisfaction when she had cleaned these of splashes and smears. Elsewhere was a beautiful marble, and the bath itself had a whirlpool fitting, as she had found out accidentally when she switched it on during cleaning and managed to drench herself in the jet. Feeling tired and dirty, she decided to allow herself a bath here. No one would ever know, she'd just leave a little later than usual.

She filled the bath, adding a small splash of the bath essence from the vanity unit. Lying back, she switched on the whirlpool, and closed her eyes. She allowed herself to use a splash of the bath essence and drawing in the scent of she became totally relaxed, enough to fall asleep. While she rested the whirlpool whipped the essence into a mass of white foam, which covered her up to her neck, filled the bath to its full depth, and formed a marshmallow mound. She was awoken by an angry voice.

"What on earth do you think you are doing young woman?"

James had returned. Her startled movement sent a cascade of white foam down and across the green marble floor, lapping at his feet in the doorway.

"Sort this mess out and then we'll speak. I'll be in the sitting room" he said, and with that a very angry man turned and stormed out of the door.

It was a very sad girl who dried herself and the bathroom floor, although both were difficult as the tears were cascading down her cheeks, threatening to undo the repair work. Eventually she was dressed, and sufficiently composed to face her employer.

As she entered the sitting room, she thought he looked less angry than when he burst through the bathroom door, but hesitating near the doorway, she did not want to put this to the test.

"Come in and sit down" he ordered, "perhaps you would like to explain your behaviour this morning and give me one good reason why I should not sack you."

Determined to show a brave face, Emma took a deep breath and after apologising for her lapse, began her sad and pathetic story, the events of the morning including eating the toast and drinking the cold coffee. She went on to talk about how she was working hard for her degree and meeting deadlines, how her father had died suddenly, and her mother was short of money and how she needed a job to keep going as she saw the degree as a way of moving to a decent job later. And she babbled on. Despite her attempt to maintain some dignity throughout, she started to cry again.

James watched her closely throughout, and silently handed her a crisp white hand kerchief to dry her face.

"You won't get far in the corporate world if you dissolve like that when things go wrong" was the dry comment.

"I won't get there if I don't get this degree" was her tart reply.

He studied her carefully. The tension was too much for her.

"Perhaps you'd like me to leave" she offered.

"No, stay there" he ordered, "I'll make us some fresh coffee, while you compose yourself."

A confused Emma disappeared into the cloak room, washed her face in cold water, and was sitting more comfortably when he returned. To her amazement, the tray he carried included a plate of chocolate biscuits.

"I thought you would appreciate these as you'd dashed here without breakfast," he said, "and assumed sitting down over coffee and biscuits would help us have a sensible discussion"

Emma did not argue.

"First, may I say that I have been impressed by you? Over the months, my home has been cared for in exemplary fashion, and you have demonstrated your honesty and integrity." Seeing the look of surprise come to her face, James continued, "I am also aware of your potential for a good degree, I see Professor Matthews fairly regularly, and am apprised of your progress. Indeed, he holds your talents and dedication in high regard."

Emma started and the reference to Professor Matthews, and looking at her watch, realised she should have been in a tutorial, five minutes ago. 'O well,' she thought, 'just another difficult interview to be had.'

James continued, "On balance, I will not sack you today, you have only 9 months to go before your finals, and I'd like to think you could come out with a first and excellent prospects of a well paid job, and it is nearly Christmas after all. But any other failing, and you will be out, and I will inform the university why."

Emma couldn't believe her luck, and garbling her thanks, gathered her belongings and fled. When she rang her professor to apologise for not attending the tutorial, he was quite relaxed about it, saying that he'd already taken a call from James Berkley and they could rearrange a time. Emma wondered how much information had been passed on, and blushed with shame at the thought of these two older men sharing the vision of her in the bath. No reference was made when she met her tutor next, so she began to put the matter behind her, and continue her life of being a good student and cleaner.

Just before Christmas, she found a note on the kitchen table, telling her that he would be away over Christmas and New Year, so there was no need for her to come in. She received this with mixed feelings, loss of income outweighed by the joy of being able to go home and share some time with her mum. She knew that there were jobs to do there, not least sorting out her father's things, which her mum had so far felt not able to do. On opening the envelope, which she assumed to be a Christmas card, she found the most beautiful card, pre printed with James Berkley's name and address, but more importantly, a personal greeting from him and a cheque for £500.

The money made so much difference to her time at home. Having set aside some cash for a new outfit suitable for possible job interviews, she was able to add some treats to their Christmas celebrations. Amongst these, both of them enjoyed a trip to the local theatre, where they laughed and cried through a very hammy production of Cinderella, starring a TV nonentity neither of them had heard of. "Who said pantomime was for children?" they laughed on the bus home.

Emma enjoyed seeing her mum more relaxed than at her last visit home. Together, they went through her father's things, sometimes surprised at the little mementos he had kept, sharing remembrances of times together, laughter and tears. Her last act before returning to university was to deliver several black sacks of clothing and books to the local charity shop.

On returning to her cleaning job, she left James a short note expressing appreciation for his gift and saying what a difference it had made to her Christmas. In the ensuing months, Emma was surprised that James was in the house, sometimes on his way out, at others, expecting an important phone call in the study. He usually stopped for a short chat, asking how her academic work was progressing, how well she is doing in the job hunt.

Towards the end of term, her tutor approached her with a special request.

"We hold a special dinner each year for senior staff and some final year students, as well as a number of the University's supporters, and local employers. It's on Friday next week, at the Majestic Hotel. I do hope you will come."

A highly flattered Emma agreed at once. It was only after returning to her flat, and inspecting her pitiful wardrobe, did she utter the cry of women everywhere. 'I haven't a thing to wear.' She shared the problem with her mum when she did her weekly contact call. Her mum came up with a solution which surprised her.

"I can see I shall have to let you into my little secret, I visit my local charity shops and find some great bargains. In fact, that camel coat you admired at Christmas had come from one."

After a trawl of the charity shops in the local high street, Emma found just what she was looking for, a smart dress in midnight blue, and they even had some heeled court shoes to match.

On arrival she was greeted by her tutor and his wife. Her nervousness on what to do and who was who was soon settled by Lorna Matthews who kindly reassured her, as well as complementing her on her new dress. After a sherry reception, they moved in to dinner, and Emma was surprised to find herself placed between an academic from the maths department and James Barkley. The evening passed quickly as they chatted about her course, the crossover with maths, applications in industry, as well as more mundane matters as music, latest books and the like. Such speeches as there were, were brief and to the point, and often witty. Emma was suddenly realised that people were rising to make their farewells, and her watch told her it was a surprising 10.30 pm. She'd had much more fun and amusement than she had expected.

Eventually, the time of her finals arrived, and she realised that she would not be able to fulfil her cleaning commitment by then and would have to return home afterwards to continue the job search. Reluctantly, she penned a note giving notice. When she next came to the house, there was a note; thanking her for her work and giving the name and contact number of a company who were seeking someone for a new R&D project.

Dressed as smartly as she could in the new trouser suit and top, Emma presented herself for interview. After a period of questioning, on both sides, the personnel officer asked her to wait outside, while they had a private discussion. Soon she was invited back to the office and offered the post, at a salary far above her expectations. She hoped she did not sound too eager or amazed as she accepted.

"If you could come with me," added the personnel officer, "the company founder and CEO, likes to meet new starters personally, his office is along the corridor."

Emma was hard pressed to prevent her jaw dropping, when James Berkley stepped from behind the desk.

"Welcome to the company", he said, extending his hand. "I understand you gave a very creditable interview, and I am fully aware of your hard work and dedication. I am sure you will prove a very creative and dedicated employee. I look forward to seeing your new project succeed."

Printed in Poland
by Amazon Fulfillment
Poland Sp. z o.o., Wrocław